THE DIDDINGTON DIAMOND

Wendy Burdess

What Readers Are Saying About THE DIDDINGTON DIAMOND

This is a wonderful period tale, with an absolutely engaging cast of characters. Ms. Burdess has a real knack for Regency dialogues and seamlessly blends together the lives of divergent personalities. -- Margo, Coffee Time Romance

Wendy Burdess writes in a delightful, entertaining style with special little tidbits that add a unique touch to the story. -- Camellia, Long And Short Reviews

Wendy Burdess

Aware of her piercing violet eyes studying him through the looking glass, he reached across for the ashtray, almost dropping it as, in one fell movement, the countess swung around on her stool to face him and declared, in the most decisive of manners: "Why, I have the solution, Toby. It is perfectly obvious."

"It is?" mumbled Toby, bracing himself for what was to follow.

"Of course it is," affirmed Caroline, with a disarming smile. "I shall allow you to marry but on one condition."

Toby's brows crept up his forehead.

"*I* shall choose your bride for you." She stood up from the stool and untied the belt of her robe. It slithered to the floor, landing in a pool of black silk at her feet. "Though you should be aware," she purred, "that I will not be choosing anyone who will divert your attentions from me."

Toby stubbed out his cigar. He had been expecting one of his mistress's infamous temper tantrums—of which he had borne the brunt more times than he cared to recall over the last two years. Other than a run-in with Mr. Wilmott, he could imagine nothing worse than having his mistress choose his future bride. As Caroline slid into bed beside him, though, obviously with other quite pressing matters on her mind, he concluded that that discussion could wait until just a little later.

Wendy Burdess

Champagne Books Presents

The Diddington Diamond

By

Wendy Burdess

This is a work of fiction. The characters, incidents and dialogues in this book are of the author's imagination and are not to be construed as real. Any resemblance to actual events or persons, living or dead, is completely coincidental.

No part of this book may be reproduced or transmitted in any form or by any means, electronic or mechanical, including photocopying, recording, or by any information storage and retrieval system, without permission in writing from the publisher.

Champagne Books
www.champagnebooks.com
Copyright 2012 by Wendy Burdess
ISBN 978-1-77155-040-6
March 2013
Cover Art by Amanda Kelsey
Produced in Canada

Champagne Book Group
#2 19-3 Avenue SE
High River, AB T1V 1G3
Canada

Dedication

For Keith.

One

England, 1815

To the genteel folk of Diddington, there were several noticeable characteristics which distinguished Miss Louisa Winchester of Hartley House from other young ladies of that pretty market town.

First, it had been reported that Miss Winchester had declined to shed a single tear upon being informed, some two years earlier, that her failing eyesight required the aid of that unbecoming apparatus known as "spectacles". And, as if that lack of tears alone were not sufficient evidence of the young lady's distinctive character, it had also been rumored that she may even have *smiled* upon the diagnosis—a suggestion immediately dismissed as preposterous by Mrs. Clark, the milliner—even for the affable Miss Winchester.

Second, unlike other young ladies of Diddington, Miss Winchester demonstrated no interest at all in the discussing of gowns, gloves, or hats preferring instead to debate the merits—or otherwise—of books. Books of absolutely any description. Excluding, which came as no surprise to anyone of the young lady's acquaintance, those of a romantic nature.

Third, in marked contrast to Diddington's other young females, the arrival of a social invitation did not inspire joy and excitement in Miss Winchester, but rather a deep sense of dread and the unfailing rearing of the question— "What was the point—unless one was out to catch a husband?" Which leads rather conveniently to Miss Winchester's final, and perhaps most singular, distinguishable feature—

Miss Louisa Winchester of Hartley House, Diddington had no interest in catching a husband.

No interest at all.

Not even the slightest scrap of interest.

A circumstance that happened to please her mother very well indeed.

Lady Eliza Winchester, the woman from whose loins the distinguishable Miss Louisa had sprung, was, this particular evening, seated on a red velvet gilded chair at the far end of Lady Mead's ballroom. Observing the proceedings with undisguised disdain, she also had about her an air of agitation, which evaporated the instant she spotted her daughter's head of raven curls through the bustling throng.

"Goodness, child, wherever have you been?" she demanded on a breath of relief, as Louisa, tripping over the shiny, buckled shoe of a footman, toppled into the empty chair alongside her.

"Just to the withdrawing-room, Mama," replied the younger woman, straightening her spectacles on her nose and swiping back an errant curl from her face. "Although, I own, it did take me quite some time to find it."

Lady Winchester narrowed her dark eyes. "Hmph. Well, I do hope you were not bothered by any…*gentlemen* during your search," she huffed, placing a particularly derisive emphasis on the word pertaining to the opposite sex.

Louisa screwed up her button nose. "Thankfully I was not, Mama," she replied truthfully, although why her mother even asked, she had no idea. In the two years Louisa had been obliged to attend such tedious social events, she had never been bothered by gentlemen—a situation for which she was extremely grateful and for which, she was well aware, she had both her plainness and her spectacles to thank. Gentlemen, it was a well-established fact, were *rarely* attracted to plain young ladies, but *never* to plain young ladies wearing spectacles, which was exactly the reason Louisa wore hers—at all times.

Eliza Winchester, seemingly satisfied with her

daughter's reply, emitted an exasperated sigh as her gaze landed on a young couple to her right. "Ugh! Just look at that ridiculous chit, Rebecca Bellingham, fluttering her eyelashes at that marquis over there. And for what? For what, I ask you? A wretched proposal of marriage—that's what. And we all know where that will lead. To a lifetime of misery, misery and—"

"Persecution, Mama," concluded a dutiful Louisa, who had heard the sentiment repeated with predictable regularity over the years.

"Exactly," affirmed Lady Winchester. "Why these ninnies are so obsessed with acquiring a husband is beyond me. As I have informed you many times, Louisa, the institution of marriage is as advantageous to women as—"

"Leeches on a corpse, Mama."

"Precisely," affirmed Lady Winchester, with a satisfactory, and very emphatic, nod of the head.

Of course to anyone aware of Lady Winchester's history—and there were few who were not—such venomous feelings toward the male species were perfectly understandable. There were, however, those that wondered at the inordinate amount of energy Lady Winchester had invested in cultivating these negative feelings over the past two decades, and also at the reasoning behind instilling these same sentiments in her young daughter. Nevertheless, few could deny that what had happened to Eliza Winchester all those years ago had been an upset of the most humiliating and devastating nature; so humiliating and devastating, in fact, that it had caused one of the greatest social scandals London had ever seen.

"Of course I have never recovered from it," Lady Winchester had been heard to profess on any number of occasions.

"How can anyone ever recover from such humiliation?"

"I am only grateful that I have had dear Louisa here for support."

For her part, Miss Louisa Winchester did not at all mind being her mother's support. Nor did she mind being clearly distinguishable from the other young ladies of Diddington. There was, after all, nothing of the remotest interest that, as far as she could see, she was missing out on. The preoccupations of the majority of Diddington females—namely who was wearing what, who was betrothed to whom, and what ball was taking place where—failed to hold her attention for more than five minutes before her mind drifted to the one great love of her life—her books.

From the moment Louisa had been able to read, she had rarely been seen without a tome in her hand. If Louisa was her mother's support, then books were Louisa's support. She relied upon them not only to improve her mind, but as a means of escaping to a host of different and fascinating worlds. There was, she had long since discovered, always a book to suit, whatever one's mood. And that was not all there was to be said in their favor. Books were controllable, dependable, and, most important of all, they were not in the least terrifying, unlike—

"Ah, Lady Winchester." A melodious male voice interrupted Louisa's musings. She jerked up her head to find Viscount Winston, a handsome widower of some middle forty years who had only recently removed to Diddington, executing a gracious bow before her mother. "I wondered," he continued, "if I may have the pleasure of escorting you and your lovely daughter to the supper-room later?"

Louisa failed to hold back a gasp as the viscount straightened. Her large brown bespectacled eyes moved swiftly from the man's expectant countenance to Lady Winchester's nonplussed one—which had turned the same shade of gray as the viscount's immaculately coiffed hair.

After what seemed like an interminable length of time, with each of the trio staring bewilderedly at one another, Lady Winchester cleared her throat and haughtily announced, "I'm afraid that that will not be at all possible, sir. My daughter and I were, er, just about to…to take our leave. In fact, we were on the very verge of it. Do come along now, Louisa."

In a flash, she sprang to her feet and began pushing her way through the swaying dancers toward the large double doors that lead out to the hallway. Several seconds later, a stunned Louisa rose from her chair, bobbed a perfunctory curtsy to the bemused viscount and scuttled after her mother in as decorous a fashion as she could muster.

She found Lady Winchester outside the front door, leaning against the wall at the top of the flight of steps. Her breath was fast and furious.

"Well," she panted, the moment Louisa joined her. "What an impertinence of the highest order. I declare, I have never heard the likes of it. Inviting us to the supper-room indeed. Does the man have no idea who I am? Of the tragedy I have suffered?" She whipped a black lace fan from her reticule and began fluttering it manically in front of her face.

"I'm sure he cannot fail to know, Mama," replied Louisa loyally. "Perhaps he was...in his cups. And not fully aware of what he was saying."

"In his cups indeed," countered Lady Winchester, with a dismissive roll of the eyes. "You know as well as I that the man was as sober as a judge, Louisa. And besides, being in his cups would be little excuse for the distress he has caused me. A woman who has known suffering as I have deserves to be treated with prodigious sensitivity. Not invited to the supper-room by all and sundry. Now come along, child. We have endured the tedium of the evening for quite long enough. I can scarcely wait until we are back at Hartley House."

Louisa silently echoed her mother's sentiment. Although why they had left Hartley House in the first place, she had no idea. She really could see no point in attending such occasions given that they both found them such a tiresome chore. But, ever conscious of Society's opinion and expectations, Lady Winchester insisted they show their faces occasionally, to avoid being considered social pariahs. Louisa could not have given a brass button whether they were considered pariahs or not. In fact, she thought she should quite like to be a pariah—never leaving the safe, tranquil confines of Hartley House—the only home she had ever known, which was as dear to her as her beloved books.

As their carriage rocked and rattled along Diddington's maze of rutted country lanes, Louisa slanted a look at her mother who was reclining against the maroon velvet squabs, her eyes closed. At nine-and-thirty, Eliza Winchester had lost little of the dark, exotic beauty so admired in her youth. In fact, however much she tried to disguise it—and she tried very hard indeed, scraping back her sleek ebony hair into the severest of buns and disguising her shapely form in the plainest of dresses—Louisa thought it unlikely her mother would ever be described as anything other than beautiful.

Yet, for all there was no disguising Lady Winchester's

beauty, there was also no denying that it existed under a large shadow of irrefutable sadness—sadness emanating from every one of Eliza Winchester's lovely pores. In fact, as she studied her now, Louisa could not recall a single moment when she had seen her mother happy.

Lady Winchester stirred and Louisa diverted her eyes to the carriage window. Peeping behind the blind, she noted that they were passing the grounds of the magnificent Diddington Hall. With warm orange light illuminating many of its windows, its imposing outline stood proud against the velvety night sky. The stunning architecture of the seventeenth century mansion never ceased to impress Louisa whatever the season, but it was at its most breath taking now, in spring; its grounds filled with daffodils, crocuses and primroses, and trees laden with lacy pink blossom, all of which epitomized the hope that accompanied this much-awaited time of year.

And it was not only spring flowers that surrounded Diddington Hall. A handful of romantic legends had become associated with it over the years, the most famous being that of the Diddington Diamond, the precious stone with wondrous magical qualities, which a gentleman had reputedly hidden in the grounds to present to his beloved when he returned from war, the tragedy of the story being that the man never did return. And so, it was said, the priceless jewel remained hidden within the grounds of Diddington's largest house.

Just at that moment Lady Winchester began snoring lightly, interrupting her daughter's reverie. Louisa turned to look at her once more, failing to suppress a sigh as she did so. Even in her sleep, her mother emanated sadness—so much sadness that Louisa doubted even the elusive Diddington Diamond would be able to work its magic on Lady Eliza Winchester. The woman was, she feared, unlikely ever to experience happiness again.

~ * ~

Gazing out of the window of the crimson drawing-room at Diddington Hall, a heavily perspiring Lord Tobias Allenby watched the distant lights of a carriage as it trundled along the lane at the bottom of the long drive. He ran a finger under the rim of his starched, pointed collar. God, it was hot in here. Spinning around, he was about to summon a footman to open a window, when he realized that none of the room's other occupants appeared the least bit hot and bothered.

His mother, Lady Arabella Allenby, Duchess of Wolsington presented the epitome of serene composure as she picked at her embroidery in a high-backed chair by the fire. Seated opposite, his father looked equally unperturbed, engrossed in a book. On a small sofa in the corner, his younger brother, Harry, with his *Gentleman's Magazine*, demonstrated no signs at all of perspiration.

Toby's gaze remained on his brother for several minutes, taking in his Romanesque nose, thick wavy chestnut hair and deep navy-blue eyes. The very same Romanesque nose, thick wavy chestnut hair and deep navy-blue eyes that Toby shared. But, even after eight-and-twenty years, Toby still found it difficult to believe that two men, only ten months apart in age and startlingly similar in appearance, could be so markedly different in character—now being a perfect example. While Toby sweated like a pig on a skewer, Harry remained as cool as an elderflower ice from Gunter's. Being thus outnumbered in his discomfiture, Toby miserably concluded that it was obviously just himself who was finding the atmosphere oppressive.

Perhaps it was because he was so worked up. Not surprising, given the enormity of what was to happen on the morrow. He resumed his pacing of the room, attempting to muster calming thoughts. No such thoughts were forthcoming. Admitting defeat, he helped himself to another glass of whiskey from the decanter on the sideboard, tossing it down his neck with a great sense of urgency.

"Do sit down, Toby dear," insisted his mother, briefly averting her own navy-blue eyes from her embroidery tambour. "All your fidgeting is not helping my nerves at all."

Your nerves! What about my nerves? Toby resisted screaming.

"Not missing London already are you, son?" muttered the duke, glancing up from his book.

"Don't be ridiculous, Charles," tutted Lady Allenby. "How on earth can the boy be missing London already? We've only been here a day. And besides, I'm sure even Toby can endure the country a little longer, given how precious Aunt Millie was to us all." She gave a fluttering little exhalation and pressed a hand to her chest before declaring, "Oh was not the funeral service today delightful? Although, I own, I do feel a little selfish keeping it such a small family affair."

"The service was perfectly charming, my sweet," smiled her husband indulgently. "And I'm sure Aunt Millie would understand perfectly that you could not cope with her legions of friends in your time of grief."

Lady Allenby set down her tambour and fished a lace handkerchief from the sleeve of her black mourning gown. "Oh, I shall miss her dreadfully," she whimpered. "She was like a second mother to me. And she always thought *so* much of the boys."

Yes, but exactly how much did she think of us? Toby wanted to shriek as he reached for the decanter again. He glanced at the ormolu clock on the mantel. In exactly twelve hours' time, he would find out the true extent of Great Aunt Millie's affection—and he only hoped for his sake that she had held him very dear indeed.

~ * ~

Several hours later, under the heavy counterpane of his four-poster bed, sleep was doing an admirable job of avoiding Lord Harry Allenby. As exhausted as he was, his mind refused to stop whirring for a single moment. He could not even blame the unfamiliar surroundings of Diddington Hall for his lack of slumber. Diddington Hall was not in the least unfamiliar to him. He had spent a great deal of time there over the years with Great Aunt Millie—God rest her soul. Despite the warmth of his bedding, Harry shivered as yet another image of the coffin being lowered into the family crypt flashed across his mind. That had been the moment realization had hit him. Great Aunt Millie, just like Clara, was gone. Behind her, she had left yet another large gaping hole in Harry's life; yet another hole that, just like the first one, he would never fill again. Nor did he wish to. Because Great Aunt Millie was irreplaceable—just as Clara had been.

Harry yanked the counterpane over his head as the ever-present knot of grief tightened in his stomach. He really should try to grab some sleep. Tomorrow was another important day. From the restless sounds emanating from the adjoining room, he was obviously not the only one having problems nodding off. He had observed how Toby had not managed to sit still for a single moment all day. Harry knew his brother well enough to recognize that, when he was so obviously agitated, it was generally because he had a great deal on his mind—most likely women or money. His brother's hedonistic lifestyle—which was, Toby constantly assured him, a source of great diversion—seemed to Harry to be overshadowed by a never-ending stream of problems. Of course, not being one of his brother's confidantes, Harry was aware that he was unlikely ever to discover the details or the extent of Toby's troubles. And for that, he was very grateful indeed—because Lord Harry Allenby had quite enough troubles of his own.

Two

Hartley House, Diddington was not an especially large abode. In fact, the agent who had sold it to Lady Winchester had aptly described it as "modest, with a particularly interesting feature of eighteenth century wood carving in the small drawing-room". Upon first viewing the property, particularly interesting features of wood carving—eighteenth century or otherwise—had not featured highly on Eliza Winchester's list of priorities. She had taken the house simply because she had had neither the energy nor the inclination to trawl around any others.

Still, some two decades on, the symmetrical, three-story dwelling, painted a welcoming shade of warm cream, continued to serve her well. Situated on the outskirts of Diddington, surrounded on three sides by fastidiously tended gardens, with an equally well-kept drive leading to the front door, the accommodation was comfortably furnished and provided more than enough room for mother and daughter. Between the two of them and their small and, for the most part, proficient staff, the household ran as smoothly as a well-oiled cog. Just as well, given that that was exactly the manner in which Lady Winchester ran her entire life.

Eliza Winchester was what was commonly known as "a creature of habit". Although several less savory variations of this phrase had been bandied about from time to time, particularly by Mrs. Potts, the cook, whose occasional indulgences with the gin bottle did not always comply with

Lady Winchester's rigid timetable.

Failing some life-threatening illness, natural disaster, or royal summons—which was, unfortunately, the least likely of the three—a typical day in the Winchester household was thus:

> 8 o'clock Breakfast
> 9 o'clock Inspection of gardens (Weather permitting)
> 10 o'clock Tea and cake (Raisin on Mondays, Wednesdays and Fridays. Madeira on all other days)
> 11 o'clock Trip to Diddington (Mondays, Wednesdays and Fridays)
> 1 o'clock Luncheon (Cold meats on Mondays, Wednesdays and Fridays. At Mrs. Potts's dubious discretion all other days)
> 2-5 o'clock Embroidery (Tuesdays and Thursdays)
> Letter-writing (Mondays)
> Reading (All other days)
> 6 o'clock Dinner

That morning, though, it soon became apparent that all was not destined to run quite as smoothly as usual.

"Begging your pardon, my lady," announced Korbett, the butler, appearing in the doorway of the drawing-room where Lady Winchester and her daughter were partaking of their tea and cake. "There is a caller."

A raisin caught in Lady Winchester's slender throat. "A-a caller, Korbett? Here? At Hartley House?"

"In the hall, ma'am."

Lady Winchester took a few seconds to absorb this information, her dark eyes growing wide in their sockets. "Well, who is she?" she eventually barked. "Has she a calling card?"

The butler glanced sheepishly at the item lying on his silver platter. He cleared his throat. "It is a, er, a, um, *gentleman*, ma'am."

Lady Winchester's china plate, complete with its remains of raisin cake, promptly slid from her lap to the Persian rug below. "A-a gentleman?" she gasped, looking imploringly at her daughter. "But it can't be. We don't have gentlemen here. At Hartley House."

Sensing her mother's distress, Louisa determined to take control of the situation, despite her own increasing anxiety. "Who on earth is it, Korbett?" she demanded. "Do bring the card here."

The butler did as she bade. Retrieving the card from the tray, Louisa's heart skipped a beat when she read the name upon it. *Viscount William Winston.* Good lord. Whatever was she to do now?

"The caller is, er, Viscount Winston, Mama," she announced, somewhat gingerly. "The gentleman who wished to escort us to the supper-room at Lady Mead's ball yesterday evening."

Lady Winchester clapped a hand to her forehead. "Heaven save us! Does the man seek to finish me off? What, in God's name, is he doing here?"

"Well, I suppose there is only one way to find out," concluded Louisa, with much more conviction than she felt. "Do show the man in, Korbett."

Disbelief settled over Korbett's round, pudgy face as he stared aghast at Louisa.

"Our caller, Korbett," prompted Louisa. "Could you please show him in."

"Of-of course, miss. If you are sure."

"Quite sure, thank you," replied Louisa, with a confidence that belied her shaking legs. Whatever was she about? She had never entertained a gentleman in her life. What did one do? Or say? Or talk about? Did they like raisin cake? Or tea, or—?

She did not have long to debate the answers to this rapidly burgeoning list, as, all at once, the man appeared in the doorway. The speed with which Louisa sprang to her feet could not have been greater if a fire had appeared beneath them. In her haste, she completely forgot about the cup and saucer that had been resting on her knee.

Silently cursing herself as both items tumbled to the rug to join those of her mother, she stammered, "Good, er, morning, Viscount Winston. How prodigiously, um, kind of you to call upon us."

Viscount Winston, immaculately attired in beige breeches, an olive-green topcoat and gleaming Hessian boots, gave a stiff, awkward bow. "Please do excuse the impertinence of my visit, Miss Winchester, Lady Winchester," he said, turning his handsome chiseled face toward the older woman. "However I wished to apologize for my behavior yesterday evening. I was given to believe that I may have caused you some distress. I was not, you see, aware of your, er, your, um—"

"Our circumstances?" offered Louisa.

"Quite," replied the viscount, with notable relief. "I have, as you may already know, only recently removed to Diddington and, not given to gossip, was first made aware of your, er, *circumstances* yesterday evening. After your rather, um, sudden departure."

"Oh," replied Louisa, empathizing with the man's evident discomfiture. "I see. Well, it is most considerate of you to call and apologize, sir. I can assure you, however, that there is really no need. My mother was a little...*indisposed* yesterday evening. Were you not, Mama?"

All eyes shifted to Lady Winchester, who had remained seated throughout the exchange, regarding the viscount as though he had a particularly nasty smell emanating from him.

"Er, well," continued Louisa, concluding there was to be no reply—or at least none of an acceptable nature—to be had from her mother. "Now that you are here, would you care to, um, join us in a dish of tea, my lord?"

At this invitation, the gurgling depths of Lady Winchester's throat projected an indecipherable sound. The viscount's cool blue eyes regarded the woman for several seconds before he lamentably announced that he had an appointment with his tailor and would not, unfortunately, be able to accept the gracious offer.

"Oh, what a great pity," remarked Louisa, with not altogether forced sincerity. "Another time perhaps?"

At which point, Lady Winchester muttered something rather vague from which Louisa caught only the words "my" and "dead body".

~ * ~

Seated in a semi-circular arrangement before the desk in

the enormous library of Diddington Hall, at precisely the same moment the unexpected visitor took his leave of Hartley House, were his grace, the Duke of Wolsington, her grace, the Duchess of Wolsington, Lord Tobias Allenby, Marquis of Yarm, and Lord Harry Allenby, Earl of Stanford.

Also present, behind the ancient oak desk, was one incongruous stuffed trout—staring disconcertingly from its glass case—and one Mr. Gerald Hinds. For more years than he cared to remember, Mr. Hinds had borne the dubious honor of acting as Great Aunt Millie's solicitor. He was a painfully thin man of some sixty-plus years with several strands of stringy gray hair stretched, somewhat optimistically, across his liver-spotted scalp. He appeared to be so engrossed in the pile of paperwork on the desk, that he had completely forgotten the room's other occupants.

"Ah-hem," Toby coughed in an unsubtle attempt to remind the man of law of their presence.

Mr. Hinds seemed not to hear.

"Ah-*hem*," Toby coughed, more loudly this time. If the wretched man did not commence the reading soon, he was concerned that his wildly thudding heart would burst out of his blue superfine jacket.

Still nothing.

"Ah-*hem*!" Toby coughed, so loudly that his mother jumped several inches from her seat.

"Goodness. Are you all right, dear?" she asked concernedly.

"Quite all right, thank you, Mother," replied Toby tartly. "I was just wondering if Mr. Hinds had *any* idea when he might start the reading." This comment was aimed directly at the solicitor whose bird-like eyes had shifted from his pile of documents and was now peering at Toby over the top of his half-moon spectacles.

"Oh, goodness. Yes. Yes, indeed," he spluttered, with a vigorous shake of his head. "Well, what on earth am I waiting for? Do you know, I really can't remember. Well, no matter. Let's crack on, shall we?"

"I should be much obliged to you, sir," said Toby, with more than a hint of asperity.

There then followed—what seemed to Toby—a

prolonged and unnecessary shuffling of papers on the desk before the solicitor eventually cleared his throat and announced, in an officious manner—"We are all aware, are we not, that we are gathered here today to hear the reading of the final Will and Testament of Millicent Phoebe Venetia O'Hare of Diddington Hall, Diddington?"

There was a collective nodding and murmured words of agreement.

"Very good," continued the solicitor. "Well, if we are all sitting comfortably, I shall commence."

Toby's heart beat a tad faster as Mr. Hinds picked up one of the documents before him, held it at arm's length and proceeded to read.

"Item Number One—To my dutiful and loving niece, Lady Arabella Allenby, I bequeath my collection of jewels, my share portfolio, and my townhouse in Grosvenor Square, London along with the entire contents thereof."

"Oh, the darling," whimpered Lady Allenby, a lone tear rolling down her powdered cheek.

Mr. Hinds cleared his throat and continued. "Item Number Two. To my two great nephews, Tobias Robert Allenby and Harold Joseph Allenby —"

Toby steeled himself, his knuckles white as he gripped the arms of the leather wing chair.

"—I bequeath the estate of Diddington Hall, Diddington, and the entire contents thereof—"

Relief seeped through him. He should have had more faith in her. She had not left him out. Great Aunt Millie had saved the day and, most probably, his life. Technically, of course, he being the elder, the share should be his alone, but Toby knew how much Great Aunt Millie had adored Harry, and it was that very fact that had been causing him so much anguish.

He had harbored a strong suspicion that the old dear may have left *everything* to Harry. Consequently, he didn't mind that the two of them were to inherit equally. That she had left them the house had far exceeded his expectations anyway. It must be worth a fortune. All he and Harry had to do now was sell it and split the proceeds. Not too difficult given how admired the place was. Come to think of it, he might know the very man. An old acquaintance of his back in London had been enquiring about the hall a few months ago. He was sure to have the cash available. The man had not long since returned to England after making a fortune in America. Toby would contact him on the morrow. Or perhaps even this afternoon if he—

Harry's voice suddenly drifted into his consciousness; it sounded strange. Turning to look at his brother, Toby noticed that Harry appeared decidedly befuddled. Immediately pushing aside thoughts of prospective buyers, he turned his attention back to the present situation.

"Would you mind repeating that, Mr. Hinds?" Harry asked.

"Of course, my lord," replied the solicitor. He cleared his throat. "To my two great nephews, Tobias Robert Allenby and Harold Joseph Allenby, I bequeath the estate of Diddington Hall, Diddington and the entire contents thereof—" he paused as before, a break of which Toby, due to his ruminations had been unaware "—to whichever of the pair marries first, on condition that their choice of bride is first approved by my niece, Lady Arabella Allenby and her husband Lord Charles Allenby."

As Mr. Hinds placed the document squarely back on his desk, a deathly silence fell upon the room.

~ * ~

Lady Winchester stood at the drawing-room window watching Viscount Winston's carriage rattle down Hartley House's immaculate drive. "A dish of tea, indeed! Whatever were you about, Louisa, encouraging the man like that?"

In her chair at the side of the marble fireplace, Louisa fiddled nervously with the ribbon at the bodice of her gown, wishing desperately that she could turn back the clock a half hour. "I own, I really do not know, Mama," she confessed. "I just thought he seemed rather, um…*nice*."

"*Nice!*" Lady Winchester whipped around to face her daughter. "Men are not *nice*. Feigned charm is merely part of their plan—their plan to lure you to them, in order that they may steal your heart, then cast you aside like a used slipper. Do not be fooled by them, Louisa. One must always, *always* be on one's guard where gentlemen are concerned. Now, that ghastly encounter has given me the most pounding of headaches. I shall retire to my chamber for a lie-down, despite the fact, I might add, that it is a Wednesday and I shall have to forego my planned trip to Diddington. You see, child, not only do men upset one's equilibrium, but also one's meticulously planned timetable. And that, you will also do well to remember, is the very least they are capable of." With that, she turned on her heel and whisked out of the room.

Louisa heaved a mournful sigh as the door swung shut. What an insensitive widgeon she had been. She should have given more consideration to her mother's feelings rather than encouraging the viscount. It would no doubt take her mama days now to calm down and, frankly, who could blame her, given the tragedy the woman had suffered at the hands of another such seemingly *nice* man—Louisa's own father.

Some twenty years before, Eliza's marriage to Lord Rupert Winchester had seemed, to all observers, including Eliza herself, an ideal match. Not only was the bride head-over-heels in love with her dashing lord, but also the Winchesters were one of the most eminent families in England. Eliza's own family consisted, rather pitifully, of only one older cousin, both her parents having been tragically killed in a carriage accident when she was thirteen years old.

An elderly aunt had cared for her well during the subsequent four years, before dropping down dead during a lively rendition of the quadrille at a spring ball in Hertfordshire. Yet, despite her lack of relatives, there had been no one happier than Eliza that day as she had pledged herself to the man she adored. And, when she had held her beautiful baby daughter in her arms ten months later, she had truly believed that things could not have been more perfect. How wrong she had been.

When Louisa was just six months old, the new Lady Winchester returned home from visiting friends one afternoon, to find a note from her husband informing her that he had fallen in love with another woman and intended traveling to the continent to begin a new life with her. As if that news alone were not bad enough, the woman in question was discovered to be one of the Winchesters' chambermaids, a buxom blonde, whose baby-blue eyes, Eliza recalled, had always held a mischievous twinkle, particularly when focused on her husband.

At first, Eliza blamed herself for her misfortune. As had her insensitive mother-in-law.

"One never," declared the dowager Lady Winchester,

"employs a girl with a bosom larger than one's own. That is a well-known and, if I may say so, rather obvious fact, Eliza."

Once she had summoned the courage to flee the suffocating, interfering atmosphere of London, though, and set up house in the tranquil surrounds of Diddington, it had not taken Eliza long to convince herself that the incident was none of her doing. She was the innocent party, a wronged wife, a deserted mother, and a tragic heroine.

All of the above, Eliza had explained to her daughter as soon as the child had been old enough to understand. And ever since then, Louisa had sympathized completely with her mother's plight. Despite the fact that her father had taken the uncharacteristically magnanimous step of ensuring they were well provided for, Louisa knew she would never forgive the man for his despicable behavior.

And she did not doubt, from what her mother had frequently told her, that *all* men were capable of such actions or worse—even Viscount Winston, who had appeared most harmless. No, the best thing she could do, she concluded, was continue to heed her mother's advice and, as she had made a point of doing for as long as she could remember, keep well away from those terrifying, complicated creatures otherwise known as "gentlemen".

Having spent enough time dwelling on the morning's unfortunate events, Louisa felt the need for some fresh air. She donned her pale yellow pelisse and bonnet, and selected a parasol. Into her wicker basket, she then neatly packed a blanket, an apple, and her favorite book of poems. About to exit the house, she noticed a letter addressed to Lady Winchester lying atop the marble table in the hall. It bore an unfamiliar Scottish postmark.

"Begging your pardon, miss," apologized Korbett, entering the hall at the very moment Louisa picked up the missive. "But given all the commotion with the, um, caller and all this morning, that letter quite slipped my mind."

Louisa set the item down. "No matter, Korbett," she said with a reassuring smile. "I'm sure it can't be anything too pressing. Please make sure to give it to my mother when she awakes."

Korbett inclined his head of thick gray hair. "Of course,

miss," he said and pulled open the front door for her.

Three

  Following the will reading, Harry Allenby slipped out of Diddington Hall at the first opportunity. No sooner had he left the house, however, than he realized he had not the first idea where he was going. He didn't care. Anywhere would be preferable to being indoors with all the furor about the will reading. He began marching briskly down the drive, the crunching of gravel under his polished boots accompanied only by the trilling of two chaffinches in a nearby oak tree. Looking about him, Harry could not help but appreciate the beauty of his surroundings, the way the lush, flower-strewn grass covering the gentle slope up to the house contrasted perfectly with the clear cornflower-blue of the sky.

  How Great Aunt Millie had loved this time of year, he recalled with a pang of sadness. That sadness, though, was immediately swept aside by another emotion. Although it was now over an hour since Mr. Hinds had announced that ridiculous condition of the will, Harry could still make no sense of it. It wasn't the fact that he was not to inherit the hall that was bothering him—although he could not deny that he loved the place—it was that he felt hurt by Great Aunt Millie; betrayed even. Knowing his situation as she did, for she had been the only person in whom he had truly confided, she must have realized that it would be Toby who would benefit. And, although she had never said so directly, Harry had always suspected that Great Aunt Millie had remained steadfastly unimpressed by Toby's high-flying lifestyle. So why then, had she added that outlandish caveat?

Reaching the wide country road at the bottom of the drive, lined on either side by thick yellow gorse bushes, Harry's attention was drawn to the vibrant patchwork of fields stretching as far as the eye could see. A bolt of inspiration hit him. Suddenly he knew exactly where to go.

~ * ~

Miss Louisa Winchester wished desperately that she had not donned her pelisse. The late April day was deceptively warm and, having removed the item some time ago, she struggled to carry it and her crammed basket and parasol. She was only grateful that she was almost upon her destination, a place she stumbled upon the very first time she had been allowed out on her own. She could have been no more than ten years old. Yet, even at that tender age, she had instantly appreciated its beauty and serenity. Her spirits lifted as she reached the old wooden stile at the entrance to Buttercup Meadow. She managed to negotiate it by dropping her parasol only once. Once in the meadow, she began heading toward the magnificent willow tree, which overhung the shallow, gurgling river there—Louisa's very favorite place in the whole of Diddington.

~ * ~

Although Buttercup Meadow was not a particularly inspired name, Harry Allenby had to confess that it was certainly a very apt one. No sooner had he reached the pertinently named field, though, and climbed over the old wooden stile, than such an overwhelming surge of memories assaulted him that he was forced to sit down. Attempting to ignore the griping sensation in his stomach, he took a deep breath and tried to focus on the impressive sight of hundreds of glistening golden flowers dancing in the barely noticeable breeze; a sight he appreciated all the more after having spent so much time in London recently.

He started as a butterfly landed with an audacious flutter upon his knee. Smiling at its effrontery, Harry studied the insect's wings—a beautiful shade of lilac veined with shimmering threads of pink. It looked far too delicate to be flying about the countryside on its own at the mercy of so many other creatures. Then again, he pondered philosophically, for all their physical size and strength, the same could be said about a great many people. Not least of all himself.

Harry's thoughts moved with practiced ease from flowers and butterflies to another glorious spring day, some twelve years earlier, when he had first made the acquaintance of Miss Clara Walpole. It had been in this very field, the site of the Diddington May Day Fair. As May Queen, at sixteen, Clara had already shown signs of the stunning young woman she was on the cusp of blossoming into. As she'd sat on her makeshift throne in a dazzling white gown, her long golden hair tumbling over her shoulders and her turquoise eyes sparkling with excitement, Harry had thought her the most beautiful girl he had ever seen.

Then, when it transpired that her parents were friends of Great Aunt Millie's and he was awarded an introduction to this ethereal creature, he had scarcely believed his luck—particularly when it became obvious that his admiration was not unrequited. So, in those awkward years between childhood and adulthood, with Harry spending every spare moment he could at Diddington, a close bond had developed between the two youngsters; a bond that had, tentatively at first, blossomed into love.

Their betrothal four years hence, following Harry's stint at Oxford, had been an emotional celebration but, just days after the festivities, Mrs. Walpole had taken ill. Clara had insisted on nursing her mother herself, leaving Harry with little choice but to respectfully postpone the wedding. Mrs. Walpole's illness had lasted for an interminable two years, during which time Harry had, rather uncharitably, thought he would implode with impatience. Then, less than three weeks after the poor woman's death, Clara herself had taken ill.

Harry wiped a bead of perspiration from his brow. He'd been so intent on reaching the meadow he'd scarcely noticed how warm the day had become. Jumping to his feet with renewed vigor, he tugged off his cravat and shoved it in his breeches' pocket, removed his jacket, rolled up the sleeves of his white linen shirt and, slinging his jacket over his shoulder, marched on toward the river and the magnificent willow tree there, under which he had tenderly kissed Miss Clara Walpole for the very first time.

~ * ~

Toby Allenby could not escape Diddington Hall quickly

enough. If his mother muttered "Well, we certainly weren't expecting that" one more time, he would not, he had silently resolved, be held responsible for his actions. Instead, mumbling some excuse about a prior commitment, he jumped into his carriage as soon as decently possible and ordered the driver not to spare the horses on the twelve-mile return to London.

Despite the clattering and jolting of the conveyance, the increasing distance between himself and Diddington had at least permitted Toby the opportunity to breathe again—and to think. His mother, despite having repeated the phrase an annoyingly unnecessary number of times, had nonetheless been correct. Not one of them had expected the bizarre condition of Great Aunt Millie's will.

Whatever could the old woman have been thinking? Particularly as she, more than anyone had been familiar with Harry's delicate circumstances concerning the fairer sex. And there remained the undeniable fact that Harry had been Great Aunt Millie's favorite. Harry had visited her regularly, even staying with her when she had sprained her ankle. Toby, on the other hand, had only ever seen her at more formal family occasions when their mother absolutely insisted upon his attendance.

And there was another, not inconsequential, consideration—Toby had always harbored a strong suspicion that Great Aunt Millie had never really approved of him and his pleasure-seeking lifestyle. Something about the way she used to look at him, with that censorious glint in her green eyes; a glint that had shone perceptibly brighter the time he had rolled up in his new, very smart, high-perch phaeton. So why then, he pondered for the umpteenth time, had she added the condition about marriage when she must have known there would be no chance of Harry fulfilling it?

Relief washed over him. Well, at least that was one thing for which he should be grateful. The house *would* eventually belong to him. It was just a damned shame the old bat had made it so inconvenient. Still, he would just have to get on with it, he concluded, banging his cane on the roof of the carriage to urge the driver on. The facts were that she *had* added the condition and that *he* would be the one to benefit from it—in only a matter of weeks if he jumped straight to it. All he had to do was break the news to Caroline, and proceed with the business of finding a wife. An image of the lovely Countess Caroline popped into his head. How would she take the news? Toby knocked on the roof of the carriage again, this time calling to the driver to take him first to his club. He had the distinct feeling that courage of a Dutch nature may well be required.

He was not wrong.

~ * ~

Lying on her back under the shade of the willow tree, the last thing Miss Louisa Winchester saw, before removing her spectacles and falling asleep, was a beautiful lilac butterfly with shimmering pink wings, which, for several minutes, had been content to sit on the puffed sleeve of her muslin gown.

The first thing Louisa saw when she awoke from her sleep, was not a delicate fluttering insect, but rather a large hazy shape, bending over her with terrifying proximity. Frozen to the spot, she attempted a scream, which, to her mounting anguish, came out as more of a whine.

The shape immediately sprang back from her. "Oh, I do beg your pardon, miss," it said, in a not unpleasant male voice. "But there was a wasp..."

Having not the first clue what was going on or what the man was talking about, Louisa jerked herself up into a sitting position and began frantically fumbling about for her spectacles.

"If you will permit me, miss, I think perhaps you are looking for these."

To her dismay, the man took a step forward and reached toward the spectacles at the very moment Louisa located them. She squealed as their hands touched. She whipped hers away in a flash. The man leaped back almost as quickly.

"I assure you I meant no harm," he insisted as she struggled to put on her spectacles with shaking hands. "I was out walking and when I spotted the wasp, which had landed on your apple core, which was, um, right next to your arm, I just thought... Well, I thought—" He broke off and cleared his throat. "Unseasonably, er, early for wasps, is it not?"

Louisa, who could now see that her suspected assailant was actually a striking man of some mid-twenty years, with the darkest blue eyes and the broadest shoulders she had ever seen, could not have found the words to agree with this wasp observation if the month referred to had been as early as January. She was, she realized, alone in the countryside with this strange man and not another soul in sight. Overcome with an urge to escape the situation, she began hurriedly scrabbling around for her belongings. Thankfully, they were all within arm's reach. With an uncharacteristic lack of regard for their welfare, she tossed her open book into the basket, crammed in her pelisse, yanked her bonnet onto her head, then sprang to her feet and snatched up her parasol and blanket.

Aware of the gentleman's gaze upon her, and still incapable of speech, she bobbed a curtsy to him before turning on her heel and, as quickly as she could without breaking into a run, scrambled across the field toward the stile.

~ * ~

Harry Allenby's twitching lips broke into a wide smile as he watched the petite female form scurrying across the meadow. Her plaid blanket was half tucked under her arm, the other half trailing on the ground behind her. What a funny little creature, he mused. And what a great deal of restraint he had had to employ not to roar with laughter when she had made that charming incongruous curtsy. Still, his behavior, too, had been somewhat bizarre. All that ridiculous babbling about wasps. He could only attribute it to the way the girl had regarded him. With those enormous dark brown eyes. He had found it most… unsettling.

As indeed, he had found his overpowering urge to protect her. This he could attribute to how incredibly vulnerable she had looked asleep, dark lashes fanning her cheeks, and that lustrous mass of long black curls strewn about the blanket. It was quite some time since he had seen such a strikingly pretty young lady, although she was not, he promptly assured himself, as pretty as Clara had been. He continued watching her retreating back and this time could not resist a snort of laughter as, in her obvious haste to escape him, she caught her shoe in the hem of her skirts, causing her yellow bonnet to slide to one side of her head. As he spun around and glimpsed a lilac butterfly, perched on a branch of the willow tree, it occurred to Harry that he had not laughed like that for quite some time.

~ * ~

Lady Caroline Levington, the beautiful Countess of

Wold, jerked bolt upright in her four-poster bed and gawped down at her lover with an expression of pure horror. *"Marriage?"* she spat. *"You? Married?* No! No! No! I will not hear of it, Toby. I will not share you with another woman."

Jumping out of bed, she retrieved her black silk robe from the back of a chair and wrapped it tightly around her slim naked form.

Toby sighed. Propping himself up against the mountain of feather pillows, he reached across to the nightstand, withdrew a cigar from the box there and lit it with a taper from the candle. "Well, that is all very fine for you to say, Caroline," he retorted through a thick cloud of smoke. "But don't forget that *I* have to share *you*. With your oaf of a husband."

Caroline stared at him aghast. "My husband, as you well know, Toby, has not been near my bedchamber for the greater part of six years. And besides, you know I cannot possibly leave him. The dullard would deny me so much as a penny."

Whisking around, she marched over to her dressing table, plonked herself down on the velvet stool there and began furiously brushing her long auburn hair with the silver-plated brush.

"That's as may be," sighed Toby, directing his comment to her reflection in the three-part mirror. "But you know more than anyone the deuced mess I'm in, Caroline. This is my only chance to get back on an even keel. If I don't get leg-shackled, I don't inherit Diddington Hall which means I can't sell it and will therefore have no brass and no hope of ever escaping this damned pickle."

The countess pouted. "How can you even consider abandoning me for such a vulgar thing, Toby? Is not what we have something special?"

"Of course it is, my darling," assured Toby, trying not to think of the other "something special" he had shared with an actress of a most disreputable, but very obliging nature, only days before. "But it's the devil's own scrape I'm in, Caroline. I am completely cleaned out."

"If it's only for money, *I* can give you money," she declared. "Haven't I helped you out more than once in the past?"

Toby inhaled another mouthful of smoke. "Everyone has helped me out more than once in the past," he sighed. "Which is why I now owe half of London an extremely large amount of money. Not least of all Jack Wilmott."

The countess gasped, stopped brushing her hair, and whipped her head around to him. "Jack Wilmott? That murderous moneylender? Oh, Toby! How could you?"

"Desperate times lead to desperate measures, Caroline," muttered Toby, raking his free hand through his disheveled mop of hair. "The cards just haven't been going my way lately."

"Hmph, that is obvious if you've been so desperate as to resort to Jack Wilmott," huffed the countess, resuming her preening. "Well, I find it most disagreeable, Toby. Infinitely disagreeable, in fact. It was my belief that we were both pleasantly served with our...*arrangement* but it appears I was sorely mistaken. One can only assume that you have grown tired of me and wish to take another mistress."

"Don't be ridiculous," retorted Toby, who feared the wrath of the fiery countess only marginally less than the wrath of the notorious Mr. Wilmott.

Aware of her piercing violet eyes studying him through the looking glass, he reached across for the ashtray, almost dropping it as, in one fell movement, the countess swung around on her stool to face him and declared, in the most decisive of manners. "Why, I have the solution, Toby. It is perfectly obvious."

"It is?" mumbled Toby, bracing himself for what was to follow.

"Of course it is," affirmed Caroline, with a disarming smile. "I shall allow you to marry but on one condition."

Toby's brows crept up his forehead.

"*I* shall choose your bride for you." She stood up from the stool and untied the belt of her robe. It slithered to the floor, landing in a pool of black silk at her feet. "Though you should be aware," she purred, "that I will not be choosing anyone who will divert your attentions from me."

Toby stubbed out his cigar. He had been expecting one of his mistress's infamous temper tantrums—of which he had borne the brunt more times than he cared to recall over the last two years. Other than a run-in with Mr. Wilmott, he could imagine nothing worse than having his mistress choose his future bride. As Caroline slid into bed beside him, though, obviously with other quite pressing matters on her mind, he concluded that that discussion could wait until just a little later.

~ * ~

"Pon my soul, mused Louisa Winchester as she staggered across Buttercup Meadow, acutely aware of a pair of navy-blue eyes watching her. What a startlingly handsome gentleman and, given the circumstances, rather nice too. *Nice.* Oh no! Her mother's words of only a few hours ago sprang into her head. Gentlemen, she must remember, were never nice. It was all an act in order that they may steal your heart then toss you aside like a worn boot. Thank goodness, she had no intention of ever becoming involved with one of them. The very notion filled her with terror; so much terror, that she caught her shoe in the hem of her gown and almost fell over, setting her precariously balanced bonnet askew.

One thing was for certain, she would not be mentioning this encounter to her mother. If her pounding heart was anything to go by, it was going to take her long enough as it was to recover from the incident without adding her mama's predictable disapproval to the equation. Gracious, what a day this was turning out to be! As she reached the stile, she dropped her parasol, tripped over the trailing blanket and landed with an ungainly thud, flat on her bottom on the dusty road.

~ * ~

Although always pleased to return to Hartley House, Louisa could not recall ever feeling quite so relieved to see its gleaming green front door as she did at that particular moment. She was quite exhausted and, having never before met with such a plethora of activity in one morning, already longing for a return to peace and tranquility. These two usually ubiquitous attributes, however, appeared to have completely deserted her. No sooner had she entered the house and abandoned her burden in the hall, than her mother came flying out of the library, flourishing the letter Louisa had spotted earlier.

"We are to have a houseguest, Louisa," she declared, in a tone that implied there could be no worse news.

Louisa wrinkled her forehead. "A houseguest, Mama? But we don't have houseguests here. At Hartley House."

"My words precisely," boomed Lady Winchester. "However I am afraid that, in this case, we have—deliberately, I might add—been left with little choice in the matter. The girl, a Miss Maria Dove, is to arrive tomorrow, which will no doubt mean yet another disruption to my meticulously planned timetable."

Regarding the letter in Lady Winchester's soft white hand, Louisa had a strong presentiment that, somehow, her mother's meticulously planned timetable would never be quite the same ever again.

Four

"Well now, is this not the most pleasant way to spend an evening?" beamed Lady Allenby, over a dinner of raised mutton pie, mashed potatoes, and French beans that evening.

Harry had to agree. He and his parents were enjoying the excellent repast in Diddington Hall's dining-room–the grandest room in the house, and one that exuded a wealth of history. Its paneled walls were a tribute to Tudor craftsmanship; its flagstone floor had been smoothed by generations of passing feet; and its two enormous stone fireplaces–one at either end– were engraved with the names and dates of all the building's previous residents. It was the most recent resident, though, who occupied Harry's thoughts at that moment.

Focusing on the empty high-backed chair at the head of the long mahogany table, Harry could clearly visualize Great Aunt Millie reigning over the proceedings, her round face with its rosy cheeks and twinkling green eyes, topped with a cluster of white curls and the ever-present lace cap. The image was so clear he could almost smell her trademark lavender scent. Could it be possible that she was in the room with them now? Watching them? Laughing at them? Relishing her new invisible role, which could well allow her to make more mischief dead than alive?

Tossing and turning in bed the previous night, Harry had still failed to make any sense of the ridiculous condition of her will. By the early hours of the morning, the only conclusion he had reached was that the old woman had actually *wanted* to leave Diddington Hall to Toby. To spare Harry's feelings she had added the clause knowing perfectly well he had no hope of satisfying it. What made that theory even harder to bear, though, was that Harry felt certain his brother had not so much as an ounce of emotional attachment to the building. In fact, he would have laid odds that the "For Sale" board would be in place before the ink on his brother's marriage certificate was dry.

Still, before any of that could happen, there remained the small matter of Toby finding a wife—and, more significantly—a wife of whom his parents approved. A potentially entertaining exercise and perhaps even the reason Great Aunt Millie had added the caveat.

His reverie was broken by a wistful sigh from his mother.

"Do you know," declared the duchess, raising her wine glass to her lips, "if I did not know better, I would swear that Aunt Millie was here, in this very room with us. At this very moment."

Harry gawped at his mother, unable to believe that she had vocalized his exact sentiments. To hide his startled expression, he picked up his napkin and dabbed at his mouth.

"Well, thank goodness you do know better, Arabella," the duke remonstrated. "And please, no ridiculous talk of ghosts. We all know they cannot possibly exist."

Just then, a cool gust of wind blasted through the room—laced with a strong scent of lavender. Harry exchanged a furtive glance with his mother. His father appeared not to notice.

~ * ~

At her writing desk in her bedchamber, Lady Caroline Levington, the Countess of Wold, was decidedly pleased with herself. She had had a very productive day. Dipping her quill in the Standish, she added one final name to her list. That made four in all. Four insipid boring prospective brides for her lover—not one of whom he could possibly fall in love with. Caroline set down the quill and leaned back in the chair, allowing herself a rare moment of reflection on her relationship with Lord Tobias Allenby...

She had first made the man's acquaintance during a dinner party at Lord and Lady Garfield's country estate. They were both included in a weekend party of some two-dozen guests. Having become bored with her latest lover's predictably tedious adoration, Caroline had dismissed the man's services some three weeks before. Since then, she had been suffering the restlessness that always consumed her during those rare periods she found herself without amusement. On the lookout for an interesting new "project", Caroline knew she had hit upon it the moment she sat down at the table and set eyes upon Toby Allenby.

Toby, however, seated at the far end, seemed to have eyes for no one other than the young widow on his right. In a scarlet gown cut even lower than Caroline's, the woman flaunted an equally desirable set of charms. Despite the sumptuous, seemingly never-ending range of dishes set before her, Caroline had scarcely eaten a thing that evening. There had been no room in her stomach for food. It had been filled with the delicious fluttering of excitement she experienced whenever she was about to conquer a new interest.

Used to men falling at her feet at a bat of her long silky lashes, Toby Allenby had appeared infuriatingly oblivious to her charms. He had paid her scant attention all weekend. In fact, it had taken Caroline several interminable weeks before the man had shown her the slightest interest. Several weeks during which she had alternately burst into floods of frustrated tears, then sent for her mantuamaker and ordered the making of yet another new gown—each one more opulent and more revealing than the last.

After what seemed like the longest month Caroline had ever endured, her strategy paid off. She had pulled out all the stops—along with a number of other things. In a pink shimmering dress, plunging to indecent depths at both back and front, very little of her indisputable appeal had been left to the imagination. She had arrived at the ball deliberately late. As her name had been announced, she had glided into the packed ballroom. All eyes had been upon her, including, she had noted triumphantly, those of Toby Allenby. It had taken almost the entire evening before he had approached her. Having anticipated the moment for so long, when he had eventually requested her hand in a waltz, Caroline's legs had been shaking so much that she had worried she may have to decline. But once in those muscular arms, she knew the wait had been worth it.

Subsequently, plucking up all her courage, she had invited Toby to call upon her the following afternoon and had been sick with nerves until the butler announced his arrival.

What followed, of course, was fairly predictable but, having suffered the torment, for the first time in her life, of fearing her desire was one-sided, Caroline's feelings for Toby Allenby were quite unlike any she had experienced before. Although not a condition she was familiar with, she could almost believe herself in love with the man. Allowing oneself to fall in love, though, was not, in Caroline Levington's opinion, an admirable trait. It epitomized vulnerability, a weak attribute with which the countess had no desire to be associated. Her feelings for Toby Allenby, therefore, remained safely locked in her heart. And there they would remain, hidden from the world and, most importantly, from Toby Allenby himself.

Yet, for all her obsession with the man, Caroline had other, much more practical, issues to consider. Toby's title, as Marquis of Yarm, meant he already ranked above her husband who was a mere earl. But, titles aside, Toby still relied upon an allowance from his father. As generous as this was, the duke might as well have placed the entire amount directly into the hands of Jack Wilmott and the like, bypassing his son completely.

No, as much as she adored him, there was no way, at the present time, Toby could even begin to keep Caroline in the style to which she had become accustomed. That was not to say, of course, that that would always be the case. When Toby eventually came into his inheritance as the new Duke of Wolsington, it would put a completely different slant on things. For that, Caroline had been content to bide her time, confident of the firm hold she exerted over her lover. Naturally, she allowed Toby the odd little dalliance. Men, after all, would be men. Her spies had informed her just last month that he had developed a penchant for a pretty little actress by the name of Francesca, at the Theatre Royal in Drury Lane. Caroline knew the affair would not last long; they never did. And they certainly never proved any threat to her long-term plans. When the time came, she would rid herself of her ineffectual husband and use every one of her unfailing charms to persuade Toby that she would make him the most perfect duchess.

Now, though, this ridiculous will business could jeopardize everything. Any solution had to be temporary. Caroline intended to find Toby a bride who not only bored him to distraction, but who could be as easily disposed of as her own husband when the time was right. A pliable little miss who could be dispatched to the country with a divorce certificate and a nice little settlement under her belt.

Caroline's guts twisted at the notion of an alternative scenario—Toby falling in love with another woman. For all titles and money vied for supremacy on her list of priorities, not far behind was her future with Toby. A mere twenty-six months of enjoying the man was not enough. She wanted another twenty-six months, and another. For, if there was one thing about which Caroline Levington was certain, it was that she would never tire of Toby Allenby. Irritate her he might with his laissez-faire attitude; infuriate her he might with his predictable unreliability; but tire her?

Never.

~ * ~

The fact that the words had been scribed over one hundred years before, and in German, was not the least bit important. King George I's written observation that Diddington was the prettiest place in the whole of England still continued to inspire pride in its residents. Their tireless efforts to maintain that image, combined with the town's natural charm and beauty ensured that, a century on, Diddington remained the envy of every one of its many visitors.

The Thames, which meandered at a leisurely pace directly through its middle, divided the town into two. At this time of year, the river's grassy banks were peppered with dazzling daisies and glistening dandelions, while elegant swans and colorful ducks bobbed about the water's surface. The town itself was a maze of enchanting cobbled streets where timber-framed Tudor buildings juxtaposed perfectly with modern shops and dwellings. Flowers abounded, spilling out of meticulously tended window boxes or crammed into minute gardens. And the air was filled with the rich, mouth-watering aromas of baking bread, roasting chickens and freshly brewed coffee.

As Harry accompanied his mother to the milliner's that morning, he noticed a palpable buzz of excitement about the town. It took him but a few moments to ascertain that it was actually his and his mother's presence that were the cause of all this heightened activity. This fact was endorsed the moment they pushed open the door to the milliner's shop and a tinkling bell announced their arrival.

"Oh my word," flustered Mrs. Clark, its stout proprietor. In a flash, she sprang to her feet, tossed aside the hat she had been decorating and sank into the deepest curtsy Harry had ever seen. "What an honor," she gushed, her chubby cheeks flushed with pleasure as she came to a standing position and began furiously smoothing down her skirts. "What an honor indeed. May I say how thrilled we all are to have you here in Diddington, your grace? And you too, your lordship." She threw Harry a broad toothless grin. "I own, Lady Allenby, the town is awash with talk of the handsome new owner of the hall. Not, I might add, that we weren't all dreadfully sorry to hear of your dear aunt's demise. Lady O'Hare was such a gracious lady—very gracious indeed. Although, I don't mind telling you, she did like her little pranks. Quite a monkey she could be at times. Do you know, she once made the poor vicar—"

Lady Allenby, regal in black bombazine, flashed the milliner her most disarming smile. "Thank you, Mrs. Clark," she said, adroitly interrupting the woman's ramblings. "I am sure my aunt shall be missed by a great many people."

The expression on Mrs. Clark's now scarlet face left little doubt that she was not at all accustomed to having her stories cut short. As if reminding herself of the eminence of her audience, she quickly rearranged her astonished countenance into one of beatific interest. She turned her attention to Harry.

"When, may I ask, are you thinking of taking up permanent residence at the hall, my lord?"

Lady Allenby gave a meaningful little cough. "It has not yet been decided which of my sons will be residing at the hall, Mrs. Clark. There are one or two...*complications* regarding my aunt's will."

Mrs. Clark's brown eyes sparkled with the obvious anticipation of one on the verge of procuring the most valuable nugget of gossip the town had had for several years. "Oh!" she exclaimed, failing dismally to feign nonchalance. "So it may well be Lord *Toby* who will be removing here?"

The duchess sailed over to a set of shelves upon which a number of hats and bonnets were displayed. "The matter is still to be settled, Mrs. Clark," she said, her tone leaving little doubt that she did not wish to discuss the subject further. "All I can tell you at the moment is that my husband and I, and Lord Harry, shall be spending a little time at the hall before we return to London." She picked up a wide-brimmed cerise hat with an ostrich feather tucked in its band. "Now, do tell me, Mrs. Clark, would it be at all possible to reproduce this delightful creation in black?"

~ * ~

The announcement of Miss Maria Dove's impending arrival had resulted in two things. The first was a flurry of cleaning activity at Hartley House. The second, as Lady Winchester herself had correctly predicted, was a deal of disruption to her meticulously planned timetable.

"It is an imposition of unpardonable proportions," she grumbled as she inspected the room she had ordered be made up for their unexpected guest. "It is not even as if we know one thing about the girl. Our connection is...*tenuous,* to say the least. We have neither seen nor heard from your old governess, Miss Wilson, in over three years. How she could possibly consider that we should be remotely interested in accommodating her niece is an assumption that defies comprehension. Not only do I find it impudent, but—"

"Well," cut in Louisa, who had heard this same speech some three times now, "Miss Wilson does say in her letter that Miss Dove is a most reserved and personable young lady, Mama, as indeed, was Miss Wilson herself. And perhaps it may even make a pleasant change to have a guest. We can... show her around Diddington. Take her to the old church at Little Hampton; and perhaps, if she is interested in architecture, the Tudor buildings at Oakhampton.

"Hmph," snorted Lady Winchester. "And when do you suggest we find time for all this gallivanting? My days are full enough as it is."

Bracing herself, Louisa muttered, "Well, perhaps you could, um, make some changes to your timetable, Mama. Temporarily of course."

The look which Lady Winchester flashed her daughter needed no vocal accompaniment.

~ * ~

Miss Maria Dove arrived at Hartley House at three

o"clock the following afternoon. Korbett announced her arrival as Louisa and her mother were busy at their embroidery in the sun-filled drawing-room.

Louisa's first impression of their houseguest, as the girl entered the room and dipped a curtsy, was that any changes to Lady Winchester's timetable to accommodate trips to churches or Tudor buildings would most likely not be necessary. Miss Dove, although undoubtedly pretty, did certainly not present the image of a young lady who would uphold an interest in such fascinating cultural relics.

At eight-and-ten, Maria Dove was some two years younger than Louisa but more than a foot taller. She had a clear peachy complexion, a halo of strawberry-blonde ringlets and a set of wide sparkling blue eyes. But the girl's obvious charms did not stop there. The moment she removed her pelisse to reveal an indecently deep-cut lilac gown and an equally indecent voluptuous bosom, Louisa's heart sank to the floor. The girl's appearance, combined with her brash air of confidence, made her the very epitome of everything Louisa knew Lady Winchester despised. Everything that reminded her mother of a previously employed chambermaid—the woman with whom her husband had run off.

Miraculously, although Louisa immediately detected the older woman's hostility to their guest, Maria Dove appeared oblivious to it. The disapproving glares, sniffs and biting comments which dominated the girl's first thirty minutes in Hartley House seemed to float directly over her ringleted head, as did the fact that she was, particularly given the tenuousness of her link to the family, being awarded very generous hospitality.

"Hmm," the newcomer sniffed, as Louisa showed her to her bedchamber—a pretty room decorated in shades of yellow and cream, with a dressing table, a writing desk, a small sofa and a stunning view out over the front of the house. "Ain't yer got 'owt bigger?"

Louisa, who had never before heard such a broad Yorkshire accent, pulled a rueful face. "Well, um, no," she admitted. "We did think this would suit you very well. There is, after all, everything you should need. And the view is quite spectacular." She gestured to the window, hoping to demonstrate her point.

Maria Dove appeared not the least bit interested in views. She plumped down onto the bed and asked, without a hint of embarrassment, "Now then, what are t" men like round these parts?"

Nonplussed, Louisa turned from the window to face the younger girl. "The-the men?"

"Aye. Yer know. Them yer amuse yerself with."

A deep flush began creeping over Louisa's cheeks. "Well." She gulped. "They are, um—"

"Mind, I'm not expecting t" meet one I'm actually going t" marry. Not *"ere*," sniffed Maria Dove imperiously. "Anyone worth marrying'll be up in London for t" Season." She heaved a rueful sigh. ""Tis a shame me aunt weren't acquainted with nobody in London. This is nearest she could manage."

"Oh," gasped Louisa, taken aback by the girl's frankness. "Well, er, never mind. I am sure you shall have a perfectly nice time here anyway. There is a great deal to, um…to see—some very interesting architecture. We have a fine example of a Norman church at Little Hampton and some Tudor buildings at Oakhampton which are particularly famed for their—"

Maria Dove began examining her fingernails. "Mind you, even though me aunt couldn't manage t" get me t" London, I wasn't idiot enough t" turn down chance t" get away. I ask yer, who would want t" waste another summer in Yorkshire? Most exciting thing that ever happens is chickens laying an extra egg. At least I'll have chance o" some fun "ere. Yer do like a bit o" fun, I take it?" She fixed Louisa with a piercing blue stare.

Louisa quailed. "Well, I, er—"

Maria Dove flopped onto her back and began laughing uproariously. "Oh, what a grand time I'm going t" "ave. And yer'll have t" introduce me t" all t" men yer know. Just "cause they'll not be worth marrying, doesn't mean they'll not be amusing." All at once, she sat bolt upright, causing Louisa to jump. "Now, when am I going t" meet "em?"

Five

The morning following Harry and his mother's visit to the milliner's, an invitation was delivered to Diddington Hall. It was to a ball being held by Lady Merchiston—one of Millicent O'Hare's dearest friends.

"Surely the woman doesn't actually expect us to go," grumbled the duke, over his breakfast of scrambled eggs. "It is, after all, only a few days since the funeral."

"But that's just it, dear," replied Lady Allenby, diligently buttering her slice of toast. "Lady Merchiston says that, as the date of the ball coincides with what would have been Aunt Millie's ninetieth birthday, and as we kept the funeral a small family affair, she has decided to hold the ball in her honor. It will, she says, permit the townspeople the opportunity of celebrating Aunt Millie's life. And we, as her only living family, are to be the guests of honor. I'm afraid we have little choice in the matter, Charles. All three of us shall *have* to attend."

Harry set down his cup with a sense of purpose. "I am sure it will suffice if only you and Father attend, Mother. I really cannot see the need for all three of us to go."

The duchess twisted her pretty features into an expression Harry found all too familiar. He awaited the arrival of two plump tears. They appeared with predictable efficiency.

"Now, Harry," she whimpered, "whatever would people think if you were not to attend? It would be the height of disrespect. It would be shunning these people's generosity. It would be disloyal to Aunt Millie. It would be…"

Harry rolled his eyes. Following her trick with the will, he was devoid of any loyalty to Great Aunt Millie but he knew his mother well enough to realize that if he did not acquiesce, he would never hear the last of it.

"Very well then," he huffed, as he pushed back his chair from the table and thrust to his feet. "I shall make a fleeting appearance. I shall *not* be staying all evening."

"Of course not, dear," murmured the duchess.

The slight hint of victory in her tone did not go unnoticed.

~ * ~

Back in London, Toby Allenby thought he should prefer to chew off one of his own fingers than attend Lady Carnaby's musical soirée that evening. Not that musical soirées ever featured highly on Toby's list of favored entertainments. This one, he had a strong presentiment, was going to be particularly hideous. Caroline, in a very strange mood, had been so insistent on his attendance that Toby harbored a strong suspicion she was up to something.

It did not take long before he discovered exactly what his mistress was plotting. She accosted him the moment he entered the long saloon of Lady Carnaby's Mayfair townhouse. Hanging onto the arm of her husband, whose impressive height and build Toby had always found a little intimidating, she was attired in a gown of silver taffeta, which clung to every one of her delicious curves.

"Ah, Lord Allenby," she gushed. "How delightful to see you this evening. We did so hope you would put in an appearance, did we not, Edmund?"

A look of bewilderment settled over the unsuspecting Lord Levington's rosy-cheeked countenance, giving Toby the distinct impression that him putting in an appearance had not so much as crossed the man's mind. Hardly surprising, given that Levington's mind was usually occupied with very little other than matters of an equine nature. Nevertheless, evidently deeming it wise to agree with his wife, the earl nodded his head of dark red hair.

"And we are not the only guests who hoped to see you, my lord," continued Caroline archly. "I have been talking to the lovely Miss Bettina Bott and, if I am not mistaken, I believe the lady quite anxious to make your acquaintance." She gazed up at her husband through a fan of silky lashes. "You don't mind if I take a moment to introduce Lord Allenby to Miss Bott do you, darling?"

The earl, who, Toby genuinely believed, suspected nothing of his affair with his wife, began chuckling. "Not at all, my love. Although you should be aware, sir," he informed Toby, "that Caroline does seem intent on a little matchmaking this evening. She has scarcely talked of anything else for the last two days."

Toby raised his eyebrows. "Really?" he said, spearing Caroline with a questioning glare.

"Do come along, Lord Allenby," chivvied Caroline, swapping her hold of her husband's arm for that of Toby's. "If I do not introduce you now, we shall have to wait until after the performances. And that, I am sure, shall be far too long for any of us."

She began steering him in the direction of a gaggle of girls in the corner. Eager not to raise suspicion amongst the other guests, Toby plastered a smile onto his face, nodding to various acquaintances as they crossed the room. "What on earth are you up to, Caroline?" he muttered through clenched teeth.

"Exactly what I told you, my sweet," replied Caroline through her own fixed grin. "I am finding you a wife."

A host of angry retorts crammed in Toby's throat but he had no time to voice any of them as they were suddenly upon the group. His spirits lifted slightly as he noticed a pretty little redhead, but his optimism was short-lived.

"Lord Allenby, may I present Miss Bettina Bott," declared Caroline, with a great sense of occasion.

The girl directly in front of Toby spun around to face him. Twice his girth, she wore a fussy gown the color of dried mud, and sported a dark shadow above her upper lip that would have put that of most men to shame. Time seemed to stand still for Toby. He was swamped by the sensation of sinking into a very deep pit of despair. Surely to God, Caroline did not expect him to marry this creature. The very thought made him—

The countess's voice jolted him back to the present moment.

"Please do forgive my appalling manners," she declared, her tone dripping with insincerity. "However, I am afraid I shall be forced to leave you two good people alone. I have just spotted Lady Ambridge, to whom I must speak on a matter of prodigious importance. Although," she tittered, "I am sure it signifies little whether I am here or not. You two will, I am certain, deal famously together." She shot them her broadest smile before whisking around and disappearing in a cloud of expensive perfume.

Now up to his neck in despair, Toby realized that not only had the rest of the group disappeared, but also that Miss Bott was staring at him with something of an expectant expression upon her piggy face. At a loss as to what else to do, he cleared his throat.

"Er, do you, um, do you enjoy musical soirées, Miss Bott?"

The girl clapped her gloved hands together. "Oh, above all things, sir," she replied in a high-pitched squeak. "I am to perform here myself this very evening—on the pianoforte."

Toby furrowed his brow. "Really? And what, may I ask, are you to perform?"

Miss Bott launched into a disconcerting mixture of giggling and snorting. "I'm afraid I can't possibly tell you, sir. Lady Levington insisted I keep it a surprise."

Toby's jaw tightened. "Did she indeed?"

He slowly turned his head until Caroline came into view, catching her eye immediately. Strategically placed amongst a group of chattering women, she was obviously watching his every move. As if to confirm this assumption, she lifted her hand and affected a very unsubtle wave. An excited Miss Bott returned it so effusively that, as Toby turned back around to the girl, she accidentally caught his cheek, slapping him right across the face.

The thing that had surprised Toby most about Miss Bott's musical performance was that he had managed to endure it for a full twenty minutes. Never had he heard anything more painful in his entire life. No sooner had Miss Bott screeched her final note, than Toby decided he had had quite enough of Caroline's ridiculous plan. He would head over to Drury Lane, where much pleasanter distractions awaited him.

Caroline's warning tone speared him just as he reached

the door. "I do hope you are not contemplating leaving, Lord Allenby."

He whipped around, preparing to tell her that that was exactly what he was about to do. But, to his grave annoyance, he discovered she was not alone.

"I was just telling Miss Bott how it was quite uncanny her performing *A Country Garden*, which, I happen to know, is one of your favorite songs, my lord."

Miss Bott broke into another fit of snorting giggles. "Oh, were you surprised, sir?"

Toby met Caroline's steely gaze. "Very surprised, Miss Bott. A most...agreeable coincidence."

Caroline's mouth stretched into a triumphant smile. "Did I mention, my lord, that I, too, am to hold a musical soirée? On Friday of this week?"

Toby's eyes narrowed. "No, you did not, madam."

Caroline's smile did not waver for a second. "And I am assuming we may count on your attendance, Lord Allenby. You would, I am sure, not wish to forgo another of Miss Bott's delightful renditions."

Recognizing this as neither the time nor the place to tell his mistress exactly what he thought of Miss Bott's renditions, Toby forced his lips into a sardonic grin. "Indeed I would not, madam," he replied, before swinging around and marching out of the room.

Outside on the pavement, Toby took a moment to collect himself. He could barely believe what he had just experienced— his own mistress plotting to find him a wife. The very notion was preposterous. Since she had first announced the idea, Caroline had refrained from mentioning it again. Consequently, Toby had given the matter no further thought, assuming she must have been jesting. He should have known better. Caroline Levington had never jested in her life.

The change in her behavior since that evening had not passed Toby by. In truth, he'd begun to find her moods unsettling. On several occasions lately, he had caught a glimmer of something disturbing in those violet eyes, something that set his nerves on edge. Initially, he could not deny that it had been Caroline's persistent air of danger that had both attracted and fascinated him. It clung to her person like an intoxicating scent.

Some two years on though, the novelty had paled. Toby had grown wary of the woman's volatile nature and afraid of what he might find if he dared to scratch beneath his mistress's unblemished surface...

Some three months into their affair, it had come to Caroline's attention that she was not the only object of Toby's desire. As munificent as ever, he had been sharing his affections with the comely widow from the Garfields' dinner party. In the ensuing confrontation, the countess had ranted and raved so much that Toby had feared not only for his own safety, but also for Caroline's sanity.

Then, a few days afterwards, a series of bizarre events had occurred. First, the lovely widow had awoken one morning to find a dead rat in her bed. Second, she became the target of a particularly venomous campaign in the scandal sheets, the outrageous claims of which completely obliterated any hope of her reputation being restored. And third, her carriage was run off the road in a very dubious "accident".

All these happenings had caused Toby a deal of concern. So much concern, that he had ended the relationship forthwith. Caroline, unsurprisingly, had denied any part in the widow's misfortunes, but not before Toby had detected a distinct shift in her mood—from spite to victory.

Ever since then, Toby had dared to stray on only a handful of occasions, always ensuring his tracks were well hidden. He was confident Caroline knew nothing of his arrangement with his little actress. That dalliance had already gone on longer than he had planned, and longer than was probably wise. Yet, the more volatile Caroline's behavior became, the more the thespian's uncomplicated company appealed. In fact, if he managed to flag down a Hackney cab, he might just fit in a visit to her this evening. At that thought, Toby immediately cheered.

~ * ~

Alone in her comfortable cream and yellow bedchamber at Hartley House, Maria Dove pinched herself. She really could not believe her luck. Her plans were progressing better than even she had expected. Not only had she managed to escape the damp, dreary, egg-laying confines of Yorkshire, but she was staying in a fine house, granted, not as fine as she would have liked, but much better than her ma's tiny, run-down cottage *and* she was off to her first ball that evening.

Since arriving in Diddington, Maria had felt compelled to pinch herself on several occasions, just to affirm she wasn't dreaming. Not that it was perfect, mind. She would have much preferred to have been in London where she could have snared herself an earl or a marquis or a viscount or, in fact, any man with a title and an income to match. But that would have to wait until next year. For now, she intended to enjoy her newfound freedom and have some fun. Nobody was going to stop her, not even that sour-faced Lady Winchester who was clearly jealous of her youth and good looks.

Maria smiled with satisfaction at her reflection in the gilded mirror above the fireplace. She pinched her cheeks and tugged down the bodice of her new gown just a shade further. She looked such a fine lady that Ned Stickleback would hardly recognize her.

Needless to say, the same Ned Stickleback had been furious when Maria had informed him of her plans. Hardly surprising, given how he practically worshipped the ground she walked on. Still, that wasn't her fault. She hadn't encouraged him—well, not much anyway. He certainly kept her amused. He'd mastered one particular trick that kept her very well amused indeed. But Maria only entertained Ned because there was no one else who remotely interested her in their boring, poverty-stricken little town. She would never dream of marrying a lowly farmer like Ned Stickleback, even though he had already asked her a half-dozen times. The last occasion had been only days before she'd left.

"Fer God's sake, Ned," she'd sneered, plucking out remnants of the haystack from her hair. "Are yer expectin" me... *me*, t" be a farmer's wife?"

"And what's wrong wi" that?" Ned had demanded, tucking his shirt into his breeches. "It were good enough fer me ma and "er ma afore that."

"*I* am not yer ma, Ned," Maria had sniffed. "Destined for bigger and better things I be."

"Oh, aye," Ned had mocked. "And what bigger and better things be they then?"

Maria had sighed dreamily. "A big house... jewels...

gowns… hundreds o" servants attending me every need-"

Ned had burst out laughing. "You mark me words, Maria Dove, yer'll be me wife within a twelve-month or me name's not Ned Stickleback." And with that he had marched out of the barn, still chuckling.

Furious, Maria had snatched up a pitchfork and launched it at the door just as it swung shut behind him. "*Your* name might be Ned Stickleback," she had screeched. "But *mine* will never be Maria Stickleback. Never."

The young Mr. Stickleback, though, was not the only one who considered Maria's ambitions well above her station. All the girls in the village thought she was hoity-toity too.

"Oh, make way fer t" duchess," they would snigger as she sailed past them in the street, her nose high in the air. "Would yer like us t" lick yer shoes clean, yer ladyship?"

Maria had long since determined that they could all go to hell—which were exactly the words her ma used. They would show them, her ma had insisted. Maria was worth ten of them. She had assets—good assets—and she should use them to her advantage. Her ma had saved every penny and every scrap of fabric she could from her job as a seamstress to make Maria an array of flattering gowns, and she'd applied every drop of her scheming ingenuity to concoct this plan. Maria's aunt, a stuck-up governess, and the only member of the family to escape Yorkshire, had been their only hope. Fortunately, Maria hadn't seen her relative for over ten years, so, when her ma had written and begged her assistance in helping them establish a better life for dear little Maria; one where a quiet, studious young lady could experience something of the world and broaden her horizons, Mrs. Dove had been able to lay it on thick.

Initially, Maria and her mother had worried the plan might not work. Miss Wilson, snooty tartar that she was, had been working at a seminary before her appointment at Hartley House, and had then moved on to a family in the wilds of Scotland. The Winchesters, being the only folk of quality with whom she was acquainted in the south, were, therefore, the Doves' only hope.

The stupid dithering Miss Wilson had written back with all manner of objections, about how she didn't feel it proper to approach Lady Winchester after so many years, and how it would seem like the greatest imposition. Maria had seen her mother's highly effective manipulative streak come into play at that point. Elsie had written back immediately that if, as her younger sister had at one time mentioned, the Winchesters held her in such high regard, then surely they could do this one small favor for a desperate young lady—particularly when they had all that space in that grand house. Worn down by her sister's incessant pleas, a reluctant Miss Wilson had capitulated and the letter had been sent to Hartley House.

Maria Dove banished all thoughts of her life in Yorkshire as she arranged her blonde ringlets. Her new life was about to start tonight at Lady Merchiston's ball. And she was so excited she could hardly wait.

~ * ~

In his dressing room at Diddington Hall, Lord Harry Allenby was not in the best of humors as he prepared for Lady Merchiston's ball. His mother really was the limit. He knew he should be firmer with her but the pathetic fact was that the woman had both Harry and his father wrapped around her little finger. Toby, needless to say, was quite another matter—but then Toby was always another matter.

Harry was angry at neither Toby nor his mother. He was furious with himself. He really should have put his foot down. The very reason he had wished to spend time in Diddington was to escape the endless round of so-called amusements the Season had to offer. He had long since had his fill of those.

Ever since their first appearance in Society, Harry and his brother had been regarded as two of London's most eligible bachelors. This accolade had never been of particular interest to Harry but, since Clara's death, he had found it an increasingly heavy burden to bear. Every woman he encountered appeared to be aware of his circumstances, but remained convinced that she would be the one to change him. That *she* would be the one with whom he would fall in love again and wander off into the sunset to live happily ever after.

Well, Harry Allenby had no intention of falling in love again. He was devoid of any inclination at all to do so. For with love came pain, and Harry Allenby had had quite enough of that.

Dismissing his valet, Harry turned to the looking glass above the fireplace and began fiddling with the folds of his neck cloth. He really was in no mood for a party. The mere thought of a stream of eager provincial mamas presenting their doe-eyed daughters to him nauseated him. All at once, a smile touched his lips as an image of another pair of eyes flashed before him—large, brown and bespectacled.

He grinned as he recalled their owner scurrying away from him like a frightened rabbit. Perhaps she would be present this evening. He thought it unlikely. She had not appeared the sort of young lady who flitted around ballrooms batting her lashes at every gentleman who came within ten feet of her. She had seemed...*different* somehow. Of course, he was being ridiculous even thinking about her. She had not uttered so much as a word to him. And all he had done was bluster on about that ridiculously unseasonable wasp. Not that any of it mattered. It didn't. Not in the slightest. Harry had no interest in young ladies. No interest at all. His heart did, and always would, belong to Clara Walpole. It had been buried alongside her and there it would remain—cold in her grave.

~ * ~

In the drawing-room at Hartley House, Eliza Winchester's dark eyes appeared to be on the verge of popping out of their sockets.

"Well," beamed Maria Dove. She picked up her skirts and twirled around. "What d' yer think?"

Louisa, who had entered the room ahead of her mother, had already absorbed the full effect of their houseguest's revealing white gown. She braced herself for her mother's cutting comments. None came. For once, Lady Winchester was speechless—a circumstance for which Louisa was extremely grateful, given the look of horror that had settled over her mother's face. Miraculously, Maria Dove appeared oblivious to her hostess's disapproval.

"A sight fer sore eyes, ain't it?" she cooed, running a disparaging eye over Lady Winchester's plain gray creation. "I don't mind telling yer, it cost a packet."

"Really," sniffed Lady Winchester, recovering something of her equilibrium. "Then may I say what a great waste of—"

Louisa cut in swiftly, anxious to avoid another sniping session. "I was just telling Miss Dove how it is likely the whole of Diddington will be attending the ball, Mama. By the end of this evening her face will be known to the entire town."

Lady Winchester sniffed. "And not *just* her face."

Six

While preparations for Lady Merchiston's ball were well underway in Diddington, Toby Allenby prepared for a much more...*intimate* occasion in the capital. His ardor strengthened with every one of the barely perceptible kisses Caroline feathered down his spine; her lips sensuously brushing against his skin.

"Now, darling," she whispered, "I do hope... that you will not... be late for my... musical soirée this evening ... I would recommend... you engage Miss Bott... in a little... conversation... before we start the performances."

Toby's ardor shriveled as effectively as if someone had dunked him in a barrel of iced water. He rolled over to find Caroline gazing down at him, a languorous smile playing about her mouth. "We must, after all, my sweet, make the most of every opportunity."

Toby sat up. He had intended broaching the matter of Miss Bott the moment he arrived but, as the countess had greeted him in a particularly effusive manner, wearing nothing more than a pair of diamond earrings, his intentions had been somewhat waylaid.

"Look Caroline, do we really have to go through with this ridiculous charade? Why can't I just marry a girl I can rub along easily with? A girl who will not turn the milk sour over the breakfast table? After all, *I* shall be the one who has to live with her."

"But darling, you agreed," pouted Caroline.

"No, I did not agree," countered Toby. "I seem to recall that you suggested you find me a wife and then completely sidetracked me, thereby ensuring we had no chance to discuss the matter further. Now, if you would just permit me to get on with the task, I am sure I can find someone in the next few days and, with a special license, have her down the aisle in a couple of weeks."

Caroline took a deep breath, quelling her panic at the mere thought of Toby walking down the aisle with a girl he could "rub along easily with"; a girl he might very well end up falling in love with. Not that she would ever dream of admitting such fears. To do so would mean she'd relinquished the upper hand—and upper hands were things upon which Caroline Levington kept a very firm grip. She adopted a different tack—much more effective and much more her usual style.

"I'm afraid that will not do at all, my sweet. If you do not permit *me* to choose your bride, then I'm afraid you shall have to resign yourself to remaining a bachelor."

Toby's brows drew together. "What does it signify, Caroline? Whoever the girl is, my marrying her will make no difference to us."

"Perhaps," murmured the countess, brushing a wayward lock of his hair from his face. "However, I have no desire to run that risk, Toby. I am exceedingly happy with our arrangement and should like it to continue *exactly* as it is."

Toby's exasperation mounted. "There's no reason why it shouldn't. You know better than anyone, Caroline, that just because one is riveted, does not mean one cannot entertain a lover."

The countess pressed her lips to his cheek. "I know that very well indeed, Toby, but nevertheless, *I* shall be choosing your bride."

He folded his arms over his bare chest. "Well, don't include me in your ludicrous scheme," he huffed. "There's no way I could contemplate so much as an afternoon in Miss Bott's company, let alone a lifetime. While you are occupied with your plans, *I* shall be occupied with my own."

Caroline sighed ruefully. "Oh, I did so hope it would not come to this."

Toby screwed up his nose. "Come to what?"

"Threats, my love."

"Threats?" An uneasy feeling wormed its way under Toby's skin. "What do you mean, *threats*?"

Caroline's countenance was one of pure innocence. "I mean, my darling, that you leave me with little choice but to inform you that, should you proceed with your own plans, then I shall be forced to involve my contacts."

Toby narrowed his eyes. "What *contacts*?"

"My very…*influential* contacts," Caroline clarified, one manicured fingernail delicately tracing a line down Toby's upper arm. "It would take very little effort on their part to ensure no decent woman of whom your parents would approve would come within a mile of you. And without a bride, my darling, you would, regrettably, lose out on your inheritance and remain up to your beautiful neck in debt. A circumstance which, I am sure, would not please Mr. Wilmott at all."

As she broke into a victorious smile, Toby's innards twisted into a very painful knot.

~ * ~

Lord and Lady Merchiston's residence, a spectacular Elizabethan E-shaped house with latticed bay windows and a thatched roof, held pride of place as Diddington's second largest dwelling–after the hall.

When their original invitation to the ball had arrived some weeks before, Lady Winchester, satisfied that she and her daughter had already put in an appearance at one social event that month, had declined, using one of her exhaustive list of excuses. Earlier that week, though, Lady Merchiston had forwarded a note informing Lady Winchester that the event was now to be held in honor of the late Lady Millicent O'Hare and, knowing in what high regard she had held Lady O'Hare, perhaps she would like to reconsider having the headache that evening and attending after all.

Lady Merchiston had been quite correct in her conjecture. Millicent O'Hare had indeed been one of the few women Eliza Winchester held in high regard. Not least of all, because she had never succumbed to that pathetic female urge of throwing her life away on a member of the opposite sex. Millicent O'Hare had been an independent soul and, although perhaps a tad too full of life for Eliza's subdued tastes, had nonetheless proved something of an inspiration to her. So, much to Lady Merchiston's amazement, Maria Dove's delight and Louisa Winchester's regret, it was decided that the residents of Hartley House would attend the ball after all.

They were not the only ones. Louisa could not recall ever having been in such a long line of carriages—nor one so slow. She could scarcely wait until they arrived at the house. Although she had no desire to attend the ball, it would be infinitely preferable to sitting in the carriage with Maria Dove's incessant questions about "'t men and "t money" interspersed with Lady Winchester's disapproving sniffs and tuts.

Louisa gazed out of the window as their conveyance trundled through the wrought-iron gates and onto the long drive leading to their destination. In the dim light, she could make out an unfamiliar navy-blue crested carriage drawing to a halt before the house. Three figures alighted. She nudged her spectacles a shade higher on her nose but the gesture did nothing to improve her vision.

A strange fizzling sensation began in the pit of her stomach—the same sensation she had experienced the evening before when an unsettling thought had occurred to her—Would the young gentleman she had met under the willow tree be attending the ball? She had quickly dismissed the thought. Of course, he wouldn't. Obviously, he was not a resident of the town or she would have seen him before. Then again, she mused, she had never seen the unfamiliar navy-blue crested coach in town either. Her fizzling increased.

By the time the Winchesters and Maria Dove entered the Merchiston residence, it was obvious that the whole of Diddington had turned out in memory of the late Lady O'Hare.

"Well," muttered Lady Winchester with some relief, "I am only grateful I saw fit to change my mind. It would not have done at all if we had been seen as the only residents of the town not in attendance. Goodness only knows what people would have thought of us."

Maria Dove, her blue eyes wide at the glittering spectacle before her, nodded her crown of glistening ringlets, seemingly, for once, in agreement with her hostess. She wasted no time familiarizing herself with her sumptuous surroundings, but whipped a glass of champagne from the tray of a passing footman. "D'yer think there'll be any titled men "ere?"

Lady Winchester shuddered. Piercing her houseguest with a frosty glare she pronounced, "Whether there are any titled gentlemen here or not, Miss Dove, is of no interest to us. And, as you are staying under our roof, I am including *you* in that observation."

Louisa steeled herself for Maria's retort but to her surprise, the girl merely drank down the entire glass of champagne, flashed Lady Winchester a disarming smile, and began weaving her way through the crowd toward the ballroom.

"That girl," Lady Winchester snarled, as they observed Maria's retreating back, "is the most indelicate little strumpet I have ever had the misfortune to—"

"Oh, look, Mama," interjected Louisa, with much more zeal than she was feeling. "There is Lady Merchiston. Do let us go and say hello."

Despite the impressive proportions of the Merchiston residence, it was clear to Louisa, as she sat on one of the rosewood chairs at the side of the ballroom, that it would have been nigh on impossible to squeeze another living soul inside the room–not even one of her diminutive proportions.

She could scarcely believe Diddington had so many residents although she had recognized several people who were not normally invited to such affairs–including Mrs. Clark, the milliner and Mr. Rivers, the owner of the haberdashery. Clearly, these usually omitted pillars of the business community had been very well acquainted with Lady O'Hare, and Louisa thought it extremely gracious of Lady Merchiston to include them this evening. She had no doubt Lady O'Hare would have been both impressed and flattered at the turnout. But she had, after all, been one of Diddington's most popular–and colorful–characters.

It was now some three years since Louisa had first made Lady O'Hare's acquaintance. Engrossed in a book under the willow tree by the river, Louisa had looked up in astonishment when Lady O'Hare, out for a stroll, had companionably plonked herself down on the blanket beside her. The old woman had remained there for several hours.

Though unaccustomed to strangers, Louisa had felt immediately at ease in Lady O'Hare's company. They had talked about all manner of things. And, for the first time in her life,

Louisa had even detailed her mother's *circumstances*. Naturally, she had also confessed her passion for books. To her immense delight, Lady O'Hare had offered her an open invitation to Diddington Hall and its enormous library. Louisa, not wishing to take advantage, and aware that she had merely a fleeting acquaintance with the woman, had only plucked up the courage to visit on some half-dozen occasions, despite Lady O'Hare's insistence that she should call more often.

She felt a flicker of sadness that she was unlikely ever to set foot in that magical room again. Immediately she scolded herself. She should be grateful that she'd had the opportunity to visit it at all. She would never forget Lady O'Hare and her exceeding kindness. She turned to her mother to voice this opinion, but to her astonishment, discovered her mother's chair empty. Evidently, she had been so lost in her thoughts that she had not paid the slightest heed to her mother's movements. Wherever could she have gone? She only hoped it was nowhere near Maria Dove.

Louisa had searched the supper-room, the withdrawing-room and even ventured to peep her head into every one of the many side-rooms. Still she had not found her mother. She had, however, discovered Maria Dove behind one of the pot plants with a wizened old man of some seventy-plus years.

"Oh, there, hic, yer are, Miss Winchester," hailed Maria, as Louisa popped her head around the plant. "Been looking f'yer everywhere, so I 'ave. Yer'll 'ave t' excuse me, Colonel." She flashed the man a rueful smile before gliding over to Louisa.

"Boring old, hic, curmudgeon," she muttered, snatching another glass of champagne from a passing tray. "Ain't there no younger ones 'ere?"

"I really wouldn't know, Miss Dove," replied Louisa distractedly. "I am looking for my mother."

Maria Dove gulped down the entire contents of the champagne flute before running the back of her hand across her mouth. "Why don't, hic, yer, hic, come with me and look fer some decent men, hic, instead? Much more, hic, entertaining than yer, hic, miserable mother."

"My mother is not miserable, Miss Dove," Louisa countered. "Through no fault of her own she has been forced to carry a great burden on her shoulders these past twenty years.

She is, in my mind, a most admirable woman."

"She ain't nowt but a sour, hic, old toad."

Recognizing that there would be little point in carrying on this discussion given Maria Dove's inebriated state, Louisa made to distance herself from the girl. "If you don't mind, Miss Dove," she declared stiffly, "I shall continue my search in the garden. It may well be my mother has slipped out for some air."

"Or, hic, maybe she's out there with a, hic, lover," Maria Dove snorted, before collapsing in a heap of hysterical laughter.

Louisa found this remark neither helpful nor diverting. She headed toward a set of French doors, praying that her drunken companion would not follow.

The doors opened out onto a large raised terrace, balustrades on three sides, the fourth one open with steps down to the extensive gardens. Three small groups of people milled about there, chattering and laughing. None of them paid Louisa the slightest heed. She crossed to the top of the steps and peered down into the grounds. A smattering of lanterns hung from various trees and bushes but otherwise she could discern nothing other than uninterrupted darkness. Surely her mother wouldn't have wandered out there alone. But, if she wasn't in the garden, then where was she? It was the only place Louisa had not yet searched. Taking a deep breath, she descended the steps.

"Mama," she called out discreetly.

There was no reply other than a muffled giggle. Louisa ignored it, confident that it would not have come from her mother. Her mother never giggled. In fact, she doubted the woman even knew how.

Louisa had covered quite an expanse when she came upon a large round pond. Several lanterns had been placed atop the stones at its edge to cast a golden glow over the water. With its thick rushes, giant marigolds and exquisite floating lilies it looked quite serene.

This serenity was broken by a pitiful croak. Louisa's heart jumped to her throat. Her eyes quickly scanned the pond until they landed upon a large green frog, stranded on a rock. Its leg was twisted at a most uncomfortable angle. It gazed at Louisa with sorrowful eyes.

"Oh, you poor thing," she whispered.

Seven

Lord Harry Allenby had to confess that the turnout at the Merchistons' ball was nothing short of impressive. He had known Great Aunt Millie had been a popular figure about the town, but quite how popular he had completely underestimated.

Still, impressive turnout notwithstanding, the occasion was every bit as painful as those he was obliged to attend in London. Perhaps even more so–courtesy of the industrious Mrs. Clark. The milliner had evidently considered it her neighborly duty to spread her limited knowledge of what had apparently become termed as The Complication with the Allenby boys' inheritance. Consequently, it now appeared the mission of every interfering tabby in attendance to discover exactly what that Complication involved.

"Dear Olivia is very accomplished on the pianoforte," one such tabby had gushed, thrusting her blushing, spotty daughter before Harry. "And there is, I believe, a magnificent pianoforte at Diddington Hall which she would be delighted to play, should you choose to hold a musical soirée there. Now, do remind me of when you said you are taking up residence there, my lord. I own, my memory is not what it used to be."

This exchange, at which Harry had merely smiled and mumbled some meaningless nonsense that even he didn't understand, was rapidly followed by—

"And Desiree does so love the grounds at Diddington Hall," a big fat ogre of a woman had enthused, as she'd pushed her daughter's unfortunate similar physique right up against

Harry's chest. "She could do wonders redesigning the rose garden when you take up residence permanently. You did say that would be in the summer, did you not, my lord? Quite the perfect time for redesigning a rose garden."

These were the only two examples Harry could recall. The stream of others had already merged into one big forgettable blur. He had endured quite enough for one evening. He would seek out Lady Merchiston, thank her for her hospitality and return forthwith to Diddington Hall. He slipped out from behind the large potted fern which had proved an effective hiding place, and had begun weaving his way through the throng when he spotted two middle-aged matrons, each with a younger girl in tow, heading directly toward him—one from the left and one from the right. Both were brandishing their closed fans in an attempt to catch his attention. They succeeded. Harry turned on his heel and spotted an open French door leading outside. Surely to God, there would be some respite there.

Resisting the urge to run, Harry marched directly across the raised terrace toward the steps. He cleared them two at a time and sought refuge in the dark shadows of the garden, where he stumbled upon an old stone bench. Confident that he was well out of sight, he plopped down upon it. The cool night air, redolent with the sweet smell of honeysuckle and evening primrose, flooded his lungs making him feel instantly better.

A muffled female giggle and an ominous rustle from one of the bushes opposite caused him to start. He smiled as, with accustomed ease, his thoughts turned to Clara. How she had loved taking a moonlit stroll with him, gazing up at the stars and making her silly wishes—wishes even he hadn't been privy to but which, one could only assume, she had been denied the opportunity to realize during her short life.

He tilted his head to the sky. There wasn't a single star to be seen. Not that it mattered. Harry had no idea what he would have wished for, other than the ability to turn back the clock several years. Sighing, he lowered his head again, only to discover a pink and lilac butterfly staring directly at him from the tip of his shoe. How very singular. Shouldn't butterflies be asleep at this time of—

A piercing shriek followed by an almighty splash brought Harry to his feet. He raced down the garden as fast as his legs would carry him. He came upon a pond and, in the middle of it, a young lady with large, brown, bespectacled eyes—and an enormous water lily on her head.

~ * ~

Miss Louisa Winchester had never been so mortified in her entire life. In the process of rescuing the injured frog, she had slipped on a mossy rock and tumbled headfirst into the water, which had proved much deeper than it looked. And now here she was, dripping wet, in the arms of the man with the darkest blue eyes and broadest shoulders she had ever seen, who carried her as effortlessly as if she were a small child. She could not decide if it was that or the fact that she was chilled to the bone, that made her shiver. She was only relieved that her teeth were chattering so uncontrollably she could not even attempt to speak.

As if all that were not humiliating enough, during their progress back to the house, she and the blue-eyed man were attracting quite an audience. Louisa began to panic at the ridiculous spectacle she was certain to create when they entered the ballroom. She was apparently not the only one to whom that thought had occurred. Approaching the steps leading up to the raised terrace, her rescuer called out to a gentleman who was leaning over the balustrade, gazing out into the gardens. So absorbed was the man in his reflections, he did not appear to notice the dripping pair, until her rescuer called out, "Excuse me, Viscount."

The man turned toward them with a start. Louisa noted with dismay that it was Viscount Winston. A shadow of horror settled over his handsome features. "Good God, Harry. And Miss Winchester! Whatever has occurred?"

"You know this young lady, sir?" asked the younger man.

"Indeed I do. She is Miss Louisa Winchester of Hartley House. But whatever is she—"

"Miss Winchester has met with an accident in the pond. As you can see, she is in dire need of a hot bath and dry clothes. I do not wish to create a stir by carrying her through the ballroom and therefore intend using one of the side entrances. I would be much obliged to you, sir, if, in the meantime, you could seek out our hostess, Lady Merchiston, and inform her of what has happened."

Viscount Winston nodded. "Leave it to me, Harry. And I shall also seek out Lady Winchester, the child's mother."

"Harry" whomever he might be, nodded in gratitude and strode around the side of the building while Louisa, to no avail, attempted to control her shivering.

Within minutes of entering the house, such a whirlwind of activity ensued that Louisa could not recall at what point her rescuer had disappeared. Nonetheless, disappeared he had, before she had had a chance to thank him. He had handed her over to a strapping footman who had deposited her in a bedchamber with an enormous fire blazing in the grate. A gaggle of maids had then appeared, whipped away her wet clothes and drawn her a hot bath. She had just been dried off and wrapped in a thick towel, when Lady Merchiston entered the room, proffering a fresh white nightgown.

"It will most likely swamp you, dear girl, but do put it on and keep warm under the bedclothes. You are most welcome to stay the night but, if you prefer to go home, I shall understand perfectly and shall find you something more suitable to wear for the journey."

Louisa had thanked her hostess for her kind offer, but had replied that, if it was not too much trouble, she should prefer to return home with her mother a little later.

Assuring her it was no trouble, Lady Merchiston had then whisked out of the room in order to organize Louisa's traveling attire. She had only been gone a few minutes when Lady Winchester entered, looking several shades paler than usual.

"Good lord, Louisa, whatever are you about?" she declared, scurrying over to the side of the bed and plumping down upon it. "I could scarce believe it when that ghastly viscount informed me you had been in the garden. The garden, I ask you! You know they are the most unsuitable places for unchaperoned young ladies. Have I not told you on several occasions that they are the hunting ground of gentlemen? That they lurk in the shadows, ready to pounce at any moment? It does not bear contemplation. Anything could have happened to you. Absolutely anything."

"But nothing did, Mama," reassured Louisa with a weak smile. "At least, nothing more than my falling into the pond."

A knock on the door caught their attention. As it eased open, a kindly round face appeared.

"Oh, I do hope I am not intruding," said the woman. "Harry has just informed me of his little rescue mission and I did so want to assure myself the young lady was being well attended."

She sailed into the room and around to the opposite side of the bed to that of Lady Winchester. "Do allow me to introduce myself," she declared, with a glowing smile. "I am Lady Arabella Allenby, Duchess of Wolsington. Lady O'Hare was my aunt. My husband and myself and indeed my son, Harry, the rescuer of this young lady, are sojourning awhile at Diddington Hall."

"And how grateful we are, your grace," Lady Winchester said. "Goodness only knows what might have happened to Louisa if your son had not come to her aid. Now, do please permit us to introduce ourselves. I am Lady Winchester. Of Hartley House, ma'am. And this is my daughter, Louisa."

Lady Allenby furrowed her powdered brow. "*Winchester*," she muttered. "Now why does that name sound familiar?" She clapped a hand to her mouth, her navy-blue eyes growing wide. "Oh my word, not Lady *Eliza* Winchester?"

Lady Winchester emitted a shuddering sigh. "I am afraid so."

"Oh, my dear," gushed Lady Allenby, shaking her head. "Such a dreadful business all those years ago. Quite shocking in fact." She broke out into another smile. "Well now, may I suggest that as poor Miss Winchester here is no doubt in need of a little peace and quiet after her ordeal, we ladies retire to the supper-room where you can tell me all about that ghastly drama."

With Louisa having assured her mother that she was well enough to be left alone and that she should like to go home in an hour or so, the two women took their leave of her.

"How ever did you cope with that appalling affair, Lady Winchester?" she heard Lady Allenby asking, just before the door swung shut.

"Well, of course I have never recovered from it," Louisa heard her mother reply. "How can anyone ever recover from such humiliation? I am only grateful that I have had dear Louisa for…"

~ * ~

Back in the library at Diddington Hall, Harry Allenby could not sit still for a single minute. After handing over Miss Winchester to the Merchistons' efficient staff, he had sent a note to his mother asking her to meet him outside the house. Having informed her of the evening's drama, he had then returned directly to Diddington Hall. He had been dripping wet after wading waist-deep into the water, but, more pressing than the need for a hot bath and dry clothes, had been his desire to escape. Holding that tiny, soaked, bedraggled girl in his arms had had rather a peculiar effect on him. Just as with the wasp incident, he had once again been overcome by the need to rescue the tiny creature. Even soaked to the bone she could not have weighed more than a bag of feathers. And, yet again, she had looked so delicate, so fragile, and so incredibly vulnerable—especially with that ridiculous water lily covering half her face.

He couldn't resist a chuckle at the image. At the same time a tingling sensation trickled down his spine as he recalled the way she had regarded him with those huge dark bespectacled eyes.

Quickly, he erased the picture from his mind. Whatever was the matter with him? During the carriage ride home, when images of Miss Winchester had insisted upon invading his consciousness, he had been forced to conclude that the matter could only be boredom. He was completely, utterly and totally bored. Why else would his head be full of some little chit who had not spoken so much as a word to him? It was simply because he had nothing in his life at the moment that remotely interested him.

He poured a tumbler of whiskey and paced around the room, the glass cradled in his hand. A vision of Toby doing exactly the same thing the evening before the will reading, flashed before him. Toby never appeared bored. Yet Harry would not have swapped places with his brother for all the riches in the world. He didn't want Toby's dissipating lifestyle. He wanted something…*useful* to do. Yes, something useful was exactly what he needed. But what? What could he possibly do without treading on other people's toes or stirring up a whole heap of gossip?

There was always the estate of course. Although Great Aunt Millie had employed a very efficient manager several years before who continued to do an admirable job. Perhaps he could do something in the town. No, it really wasn't the done thing and would only create a ludicrous fuss. No, what he needed was something solitary; something that would completely absorb him. He slumped down in the chair behind the ancient oak desk and glanced about the book-lined room.

At the same moment the light scent of lavender hit his nostrils, a bolt of inspiration shot through him. Suddenly he knew exactly what he could do.

~ * ~

In Caroline Levington's elegant music-room, Lord Toby Allenby was decidedly hot under his high-pointed collar. Although he had not considered it possible, Miss Bott's screeched rendition of something resembling *A Country Garden* had sounded even more ghastly the second time around. Or perhaps it was the nauseatingly knowing looks the girl had thrown in his direction that had made it appear so.

Toby felt sick to the core–and not only because of the dreadful performance. Using another of her devious ruses, Caroline had again manipulated him into being alone with Miss Bott earlier. Prattling about a new collection of china she had acquired, the countess had steered them both into the little room in which the service was displayed. Before they had had time to examine so much as a cup, Caroline had suddenly "remembered" that she was to check on the refreshments and would, therefore, have to leave them to it. Toby had spent an awkward few minutes muttering some inanities about handles, plates and floral designs. Miss Bott's piggy eyes had regarded him expectantly all the while. Toby could almost have kissed the stout old dowager who had entered the room shortly afterwards, permitting his escape.

He would have to put an end to this nonsense, he resolved. But how? Caroline had made her intentions perfectly clear. And the knowledge that she would not hesitate in carrying out every word of her threats had Toby's nerves jangling.

"Ah, there you are, Lord Allenby." Caroline's voice sliced through his thoughts as effectively as a cold steel blade. "I was just telling Miss Bott how I have an appointment in

Diddington in a few days' time and, given how delightful the town is at this time of year, the most marvelous thought occurred to me—"

Toby steeled himself.

"You recall you mentioned recently how keen you were to pay a visit to your dear mother at Diddington Hall, my lord? Well—"

Toby's eyes narrowed.

"—I thought to myself, why don't all three of us go together? In my carriage. I can drop you both at the hall, then go onto my appointment. While you, my lord, can show Miss Bott the house. And, of course, she shall have the added advantage of becoming acquainted with your parents. Is that not the most splendid idea?"

Toby could think of a great many words to describe Caroline's plan. Splendid was not amongst them.

~ * ~

Alone in the drawing-room of Hartley House, Lady Eliza Winchester debated the merits of a meticulously planned timetable, when no one but herself took the slightest notice of it. She glanced, for the umpteenth time, at the clock on the mantle. Almost ten o"clock. According to her timetable, everyone should be up, washed, breakfasted, and completing a tour of the gardens by now. But no one, apart from herself, seemed remotely interested in any of these activities. Neither her daughter nor their houseguest had even made it down the stairs.

The lack of regard for her schedule notwithstanding, Eliza had to confess to being more than a little relieved that Maria Dove had not yet appeared. She could not have cared less if she never set eyes upon the wretched hussy again, particularly given the embarrassing debacle of transporting the girl home from the ball the previous evening.

The chit had imbibed so much champagne that it had taken six footmen and three attempts before she was deposited in the carriage. Fortunately for all, once she was inside, she had immediately fallen asleep. The girl really was the outside of enough. Eliza intended to write to the chit's aunt, Miss Wilson, about her behavior just as soon as a little normality was resumed to the household. Although quite when that would be, she had no idea. She was about to despair completely when Louisa entered the room looking as fresh as a daisy in a soft blue day gown.

"Oh, I am so sorry, Mama," she gushed. "I had not realized the time and I was so tired after all the events of yesterday evening that I—"

"It really does not signify, Louisa," said Eliza briskly, sensing a glimmer of hope as her eyes wandered, once again, to the clock. "If you do not dilly-dally over breakfast, we shall still have time for today's planned trip to Diddington."

Louisa, who had feared serious repercussions given the lateness of the hour, had no intentions of dilly-dallying. She was about to dash off to the breakfast-room when she spotted a navy-blue crested conveyance drawing to a halt outside the front door. Out of it stepped Lady Allenby.

"Please do tell me if I am imposing," insisted their charming visitor a few minutes later. "I know it is grotesquely early, but I spotted these delightful violets in the garden this morning and thought immediately of dear Miss Winchester."

"That is most kind of you, ma'am," Louisa smiled as she accepted the pretty posy, neatly tied with a white silk ribbon. "There was really no need."

"Well, as you have no doubt deduced by now, I am the world's worst fusspot," declared Lady Allenby, sinking onto the sofa. "I'm afraid, Miss Winchester, that once one is a mother, one never stops fussing–nor indeed worrying. Even though my two boys are grown men, I do not mind admitting that their antics still cause me many a sleepless night. Toby is a law unto himself. He spends most of his time in London and gets up to goodness only knows what. And Harry—Well, what can one say about Harry?" Her smile faded.

"How long do you intend to stay in Diddington, your grace?" asked Louisa.

Lady Allenby beamed at her. "I'm afraid it is all rather up in the air at the moment. Just between us–and I know this will go no further—" Her navy-blue eyes flitted about the room, ensuring no servants were present. "Aunt Millie added a rather...*strange* clause to her will. She has bequeathed Diddington Hall to one of the boys–whichever one of them marries first."

Louisa, momentarily distracted by a glimpse of Maria Dove hovering in the hallway, furrowed her brow. Had she heard correctly? "So whichever one of your sons marries first, Lady Allenby, will inherit Diddington Hall?" she confirmed.

"That is quite correct, my dear Miss Winchester. The bride must first be approved by my husband and myself. Of course, it will go to Toby. Harry has no intentions of ever marrying. Not since he lost dear Clara. The boy has quite resigned himself to never finding love again. And, I own, he is certainly making no effort to do so, despite my best endeavors to steer him out of the house and into female company. He has not the slightest interest in returning to London for the Season and tells us he plans to remain in Diddington for as long as the fancy takes him."

"I can't say I blame him," uttered Lady Winchester. "I, for one, would certainly never contemplate marriage again. In my opinion, the institution is as advantageous to women as leeches on a corpse and, thank goodness, Louisa shares my sentiments. I have told her on many occasions that, rather than chasing after gentlemen, she is much better engaged indulging her passion for books."

Lady Allenby clapped her hands together. "Miss Winchester has a passion for books? Oh, how very serendipitous. Do you know, Miss Winchester, Harry has just announced to us this morning that he intends to catalogue the whole of the Diddington Hall library? My aunt had often talked of employing someone to do it but never seemed to have time to arrange it— far too busy with her hectic social life, one can only assume. Of course, it must be done at some stage. There are, unquestionably, some very valuable works there. It is a mammoth task —quite colossal in fact. Harry will definitely be in need of some assistance. And, if you are as passionate about books as your mother suggests, Miss Winchester, you would be the most perfect person to help him."

Louisa's brows shot to her hairline. Help the man with the darkest blue eyes and broadest shoulders she had ever seen? The very notion was too terrifying to contemplate. Thank goodness her mother would never allow it.

"Oh, what a marvelous idea, your grace," declared Lady Winchester. "Louisa did so love her visits to the library when your aunt was alive."

Louisa gawped in amazement.

"Well, then that is settled," declared a beaming Lady Allenby. "Shall we say—"

At that moment, Maria Dove, a charming smile on her face, glided into the room. "Good morning, Lady Winchester, Miss Winchester," she said, in a voice that bore no trace of her usual Yorkshire accent.

Louisa stared at the girl in astounded silence. Lady Winchester's eyes grew wide in astonishment. At a discreet cough from the duchess, Lady Winchester regained a little of her composure. "Lady Allenby, may I, er, present our, um, houseguest, Miss Maria Dove. From Yorkshire. Miss Dove, Lady Allenby, Duchess of Wolsington."

Maria sank into a gracious curtsy.

"All the way from Yorkshire, you say? How very splendid," enthused Lady Allenby. "I do so love the north. Now tell me, how are you enjoying Diddington, Miss Dove?"

"Very well, thank you, ma'am," replied Maria, settling herself down on the sofa alongside their guest. "Lady Winchester is a most cordial hostess.
And dear Louisa and I have become quite inseparable."

"Well then, if the two of you are inseparable," beamed Lady Allenby, "then you, too, must come to Diddington Hall to help with the cataloguing of the library, Miss Dove. If, of course, you are as passionate about books as your friend here appears to be."

"Oh, I can assure you, ma'am," replied Maria Dove, with a victorious grin, "I am very passionate indeed."

~ * ~

Eliza Winchester did not enjoy her scheduled trip to Diddington one bit. Maria Dove's peculiar behavior had quite unsettled her nerves. Not only that, but with the girl so clearly obsessed with the opposite sex, Eliza was terrified she may attempt to exert some influence over Louisa in that regard, thereby undoing two decades of her own hard work. The moment Lady Allenby had suggested Louisa assist in the cataloguing of Diddington Hall's library, Eliza had grasped the opportunity with both hands.

Surely Maria Dove would have no wish to spend time in a library. Eliza would have thought the idea completely abhorrent to her. But, to her immense irritation, Maria Dove had seemed only too eager to help. Eliza was sure she was up to something. She would not trust her as far as she could throw her. She intended to write to the girl's aunt that afternoon–during her designated letter-writing hours–and inform her that the situation was not in the least satisfactory. Maria Dove should be returned to whence she came, forthwith.

As the clock struck two, Eliza's heavy eyelids appeared to have ideas of their own. Perhaps even she may be forced to deviate from her meticulously planned timetable this afternoon and submit to a little repose. She was about to inform Louisa of her decision, when her attention was drawn to a green carriage trundling up the drive.

Good heavens. There had never been so many visitors to Hartley House. If she was not mistaken, it was that ghastly viscount again. Well, she would tell him exactly what she thought of him calling upon people in the middle of the afternoon. It was not at all the done thing.

To her surprise, though, it was not the viscount who appeared in the doorway a few minutes later, but an enormous bouquet of flowers–a breath taking bundle of roses, lilies and carnations—behind which only Korbett's short legs were visible.

The butler cleared his throat. "Begging your, er, pardon, my lady, but these are for Miss Winchester. From Viscount Winston. The gentleman says to say that he hopes she has fully recovered from her ordeal yesterday evening."

"Oh, how very thoughtful of him," beamed a delighted Louisa. "Do show him in at once, Korbett."

"I'm afraid that will not be at all possible, miss. He has already left."

"Left?" echoed Louisa. "Whatever for?"

"He said that he did not wish to disturb you, given the unsociable calling hour."

Louisa flopped back in her chair. "Well," she exclaimed. "Was there ever such a kind and considerate man, Mama?"

"Hmph," huffed Lady Winchester, evidently unimpressed. "Do not be fooled, Louisa. Flowers are simply another tool in a gentleman's repertoire. Another tool they can employ to—"

"Nevertheless, Mama," broke in Louisa irritably. "I

believe I have never seen such a beautiful bunch of tools in my entire life."

~ * ~

Louisa's excitement at receiving her first bouquet did not last long. By that evening, she had succeeded in working herself up into an enormous flurry. The notion of spending time in the Diddington Hall library with Lord Harry Allenby was terrifying enough. To make matters worse, she would be obliged to thank the man for rescuing her from the Merchistons' pond, thereby dragging up that whole unfortunate incident. Still, despite her mounting anxiety, she'd had what she considered an inspired idea. She would write him a note. That way, she need make no mention of the embarrassing occurrence when she did come face-to-face with him. And, at the same time, she could use the opportunity to rectify his indubitably poor impression of her.

With her nerves a little calmer, she sat down at her writing desk, dipped her quill in the Standish, and began to write:

> *Dear Lord Allenby*
>
> *I am sorry that circumstances did not permit me to thank you personally for coming to my aid at the Merchistons' ball. I am therefore writing this note to express my gratitude. I realize that you may be wondering what on earth I was doing beside the pond that evening. Well, I was attempting to rescue an injured frog. It had, you see, damaged its hind leg and hind legs are particularly crucial to frogs. They are specially designed for jumping and leaping and are split into the shinbone (tibiofibula), the thigh (femur) and two elongated anklebones (tarsals). I believe this particular frog had damaged its femur. Should you wish to study it in more detail, I am sure you will find the anatomy of amphibians most interesting.*

Her quill hovered over the paper. Should she add something about seeing him soon at the library? She decided not. After all, she had not yet fully made up her mind to go. It was not too late to feign some excuse, some illness and, by the time she "recovered", the task would hopefully be so far underway that the man would no longer be in need of assistance—or else had sought some elsewhere. With that heartening thought, she signed off.

Yours sincerely,
Louisa Winchester (Miss)

Eight

In Diddington Hall's crimson drawing-room, his grace, the Duke of Wolsington and her grace, the Duchess of Wolsington did not know what to make of the scribbled note they had received from their eldest son the previous afternoon, informing them of his intended visit—with a young lady by the name of Miss Bettina Bott.

For the third time that morning, the duchess rearranged the pile of cushions on the sofa. "I declare I am at a loss what to make of it," she flustered. "In all his nine-and-twenty years Toby has never given marriage a thought. And one can only assume he *is* now contemplating marriage. What other reason could there possibly be for him to invite this Miss Bott to take tea with us?"

"Perhaps it has something to do with the condition of Aunt Millie's will," muttered her husband as he glanced up from his book.

"Aunt Millie's will?" Lady Allenby repeated. "Are you suggesting, Charles, that Toby would marry simply to inherit Diddington Hall?"

"Stranger things have happened," replied her husband, his free hand stroking the end of his moustache.

The duchess gave a dismissive tut. "I have no doubt they have," she said, bustling over to the vase of roses on the table before the window. "However, the very notion of such a thing is ridiculous. Whatever would Toby want with Diddington Hall? You know the boy cannot abide the country." She snapped off a yellowing leaf.

"Haven't the slightest idea what he would do with it," Lord Allenby confessed. "Perhaps he intends to sell it off and pocket the proceeds."

The duchess slanted her husband a withering look. "Really Charles, you do say the most outrageous things. Neither of the boys would dream of selling the house. We are all far too attached to it. Besides, what would Toby want with a load of money? His allowance is more than generous and he has never so much as hinted at your raising it."

"That's because he knows he would be flogging a dead horse."

The duchess quivered with exasperation. "We are all fully aware of your feelings on that matter, sir. Although I do still consider it a little harsh of you, insisting Toby sign that agreement when he became of age."

The duke jerked up his head and glared at his wife. "*Harsh?* It was nothing of the sort, Arabella. Toby is awarded a very generous allowance—very generous indeed. If he can't prove to me that he can manage it, then I've no intention of leaving the dukedom to him. The boy has to be made aware that, along with a title, comes a great deal of responsibility, not only for oneself, but for future generations. If Toby ever asked for a raise, or a hand out, he knows fine well I would consider such a request as proof he is unworthy of his birth right."

"But by doing so, Charles, you are making poor Toby suffer for the mistakes of your grandfather."

"My grandfather was a heedless, womanizing coxcomb," countered Lord Allenby. "You cannot conceive how hard my father had to work to rebuild the estate after that lack wit squandered our entire fortune on wine, women and gambling. I refuse to have the family name falling into such disrepute again, Arabella. Or, for that matter, have Toby's sons suffer the same depressing fate as my own father."

The duchess rolled her eyes, having endured the same speech on a great many occasions during her thirty-year marriage. "Of course you do realize, Charles," she declared, as a sudden thought occurred to her, "that you are making the rather large assumption that Toby will marry and produce a son."

"Well, I suppose, my dear," he sighed, "that brings us neatly back to where we started this discussion. What we make of this, rather unfortunately named, Miss Bettina Bott."

~ * ~

The moment Bettina Bott tinkled the last note of *A Country Garden* on Diddington Hall's magnificent pianoforte, Lady Allenby's hand automatically reached for her vinaigrette. Remembering her manners, she promptly withdrew it.

Miss Bott, meanwhile, swung around on her stool and beamed at the three members of her audience, all of whom stared back at her with unfathomable expressions about their faces.

"I was a little nervous," she giggled, in her own inimitable fashion.

It was the duchess who first managed to recover something of her composure. "Not that we could, er, tell, my dear. It was quite...delightful. Was it not, Charles?"

Following a sharp jab of his wife's elbow between his ribs, the duke muttered, "Oh, er, yes. Quite, um...delightful indeed."

To the duchess's horror and, she was certain, that of both her husband and son, Miss Bott swung back around to the instrument, her pudgy fingers hovering over the keys. "I can play another if you like. Are you familiar with—"

"No!" snapped Toby. Then, modifying his tone, "That is, I, er, think perhaps you had best sup your tea first, Miss Bott. Before it goes cold."

"What an excellent idea, Toby," agreed Lady Allenby. "And then, er, perhaps after tea, Miss Bott—"

The girl giggled. "Oh, after tea I should like to see the grounds, if I may." She cast an adoring glance toward Toby. "I have been reliably informed—by my dear friend, Lady Caroline Levington, the Countess of Wold—that your son gives an excellent tour of the grounds, Lady Allenby."

"Well, I'm afraid the countess has misinformed you, Miss Bott," countered Toby. "My knowledge of the grounds is nowhere near as extensive as that of my mother. I am sure she would be only too delighted to show you around, would you not, Mama?"

A bemused Lady Allenby threw a questioning look at her son. At the meaningful one he returned, she replied, "Of, er, course. I should be only too delighted, Miss Bott."

~ * ~

As planned, Caroline Levington's carriage arrived at Diddington Hall a little after six o"clock with the intention of returning Toby and Miss Bott to London. Having spent the entire afternoon in Miss Bott's irritating company, Toby found he was devoid of any desire to suffer more of the same in the close confinement of a carriage.

Equally as daunting, was the idea of Caroline's inevitable interrogation of the afternoon once they were alone. To this end, ensuring there was a decent audience about them, Toby casually informed the countess that his plans had changed. He would not now be returning to London, but spending the night at Diddington Hall instead. The look upon Caroline's face left little doubt as to her feelings. With the announcement being made in front of the duke and duchess, Miss Bott, and a handful of servants, though, she could do nothing more than wish him a very pleasant evening.

"I do hope I shall be seeing you…*soon*, Lord Allenby," had been her parting words, as the carriage pulled away. Knowing it would add greatly to her displeasure, Toby had not deigned to reply.

Toby's triumph in trumping Caroline did not last long. Only minutes later, it had paled into insignificance as the stark reality of his situation seeped through him. He remained on the steps of the hall, watching the countess's carriage until it disappeared from view. Then, taking a deep breath, he made his way back to the crimson drawing-room.

His parents had already resumed their seats there, each in a high-backed chair either side of the marble fireplace. The duchess was intent on her embroidery, while the duke flicked through the newspaper. With his heart pounding, Toby assumed a position between the two of them, his back to the fire. He must, he resolved, give no indication of his true feelings.

After all, if his parents did approve of Miss Bott, he could whisk her down the aisle in a matter of weeks and that would be an end to this whole ghastly business. He would sell the hall, pay off his debts, be free of Jack Wilmott–and…have Miss Bettina Bott as a wife. He ignored the bile rising in his throat at the very idea of the latter.

Feigning nonchalance, he asked, of no one in particular, "What, um, did you think of Miss Bott?"

The mystified look his parents exchanged did nothing to ease his nerves.

"I thought her perfectly, um...nice," mumbled the duchess, reverting back to her embroidery. "If not a little young."

"She is eight-and-ten, Mama. A perfectly respectable age for a young lady to marry."

Lady Allenby snapped up her head. "Please tell me you are not intending to marry that girl, Toby."

"Why shouldn't I?" Toby retorted. "She is very well accomplished and I have it on good authority that her family is—"

The duke shook his head. "Don't care about any of that. It wouldn't do. Wouldn't do at all. She would bore you rigid in a matter of days, man. That's assuming she didn't drive you to Bedlam first with that irritating giggle."

The duchess nodded her agreement. "Your father is right, Toby. Miss Bott does not seem the type of girl who would hold *your* interest for more than five minutes."

"I—I find her most...interesting," mumbled Toby.

"You have not the first thing in common with her," pointed out the duchess.

"And that giggle." The duke shuddered. "Man can't live with that. No indeed."

"Well, I believe myself a little, um, in love with her," Toby declared.

His mother fixed him with a disbelieving stare. "Really, Toby dear, after that dreadful performance on the pianoforte, it would be hard enough for the girl's poor mother to love her."

~ * ~

Harry Allenby had not slept well. He had retired to bed the previous evening with a splitting headache, which had remained with him ever since he had caught that painful rendition of *A Country Garden* the previous afternoon. Having subsequently received an introduction to the perpetrator of the warbled tune, and learned that she was a friend of his brother's, Harry could not help but wonder what Toby was up to.

Miss Bettina Bott appeared the very antithesis of the type of woman with whom his brother normally associated. Something was most definitely amiss but, with enough issues of his own to occupy him, Harry found himself devoid of both the energy and the inclination to worry about exactly what that something was.

Harry had not been at all impressed when his mother had first informed him that she had invited Miss Winchester and her houseguest to the hall today, to help him catalogue the library. One of the main reasons he had chosen the exercise was because it was something he could do alone; something in which he could absorb himself completely. Now, thanks to his mother's interference, he was destined to spend the majority of his time with two simpering females. Although, he reminded himself, Miss Winchester, for all her scrapes, did not look like a simpering female. There was something different about her; something…distinguishable–and it was certainly not just her charming spectacles.

As Harry descended the stairs to the breakfast-room, he could not recall the last time he had been so nervous. If he were a betting man, he would have laid odds on it being the first time he had climbed atop a horse, when he was seven years old. For heaven's sake, he scolded himself, he was a grown man. Surely he could cope with the presence of one little bespectacled chit and her friend in the library for a couple of hours.

He bit back a smile as he recalled the note he had received from Louisa yesterday, thanking him for coming to her aid in the pond. It had included a rambling description of amphibians' limbs. Not the least bit interesting, but extremely endearing nonetheless. And now, this morning, that endearing slip of a girl, with her charming spectacles, would be spending time in the library with him.

As he entered the breakfast-room and discovered his brother tucking into a pile of ham and eggs, Harry concluded that he could not face so much as a mouthful of food. He settled for a cup of coffee instead.

~ * ~

Even with the help of her maid, it had taken Louisa Winchester twice as long as usual to dress that morning. Not only was she all fingers and thumbs, but also she had, for the first time she could recall, taken more than thirty seconds to choose which gown to wear. From her limited selection, she had chosen one in primrose muslin with two rows of ruching about the bodice. Or was that too much? Should she have gone for the plainer one with the—Or perhaps she should have feigned an illness after all. A sore throat or a—Oh, for heaven's sake. What was she worrying about?

But Louisa was all too aware of what she was worrying about. The fact that Lord Harry Allenby was, quite obviously, a man. One of that terrifying breed whose devious, manipulative behavior her mother had spent years warning her against. One of that terrifying breed who concealed an efficient weaponry up their sleeve in order to tempt a lady and trick a lady, before tossing her aside like a used rag.

The strange thing was, though, despite her mother's vociferous lecturing over the years, Louisa could not, for one moment, imagine Harry Allenby treating anyone with such careless disrespect–particularly not a woman. Even during their first encounter in Buttercup Meadow, when he had scared her half to death, she had no doubt now his intentions had been anything other than honorable. His obvious remorse over her alarm had been written all over his concerned–and, she had to admit—extremely handsome face.

Then there was the occasion he had rescued her from the pond. Despite the fact that she must have presented an absurd picture, he had not once laughed at her. Although she did harbor a niggling suspicion that his cough, as he had removed the water lily from her head, may have been affected in an attempt to disguise his mirth.

Louisa was aware, of course, that her mother would dismiss such perceived consideration and gallantry as nothing more than tools in Harry Allenby's armory. Tools with which he could tempt and trick Louisa before the inevitable tossing aside. Perhaps her mother was right. What, after all, did she know of gentlemen?

Nothing, she concluded with some panic. She knew absolutely nothing of them.

Was she allowing herself to be tricked by Lord Harry Allenby?

Was he merely feigning charm and heroism, in order that she would lose her heart to him?

Not that she intended losing her heart to anyone. Ever.

That point notwithstanding, she must continue to keep

her wits about her. She must continue to heed her mother's advice.

And she must, she resolved, as she descended the stairs to the breakfast-room, show Harry Allenby that she was not some simpering wet-goose who needed a gentleman to help her out of her scrapes–although that might be somewhat difficult to disprove given the situations in which he had so far encountered her. Nonetheless, she did hope she had already gone some way to changing his perception of her. She had included a very detailed description of amphibians' limbs in her note thanking him for rescuing her from the pond. That must, surely, have given him some idea of the level of her intelligence.

She would go to Diddington Hall today and she would be strong and clever and helpful and…most likely hungry, she concluded as she caught a whiff of bacon and realized she could not face eating a single thing. She settled for a cup of coffee instead.

~ * ~

Miss Maria Dove had given herself a very—*very*—strict talking to following Lady Allenby's visit to Hartley House, and the revelation regarding the inheritance of Diddington Hall. Having never imagined she might find a rich and titled husband in boring old Diddington, Maria had deemed there to be little point in affecting her airs and graces. Now, though, things were different–very different. Her quest for fun would have to be shelved until she had implemented her new plan. There would be no more flirting until she had snared Lord Harry Allenby. And as for champagne… she would not, she vowed, touch another drop until their wedding day.

~ * ~

Miss Louisa Winchester and Miss Maria Dove arrived at Diddington Hall shortly after eleven o"clock. The butler showed them to the morning room where they were, so he informed, to meet first with the duchess.

Despite all her positive resolutions, Louisa's legs were shaking at such a pace, she was surprised she could follow the servant. Maria Dove, conversely, appeared not the least bit over-awed by the occasion nor, indeed, by the opulent surroundings. The butler had been forced to stop five times *en route* to their destination while the younger girl had admired some artifact or other before pressing him as to its value.

Louisa's heart was in her mouth as the butler pushed open the door to the morning room. Spotting only Lady Allenby, she experienced a shudder of relief.

"Ah, my dear Miss Winchester," gushed the duchess, springing out of her chair and bustling over to Louisa with her hands outstretched. "And Miss, er, Dove," she added, her eyes drawn to Maria Dove's ample cleavage displayed, in all its usual glory, in a low-cut, apple-green gown.

Maria Dove dropped a deep curtsy. "May I say what a great honor it is to be here, ma'am."

"Now, now, there is no need to stand on ceremony," Lady Allenby said with a dismissive wave of her hand. "Do come and sit down. Harry will be joining us shortly."

At this announcement, Louisa's shaking increased tenfold, while Maria Dove tugged down her bodice just a tad further.

It took a moment for Louisa to realize quite what had happened. In the armchair opposite her hostess, she had just reached for the milk jug on the table before her, when the door opened and in came Harry Allenby. That she had been fully expecting his presence, and had been keeping a wary eye on the entrance, had not eased Louisa's nerves one jot. Nor had the fact that, at exactly that same moment, a large white Persian cat had sprung onto her lap causing her to squeal, the milk to go flying, and the incensed pet to meow vociferously.

"Oh, g-goodness," stammered Louisa, gawping helplessly at Lady Allenby. "I am so sorry, your grace. I really didn't mean to—"

"It is quite all right, my dear," an equally abashed Lady Allenby apologized, summoning over the footman in attendance. "It is my fault entirely. Kitty can be a dreadful nuisance, I'm afraid. I should have warned you."

"Perhaps I should have warned you about Miss Winchester, ma'am," piped up a sanctimonious Maria Dove. "She is somewhat prone to accidents. Only yesterday she tripped over her own feet and flew headlong into the path of a carriage. It missed her by half an inch."

As the cat continued its hysterical mewing, Louisa flushed a deep shade of pink. So much for her efforts to prove to

Harry Allenby that she was not a clumsy muttonhead, but an intelligent, capable young woman. She slanted him a look as he remained standing in the doorway, observing the scene. With yet another pang of humiliation, she noted, by the twitching of his lips, the great deal of effort he had to employ not to laugh at her.

~ * ~

In the library some forty minutes later, Maria Dove had rarely been in better spirits. Yet again, she had to pinch herself. Naturally, it made no difference to her what Lord Harry Allenby, Earl of Stanford looked like. She planned to marry him even if he resembled that old stuffed trout in the glass case behind the desk. Yet the man bore no resemblance at all to a dead fish. He was, in fact, quite the most dashing man Maria had ever set eyes upon. This, combined with the fact that he was also the richest, would make her task very pleasant indeed. If ever there was a girl blessed with the most prodigious good fortune, it was, she concluded, Maria Elsie Dove.

Two hours later, Maria had begun to suspect her task may not be quite as simple as first envisaged—particularly given her strong aversion to books. She did, in fact, detest them. And she could certainly see no point to them. Not only were they boring and dusty, but they were full of stupid words. And there was the pathetic Miss Winchester, now evidently fully recovered from her embarrassing cat and milk incident, practically salivating over them.

Clearly the girl hadn't the first idea about gentlemen.

Gentlemen, it was a well-established fact, did not favor ladies who exhibited an interest in books. Nor did they favor ruched gowns, flat bosoms or spectacles. With her limited knowledge of the opposite sex, Miss Winchester would, naturally, be aware of none of this. Nonetheless, the color that rose in the older girl's cheeks whenever Lord Harry addressed her, had not escaped Maria's attention. If she was not mistaken, Miss Winchester had developed something of a *tendre* for Lord Harry.

Well, the girl was to be pitied. An earl would never be interested in a pea-goose like her. She wouldn't have the first idea what an earl needed. Whereas Maria…she knew exactly what men needed–earls or otherwise.

Nine

Lady Caroline Levington spent twenty minutes examining her exquisite face in the three-part looking glass atop her dressing table. During that time she discovered two faint lines either side of her eyes and the beginning of a small pimple on her chin. Consequently, she was not in the best of humors when Toby arrived. Nor, it appeared was he.

Upon entering her chamber, he did not even bother to bid her good day, but flopped straight down into the armchair at the side of the bed. Caroline regarded him through the looking glass. His refusal to return to London with her and Miss Bott had annoyed her intensely. But she refused to dwell upon the matter. There were topics of much more import to discuss–namely whether the duke and duchess had considered Miss Bott a suitable wife for their son. Caroline was optimistic. She had, after all, invested a great deal of time and attention in compiling her list of potential brides. And she had not put Bettina Bott at the top of that list without good reason.

"Well?" she demanded, with a lift of her perfectly arched brows. "What did they think of her?"

Toby emitted a heavy sigh. "They did not think her suitable, Caroline. Which is hardly surprising."

Caroline sprang to her feet, kicked the stool aside and began pacing about the room like a caged animal. "Not suitable? The girl is perfectly suitable. She would make a most obedient wife and, when the time was right, would not dare to demur when I—"

She stopped her pacing directly in front of Toby and placed her hands on her narrow hips. "What reasons did they give for arriving at this ludicrous conclusion?"

Toby's hackles rose. "They did not have to give any reasons, Caroline. The girl insisted upon singing for them."

The countess stamped her foot in frustration, then stomped over to her writing desk. She plopped down on the chair there. A heavy silence fell over the room, broken only by the tapping of one manicured fingernail on polished wood. The sound reverberated through Toby's bones. In an attempt to block it out, he rested his elbows on his knees and covered his ears with his hands.

The tapping stopped abruptly. Toby jerked up his head to see Caroline removing a piece of paper from the middle drawer of the desk. It contained, he noticed, a short list.

"Well," declared his mistress, in much more measured tones, "if Miss Bott is unsuitable, then we shall be obliged to move onto our next candidate…Miss Lucinda Fothergay.

~ * ~

In Diddington Hall's magnificent library Maria Dove was no nearer to comprehending the point. Who cared if the blasted books were catalogued or not? Certainly not her. Not that she would dream of voicing such a sentiment. That would not do at all, particularly given the ridiculous amount of interest Miss Winchester expressed in the task. No, Maria knew exactly what her role was to be. She would breeze about the library displaying her assets and driving Lord Harry wild with desire.

She discreetly adjusted her assets before pulling out a set of five small, dusty, hard-backed books from the shelf in front of her. They were so old their titles had completely faded. Had it been left to Maria, she would have happily tossed them into the bin. Instead, she sailed over to the desk where Louisa and Harry were seated side-by-side, scribbling away.

"Ah-hem."

Both heads tilted upwards.

Maria affected her most charming smile. "What would you like me to do with these, my lord?" she asked, proffering the books at exactly the same level as her chest.

The innuendo was every bit as effective as she intended. Harry dropped his quill. Beads of perspiration began sprouting from his forehead. He fumbled in the pocket of his breeches and drew out a handkerchief.

"I, er, um—" he stammered, and dabbed at his brow.

"Why don't you leave them on the table in the far corner, Miss Dove," Louisa suggested, far too helpfully for Maria who had been savoring the moment. "We will look at them when we are ready. In the meantime, if you wouldn't mind trying to ascertain into which category they should be logged, that would be most helpful."

Maria fixed Louisa with a frosty glare before turning another dazzling smile to Harry. "Very well," she said, before spinning around and sashaying over to one of the leather wing chairs around the fireplace.

Blast that Winchester girl, she fumed. She really would have to think of some way of ridding herself of her and getting Lord Harry alone. Then she could show him exactly what needed logging–and where.

About to toss the books onto the table, she idly flipped one open and scanned the first few lines. Slowly, filled with disbelief, she sank down onto a chair and began to read in earnest. She could scarcely give credence to what the book in her hands contained and, when she noted the time, was equally hard-put to accept that she had been reading it for so long. These small volumes had turned out to be quite a find—quite a find indeed. All dated within the 1730s, Maria could hardly believe folk had known about such things back then, let alone been allowed to write about them. So explicit were they, she had come over quite peculiar.

Hearing Miss Winchester muttering something about them taking their leave shortly, Maria surreptitiously slipped one of the books into her reticule. She could hardly wait until she was tucked up in bed that night so she could continue reading it in peace.

~ * ~

Back in London, Lord Toby Allenby had spent a very pleasant evening at his club. Actually, he had spent a very pleasant *afternoon* and evening at his club. Time well spent, he concluded. His consumption of a large amount of alcohol had assisted greatly in helping him see things clearly. He would call Caroline's bluff. He would tell her, in no uncertain terms, that he would choose his own bride. He would tell her that, if she wished to inform her "influential contacts" of his decision, then she was perfectly free to do so. She had already contrived another meeting with a prospective bride for the morrow.

Well, he would tell her that she would be meeting the girl alone. Lord Toby Allenby would not be there. And he would tell her all of this right now. He stood up from the wing chair which had housed him very comfortably for the last eight hours. His head swam but, with practiced skill, he managed to steady himself, slur a few goodbyes and stagger out into the street.

In his drunken stupor, Toby had no idea of the time. He knew only that the lighted flambeaux meant it must be late. The cool night air cut through his topcoat causing him to shiver as he attempted to collect his bearings. He marched, in as purposeful a fashion as his legs would allow, in the direction of the Levingtons' townhouse.

Due to the copious amount of whiskey sloshing about his veins, and the obscene amount of concentration he was employing just to stay upright, Toby failed to notice the two men behind him. And the fact that they were following him completely passed him by. It was only when a sharp blow struck the back of his head and two sets of arms dragged him into a nearby alley, that he realized anything was amiss at all.

In a misty, painful haze, he could just about discern a ruddy, whiskered face. It was so close to his that the man's warm, fetid breath flooded Toby's nostrils. He retched, just before something cold and sharp was pressed to his windpipe.

"Just a little reminder from Mr. Wilmott, sir. He says he hopes to be hearing from you soon. Otherwise, he'll be forced to send you another…reminder."

The men's fading jeering laughter was the last thing Toby heard before he passed out.

~ * ~

As he supped a glass of whiskey in his bedchamber that same evening, it occurred to Lord Harry Allenby that he had to give his mother credit. It had been an inspired idea asking Miss Winchester to help him catalogue the library. He had been naïve to even contemplate such an undertaking on his own, particularly as he hadn't had the first idea where to begin. In a bid not to look completely stupid in front of his two assistants, he had cobbled together some notes on a system he had devised—a system even he wasn't convinced would work.

Miss Winchester, conversely, had only been in the library a few hours and had already designed such an effective and simple method that had far surpassed his pathetic offering. Despite the incident with the cat and the milk earlier, which he had actually found most diverting, Miss Winchester, just as he had suspected, had proved delightful company. It was her intelligence and lack of affectation, he realized, that made her distinguishable from other young ladies of his acquaintance. Harry did believe he would enjoy her presence at Diddington immensely.

The only fly in the ointment was the terrifying Miss Dove. Harry had a strong suspicion that, although she proclaimed otherwise, books did not feature highly amongst Maria Dove's interests. He would wager that she would tire of the task in a week and find something she deemed more amusing to occupy her—which would suit Harry Allenby very well indeed.

~ * ~

Lying in her bed, gazing at the ceiling, Louisa Winchester could scarcely believe herself. Not only had she dared to suggest a cataloguing system to Lord Harry—but the man had actually seemed impressed with it. What surprised her most, though, was that, once she had grown accustomed to his presence, he had not seemed the least bit terrifying. Nor had she felt half as awkward around him as she had imagined. That fact, she could only attribute to being surrounded by all those wonderful books; books she could enjoy for several more weeks—months even.

The familiar fizzling, which she now recognized as excitement, began in her stomach; excitement that was due purely, of course, to the privilege of being able to spend more time with Diddington Hall's wonderful literary collection.

~ * ~

The following morning, due to the nature of her new reading material, Maria Dove was in a peculiar mood. So hot and bothered was she, she could not sit still for a single minute. She experienced the most vivid dreams the night before, which had made her all the more determined to be alone with Harry

Allenby. To her immense irritation, though, the man appeared not to even notice her that morning as she seductively peeled off her pelisse to reveal one of her most provocatively cut day gowns.

An hour later, as part of Miss Winchester's annoyingly efficient cataloguing system, each of the trio had been allocated a section of shelves to log. Louisa, having dealt with those she could reach, was halfway up the library ladder.

To Maria Dove, the whole exercise was exceedingly tedious. Thankfully, a rather clever idea had occurred to her. One which would not only make things more interesting, but would also further her plan.

She smoothed down her skirts and cleared her throat before asking, in a most affected voice, "Would it be awfully rude of me to suggest some refreshment, my lord? My throat is dreadfully dry today."

To her annoyance, Harry did not even turn to look at her, his eyes firmly fixed on the bookshelves.

"Oh, how very remiss of me, Miss Dove," he muttered, completely absorbed in his task. "Please do feel free to order some refreshment. I'm afraid you shall have to go out and find a servant, though. You may recall I told you yesterday that the bell-pull in this room no longer works."

Maria had recalled exactly that. "I, er, thought perhaps Miss Winchester should like to go," she suggested sweetly. "After all, Miss Winchester, you must be extremely tired spending so much time up the ladder. A walk would no doubt do your little legs the world of good."

"Oh, don't worry about me, Miss Dove," Louisa replied affably from the ladder. "I am not the least bit tired. It is very kind of you to consider my little legs, but I shouldn't mind at all if *you* order the refreshments. Now that you have mentioned it, I think a dish of tea would be just the thing."

Maria's narrowed eyes burned into Louisa's back. It wouldn't take much for her to yank the girl from the ladder, open the door and toss her outside like that irritating cat of Lady Allenby's. But that would never do. And was certainly not the behavior of a future countess. Instead, she would turn the situation to her best advantage.

"Very well, I shall go," she announced breezily. She

sashayed over to Harry who was now on his knees, examining the books on the lower shelves.

Maria bent directly over him. "Have you any particular request, my lord?"

At the unexpected expanse of wobbling flesh thrust before him, Harry's breath caught in his throat. He began coughing uncontrollably.

"I think, perhaps, a glass of water may be called for, Miss Dove," suggested Louisa, still avidly scanning the shelves.

Maria ground her teeth. She really would have to think of a way to rid herself of that irritating chawbacon soon. There was a limit to how much time Maria Elsie Dove could endure in a library–and that limit was fast being approached.

~ * ~

No sooner had the library door closed behind Maria Dove, than Louisa spotted the very book she and Harry had been discussing yesterday.

"Oh, look," she exclaimed. Pulling out the weighty, leather-bound tome with her free hand, she held it out to the approaching Harry.

"Do be careful, Miss Winchester," he begged. "It looks extremely heavy."

"It is," agreed Louisa, pulling a rueful face. "Would you mind taking it from me?"

She bent slightly to hand him the book but, in doing so, her thin sole slipped on the rung, causing her to lose balance. Bracing herself for a hard landing on the floor, she was amazed to find herself swept up, yet again, in Harry Allenby's strong arms—arms that seemed to be making a habit of rescuing her. Neither of them spoke but, with their gazes locked, Louisa was aware of nothing other than the hammering of her heart and a very pleasant melting sensation sweeping over her. The moment was broken as the door burst open and in charged Maria Dove.

Ten

The combination of a blow to the head, an excessive amount of alcohol and spending the entire night in a stinking alley, had not made for one of Toby Allenby's better experiences. A large rat scurrying over his chest had jerked him back to consciousness just as dawn had broken. Toby shuddered at the memory of the filthy rodent crawling over him. The fact that it had had a pair of piercing violet eyes had somehow made it all the more terrifying. Of his assailants' appearances, he could recall nothing, but the gouge in his throat had left a chilling reminder of the weapon one had obviously been brandishing.

For all this inauspicious start, Toby had the distinct impression that the day was not about to improve. Caroline had instructed he meet her around the corner from the Church of St. Bartholomew, on Shiphall Street. Courtesy of an hour lying in a tub of hot soapy water, and a set of clean clothes, his spirits were somewhat revived as he set off in his carriage. His relentless headache, though, showed no signs of abating. Caroline was already there when he arrived. She looked much less striking than usual. There were no jeweled trimmings on her cloak, and her normally abundant mane of glossy auburn hair was constrained in a conservative snood.

Of course the idea of conveniently "forgetting" the meeting had occurred to Toby several times. With the events of the previous evening weighing heavily upon him, however, he had not considered it a wise move. Just as he had no doubt Jack Wilmott would carry out his threats, Toby was equally sure

Caroline would not hesitate in carrying out hers. No, if he was going to outwit Caroline Levington and find his own bride, he would need to give the matter a great deal more sober consideration. For today, though, it was as much as he could do to remember the name of the street on which he was to meet her.

"Good lord," exclaimed Caroline, taking in Toby's deathly gray pallor and the dark shadows beneath his bloodshot eyes. "You look absolutely dreadful."

Not half as dreadful as I feel, Toby resisted saying. Yet, as terrible as he both looked and felt, sufficient sense still prevailed for him not to recount anything of the previous evening's happenings to Caroline. If she knew Jack Wilmott was turning up the heat, it would add more fuel to her ridiculous campaign. "I, er, didn't sleep well," he muttered.

"Well, you are certainly not helping matters turning up in that state," she chided, half turning to glance at the church on the corner. "I would recommend your being a little more civil. *And* putting a smile on your face."

Toby had just opened his mouth to protest about being spoken to as though he were a child, when Caroline's attention was abruptly diverted.

"Ah, there they are," she exclaimed, clapping her hands together. "Exactly as I was informed they would be. Do come along now, Toby." She grabbed his arm and dragged him to the corner.

Toby spotted two tall, thin women picking their way down the church steps. They were dressed in identical plain gray cloaks and bonnets which did nothing to flatter their pale complexions and pointed noses.

"Ah, Lady Fothergay," gushed Caroline, as she and Toby reached the bottom of the steps at exactly the same moment as the countess's unsuspecting prey. "And dear Miss Fothergay. I declare it is a positive age since I saw you both."

"We have been to morning service," informed Lady Fothergay stiffly. "Hearing the Lord's words helps us prepare for the work ahead of us each day."

"And permits us the opportunity to pray for those less fortunate than ourselves," added Lucinda Fothergay. "Of which there are many, Lady Levington."

Caroline's beatific expression faltered very briefly.

"Well, of course. Of course there are–a great many indeed. And it is…the very greatest of pities."

Lady Fothergay pursed her thin lips. "*Pity*, I'm afraid, does not help anyone's cause, Lady Levington. The poor are in need of a great many things. *Pity* is not amongst them."

Toby bit back a smile at the annoyance which briefly hovered over Caroline's countenance.

"In…er, indeed," she faltered. Then, brightening her tone, "Still, the Lord does, as they say, work in very mysterious ways. Like bringing us together today. How very fortuitous that I happened to be walking by at this particular moment–and with my *dear* friend, Lord Allenby. Are you already acquainted with Lord Allenby, Lady Fothergay?"

Lady Fothergay turned her cool gray eyes to Toby. "We are not," she snapped.

Caroline beamed. "Well then, I consider myself most fortunate in being allowed to rectify that situation. Particularly as you all have so much in common."

At this astonishing declaration, Toby made an attempt to raise his eyebrows. At the piercing pain that shot through his head, he promptly lowered them again. The Fothergays, meanwhile, were regarding Caroline with an air of suspicion.

"Why, your good work, of course," declared Caroline triumphantly. "I know Lord Allenby would love to hear *all* about it. He is quite intent on easing the plight of those less fortunate. Now, I have just had the most marvelous idea. Why don't we all go for a cup of coffee and we can discuss the matter further."

~ * ~

"How are you enjoying your time at Diddington Hall, Louisa?" asked Lady Winchester when the two of them were alone at their embroidery that evening.

Louisa attempted to quell the guilty flush that spread over her cheeks. Since her fall from the ladder, when she had, once again, found herself in Harry Allenby's arms, she had felt decidedly peculiar. In fact, she could scarcely wipe out the image of his face so close to hers and the gloriously warm sensation that had suffused her entire body. None of this, however, she thought it prudent to confess to her mother.

"I am, er, enjoying it very well, Mama," she replied. "It is a fascinating, um, collection they have there."

Lady Winchester smiled as she re-threaded her needle. "How very kind of Lady Allenby to ask you. I do not mind admitting, Louisa, that the acquaintance of that charming lady is one I would not mind furthering in the least."

Louisa stopped mid-stitch and regarded her mother in astonishment. She had never before heard her speak so favorably of anyone—with the exception of the late Lady O'Hare. But what was even more remarkable, was the fact that Louisa spending every day in the presence of Lady Allenby's equally charming son, seemed to have passed her mother completely by. And Louisa had no wish at all to bring it to her attention.

~ * ~

Unfortunately now a regular occurrence, Harry Allenby was having difficulty sleeping. The image of Louisa Winchester's face, just inches from his, insisted on invading his conscience every time he closed his eyes. As he had held her in his arms, her delicious scent—a mixture of roses, vanilla and cinnamon—had tickled his nostrils, making him pleasantly light-headed. Gazing at the ceiling, Harry chuckled as he recalled the incident with the cat and the milk. Never before had he met a woman who made him smile quite as much as the tiny Miss Winchester. Except, of course, Clara. And just as Clara was dead, he swiftly reminded himself, so, too, was Harry Allenby's heart.

~ * ~

Still to be convinced of the existence of The Almighty, Lord Toby
Allenby had no reservations in praying to the man that he might wake up to discover it was all a hideous nightmare. He imagined the euphoria—he'd open his eyes in his warm comfortable bed and realize it had been nothing more than a figment of his active imagination. He may even have found it somewhat amusing. But it was, unfortunately, no figment of his imagination. Nor was he the least bit amused. And if word of it got out in his club, the resultant jibes and jokes would be guaranteed to last far longer than Toby himself.

Following their "fortuitous" meeting with the Fothergays the previous day, Caroline had insisted on dragging the little party along to a coffee house. Toby had been desperate for a hair of the dog. Instead, he had imbibed several cups of weak black liquid and listened, with a pounding head, for ninety minutes while Lady Fothergay and her daughter explained in great—and to his mind unnecessary— detail, their efforts to help the less fortunate. Of course, even Toby could not deny that it was an admirable undertaking. And he was immensely grateful that such selfless people as the Fothergays existed to perform such necessary work.

But Lord Toby Allenby did not pretend to have one altruistic bone in his body. He was not afraid to admit that, just like the majority of his class, his life revolved solely around his own egotistical pleasures. With the lump on his head providing a throbbing reminder of his own plight, though—namely his desperate need for a bride, a murderous moneylender breathing down his neck, and a scheming mistress manipulating his every move—he had confessed nothing of this selfishness to the Fothergays.

Consequently, because of that lack of admission, he was now, at the ridiculously unsociable hour of eleven o"clock in the morning, in a cold wooden building adjoining the side of the Church of St. Bartholomew, preparing to dish out cracked bowls of broth.

Toby's only consolation was that, to ensure her plan ran smoothly, Caroline had been forced to accompany him. Not that there was any pleasure to be had from the woman's company. Quite the opposite in fact. He watched as she set out the bowls, chatting merrily to the Fothergays all the while. Behind her cheery self-sacrificing façade, Toby knew the countess well enough to recognize she hated the experience even more than he did. Which was some feat.

"Unfortunately, the Lord's work is never done," declared Lucinda Fothergay as she prized the lid from an enormous vat of broth. The smell washed over Toby like a tub of dirty water.

"Indeed it is not, Miss Fothergay," agreed Caroline. "And the more hands there are to help Him, the better. Do you not agree, Lord Allenby?"

Toby pretended not to hear. He busied himself with some spoons.

"You say you do this every day of the week, Miss Fothergay," confirmed Caroline, her nose wrinkling slightly at the very notion.

"Every day except Sundays, ma'am. On Sundays the Lord permits us a little rest."

"Sundays are spent in prayer and Bible studies," chipped in Lady Fothergay. "It is a day of rest for the body, not the mind."

"Of course it is," beamed Caroline. "Well, Lord Allenby and I shall be only too delighted to help you for the remainder of this week. Shall we not, sir?"

Toby tossed Caroline an icy glare.

She returned it with a beatific smile. "And then," she enthused, "on Sunday, why don't we have a little trip into the countryside? I am sure the fresh air would do us all the world of good. In fact, we could ride out to Diddington and attend morning service at the lovely little church there."

She clapped a hand to her forehead. "Oh, silly me. I quite forgot my husband has made other plans for Sunday. But I'm sure that does not signify in the least. Lord Allenby would, I am certain, be more than happy to ride out with you two ladies. Now is that not a marvelous idea?"

Neither the Fothergays' lack of response, nor Toby's murderous expression, deterred the countess.

"And perhaps, my lord, Lady Fothergay and Miss Fothergay may even have the added pleasure of making the acquaintance of your parents there."

It was all Toby could do not to pick up the vat of disgusting broth and pour it all over Caroline's smug face.

~ * ~

The small wooden gate, made smooth by years of weathering and hundreds of hands, opened without so much as a creak. Harry stood for a moment in the warm April sunshine, steeling himself before he stepped through it. The scene before him had hardly changed at all in the five years he had been coming here. Not that he came with any great regularity. He couldn't. The whole experience left him drained for days afterwards. Today, though, from the moment he had opened his eyes, he had been flooded with a strange compulsion to visit; a compulsion he had never before experienced.

He had been at the church only days before, for Great Aunt Millie's funeral. The imposing family crypt in which her remains had been interred was at the front of the building.

Clara's grave was at the back, marked with just another unremarkable headstone like the sixty or so others laid out in their neat, ordered lines.

The majority were well tended—flowers changed weekly, weeds removed diligently and granite and marble tributes scrubbed of moss when necessary. There was a handful that bore no such evidence of loving care. One of these never ceased to exude a peculiar effect over Harry. For some inexplicable reason, he was always drawn toward it. It was situated at the end of the first row, which meant the ivy growing freely over the boundary wall could impinge upon it with wild abandon. The headstone itself was so old and weather-beaten it was no longer possible to read its inscription. *Loving* was the only decipherable word. It provided no clue to its occupant's identity.

Harry crouched down and tore away the ivy. He then pulled out a pink rosebud from the bunch of twelve he had brought for Clara and propped it up against the stone. He traced the one remaining word with his finger. Whoever it was, who lay beneath the earth here had been loved by one person at least. That was some consolation. Perhaps they had been reunited with that person in death. Or perhaps not. Perhaps there was only our brief, transient time on earth to love and after that we were on our own, a flock of lonely, detached souls drifting aimlessly about eternity. It was a sobering thought. And one Harry had no wish to dwell upon.

He made his way over to Clara's grave. By contrast it was scrupulously well cared for by her family. As Harry busied himself arranging the remaining eleven pink rosebuds in the vase there, he glimpsed a pink and lilac butterfly settling on the twelfth.

~ * ~

As Louisa entered Diddington Hall's library later that morning and spotted Harry Allenby behind the desk, her heart skipped a beat. Not only did he look even more handsome than usual, but another idea about the library had occurred to her during the long hours she had lain awake the previous night. Again it was simple, but it should significantly speed up their already efficient system. Bubbling with nervous excitement, she could scarcely wait to explain it to him.

The moment she finished, Harry exclaimed with enthusiasm, "Good lord, Miss Winchester, what an inspired idea. I only wish I had thought of it myself."

Louisa flushed with delight. "It's a very simple idea, sir."

"Simple!" Harry echoed, his navy-blue eyes twinkling. "It is quite brilliant. Do you not agree, Miss Dove?"

Maria Dove, absorbed in her little hard-backed book, jerked up her head at the mention of her name. "Wh-what?"

"I was just saying, Miss Dove," repeated Harry, his tone lilting with impatience, "what a brilliant idea Miss Winchester has had to help us with the cataloguing. And I'm sure," he continued, not even bothering to wait for Maria's response, "that while Miss Winchester and I begin implementing her idea, you would not mind in the least arranging some refreshment."

~ * ~

Mr. Gerald Hinds, Great Aunt Millie's long-suffering solicitor, happened to be visiting Diddington Hall that morning to go over one or two business matters with the duke and duchess regarding the estate. He also happened to be passing the door to the library at exactly the same moment a young lady, displaying a great deal of bosom, just happened to storm out of it. Her pretty face clouded with fury, she did not even bother to acknowledge Mr. Hinds's presence as she stomped along the corridor.

Curious as to the cause of the young woman's disgruntlement, Mr. Hinds peeped around the door of the library. There he saw two heads bent over the desk—that of Lord Harry Allenby, and that of an extremely sweet bespectacled young woman with a long shiny mane of dark curls. Deep in conversation, neither of them noticed him. But Gerald Hinds noticed them. He noticed everything about them. He noticed how close they sat and he noticed the unmistakable sparkle in their eyes as they regarded one another.

He smiled fondly as he recalled exchanging similar sparkling looks with the late Mrs. Ruby Hinds. Those had been the days. At the age of forty, Gerald Hinds had given up hope of ever marrying. Then Millicent O'Hare had introduced him to Ruby and that, as they say, had been that. Recalling Lady O'Hare's matchmaking efforts, an alarm bell began ringing in his head. Wasn't there something Millie had wished him to do if he had the slightest inkling of this very occurrence?

He scratched his bald head trying desperately to remember. No—it completely failed him. He would have to go back to his office and re-read the long list of instructions she had left him. He retreated into the corridor, shaking his head. Even in death, the remarkable Millicent O'Hare managed to keep him just as busy as she ever had when she was alive.

~ * ~

Maria Dove was in extremely high dudgeon. Lord Harry Allenby–the man she intended to make her husband—treated her as though she were nothing more than a servant. This was the second time in as many days that she had been dispatched for refreshments. She had a good mind to demand the presence of a footman in the library although that would not help matters in the least. Maria's plans involved catching Harry Allenby alone; a difficult enough task given the ever-present Miss Winchester. To add servants to the equation would merely complicate the exercise further.

Maria could not resist a smile at the thought of the delights she had in store for Harry. She had been proud of what she considered an extensive repertoire of tricks but, since acquiring the set of little hard-backed books, she realized her knowledge had been distinctly lacking. Those books had proved extremely educational. In fact, she could hardly wait to start on the third one that evening. The very prospect lifted her spirits and left her feeling deliciously naughty.

~ * ~

The following day, in an increased state of agitation courtesy of the third little hard-backed book, Maria Dove applied particular care to her appearance. No one would treat her like a serving wench, she resolved, as she applied a large dollop of rouge to the center of both cheeks. Maria Dove was nobody's servant. She had assets–good assets—and she intended to use them. Her maquillage complete, she turned her attention to her wardrobe.

From her vast collection of gowns, she selected a burnt-amber silk edged with delicate lace. It was much more fitting for a ball than a day spent cataloguing a library. Maria didn't care. She was sick of waiting, desperate for some action. Today she intended to make a striking impression. Today she intended to tantalize every one of Harry Allenby's senses and drive him wild with so much heated desire that he would kick the boring, bookish Miss Winchester out of the room, lock the door and ravage Maria over the desk–after, naturally, she agreed to be his wife.

To Maria's vexation, she found Harry Allenby in an already heightened state of excitement that morning before she had had a chance to remove so much as her cloak. He was seated behind the large oak desk.

"Ladies," he pronounced animatedly, as the two girls entered the room. "You will never guess what I have found this morning."

Louisa's brown eyes lit up behind her spectacles. "Is it the sixteenth century edition of Italian poetry we spoke of yesterday?"

Maria rolled her eyes.

"No, it is not, Miss Winchester," said Harry, holding up a piece of paper. "It is something much more exciting."

Louisa, obviously intrigued, scurried over to the desk. Maria, on the other hand, did not even attempt to disguise her lack of interest. She flung her cloak over the back of one of the wing chairs before following at a much more subdued pace.

"Is it a letter?" asked Louisa, pushing her spectacles a shade higher on her nose as she peered at the paper.

Harry beamed at her. "Of sorts, Miss Winchester. It is a very strange note from my great aunt. A note requesting that I undertake a search for the Diddington Diamond."

At the mention of jewels, Maria Dove's ears pricked up. "What is the Diddington Diamond?" she asked.

"It is a precious, magical stone, Miss Dove. According to rumor, a lover had intended to present it to his betrothed when he returned from war. He hid it in the grounds of Diddington Hall for safekeeping. But he never returned and so no one knows where the stone is hidden," explained Harry.

A bolt of inspiration struck Maria. "Well, then," she purred, running a seductive finger along the laced edging of her bodice, "perhaps we should try and find it—together."

Harry leaned back in his chair, his long legs stretched out before him. "I think, Miss Dove—" He broke off, momentarily distracted by the pink and lilac butterfly fluttering at the window, "—that that is exactly what we should do."

Eleven

Alone in his London lodgings, Toby Allenby imbibed a large slug of whiskey and concluded that he did not wish to so much as smell another spoonful of broth as long as he lived. He had now spent a total of five days dishing out the slop. How anyone could even consider eating it was beyond him. But eat it they did—dozens of them—greasy-haired women with a clutch of grubby children about their skirts; men in ill-fitting clothes, their worldly belongings concealed in a dirty neckerchief; ragged orphans, all alone in the world, abandoned to the mercy of the crime-ridden streets. Amongst others.

Toby had never seen anything like it in his life. Obviously he had known such suffering existed. How could he not with beggars thrusting a filthy hand in his face every time he walked down the street and women of the night thrusting other things, pleading a pitiful sum for the use of their filthy, emaciated bodies? Other than tossing them the occasional farthing during a rare moment of magnanimity, Toby had never really dwelled on the plight of anyone other than himself.

Now, though, was not the time for Toby to be engaging in altruistic activities. He had enough problems of his own to deal with—one of them in the bony, sanctimonious form of Miss Lucinda Fothergay. The girl was so infuriatingly pious that, on more than one worrying occasion, she had made even the porcine Miss Bott seem desirable. For all his increasingly urgent need for a wife, Toby thought he would rather face another visit from Jack Wilmott's lackeys, than a lifetime with the dour Miss

Fothergay. How Caroline could even contemplate him marrying such a self-righteous creature was absurd. Clearly, Caroline had her own agenda—to ensure Toby's bride would prove no threat to her.

At the thought of his mistress, Toby felt a stab of anger. Caroline was so obsessed with her own egotistical motives that there was no consideration at all of his needs. He would, after all, be obliged to live with the wretched woman. Caroline's game was tantamount to blackmail and, as desperate as he was, Toby Allenby did not appreciate being its main pawn. If only he could think of some way of outwitting her, of choosing his own bride and whisking her down the aisle before Caroline had even a sniff of his intentions. He reached, yet again, for the whiskey bottle. Yet again, he found it empty.

~ * ~

Alone in Diddington Hall's library that same evening, Harry Allenby re-read Great Aunt Millie's note for what must have been the twentieth time. He had to confess to being somewhat mystified when he had found the missive—clearly marked for his attention—lying atop the desk first thing that morning. How it had come to be there, he had no idea. In the same way he had no idea exactly what Great Aunt Millie was about.

Ever since the will reading, Harry had concluded that the close bond he and his deceased relative had shared, had obviously not been half as significant to her, as it had to him. Great Aunt Millie had evidently thought a deal more of Toby and, to that end, had wished him to inherit her ancestral home. Then, just as Harry was coming to terms with that realization, this note appears.

What difference it made to anything, he didn't know. Did Great Aunt Millie wish Toby to inherit the hall and Harry the Diddington Diamond? Why though, if that was the case, had she not made things simpler? What he was certain of was that, even from the grave, Millicent O'Hare's mischief making continued; this particular prank stirring Harry's interest, making him feel more alive than he had for a very long time. He only wished he had had the foresight to break the news of the note to Miss Winchester without the ubiquitous, overly-painted Maria Dove present. That way, he could have had the added bonus of spending a little time alone with the girl—purely, of course, to concentrate on the note.

~ * ~

Millicent O Hare's note could only be described as cryptic. After the initial paragraph informing her great nephew, Harry, that she wished him to search for the jewel, there was a list of four locations, with an instruction that these be visited in strict numerical order and at the specific times noted. The first was the old Norman church at Little Hampton, to be visited at eight o"clock in the evening.

"How very intriguing it all is," murmured Louisa as she re-read the missive.

Maria Dove did not share this sentiment. "Hmph," she snorted. "I don't find it the least bit intriguing. In fact, I find it most odd. This O'Hare woman must have been as mad as Bedlam."

"I can assure you my great aunt was far from mad, Miss Dove," countered Harry. "A little eccentric perhaps, but then so are a great many intelligent people. Perhaps, if you feel so strongly on the matter, you would prefer not to assist Miss Winchester and myself."

Louisa noted a distinct shift in Maria Dove's tone as the girl affected an ingenuous smile and said, "Of course I wish to help. Nothing would give me greater pleasure, my lord."

By the look which flittered across Harry's face, Louisa did not think
he was convinced. She turned her attention back to the note. "I can only assume that there will be more clues to be found at each of these locations," she said, nudging her spectacles higher upon her nose. "Although why we are instructed to visit at specific times is a little puzzling."

"Puzzling indeed, Miss Winchester," concurred Harry. "And yet another adjective that can be aptly attributed to my great aunt."

~ * ~

Due to the late hour of the instructed visit to Little Hampton, Louisa suggested her mother accompany the party in the role of chaperon. With the excursion involving an enormous digression from Lady Winchester's meticulously planned timetable, the invitation had not, as Louisa expected, been greeted particularly effusively. It was for that reason that Louisa had kept something up her sleeve which might make the proposal a tad more appealing.

"Really, Louisa, you know very well that I do not have time to gallivant about the countryside looking for a ridiculous stone," Lady Winchester had protested.

"I thought it might be rather exciting, Mama," Louisa countered. "And I thought, perhaps, we could ask Lady Allenby."

At this suggestion, Lady Winchester suddenly acknowledged that she might find time for a little gallivanting after all.

The old Norman church, surrounded by rolling countryside just outside the village of Little Hampton provided a classic example of Romanesque architecture. Its thick stone walls, vaulted ceiling and decorated arches were a lasting tribute to its highly skilled workforce. Built in 1184, the church had recently become something of a tourist attraction. It was unfailingly included on the itineraries of Diddington's many visitors, a handful of which were still milling about when the Allenby carriage pulled up and its five occupants alighted.

"Well, what are we looking for?" demanded Maria Dove. The impatience in the girl's tone did not pass Louisa by. And why she had donned such an inappropriately revealing gown for the expedition, she could not begin to imagine.

Harry rubbed his chin. "I really don't know, Miss Dove. Perhaps some of us should take a look inside and the others outside. See if we can spot anything that might be contrived as a clue."

"What a splendid idea," concurred Lady Allenby. "Lady Winchester and I shall search inside, and if we don't find anything we shall have a little gossip in the pews."

Maria Dove spotted a chance. "In that case, perhaps you and I can search the back of the church, my lord. While Miss Winchester remains at the front."

Harry shook his head. "I, er, think it perhaps best if we all stick together, Miss Dove."

A look of what Louisa could only describe as fury, settled over Maria's face. "As you wish," huffed the girl, before flouncing off toward the back of the building.

Harry turned to Louisa. "Would you, er, like to accompany me, Miss Winchester?" he asked diffidently. "You may, of course, go with your mother if you prefer. Or even stay in the carriage. Or—"

"I should very much like to accompany you, sir," replied Louisa. "What do you suppose we are looking for?" she asked, as the two of them wandered along the side of the church.

Harry shrugged his shoulders. "I have no idea, Miss Winchester. I had thought that I knew my great aunt very well but, since her death, I'm beginning to think I didn't know her at all. Quite what she intends us to find this evening, I have not the first idea. I am only hoping that all will soon become clear."

Louisa did not share Harry's optimism. Unlike the churchyard at Diddington with its neat, ordered rows of graves, Little Hampton's offering was sadly lacking. The grass was unkempt and in imminent danger of overtaking the half-dozen crumbling headstones scattered about. Maria Dove, having given the scene a cursory glance, was already retracing her steps, muttering something about being cold.

"Well," sighed Harry, looking about him. "I really don't think we are going to find anything out here, Miss Winchester. Perhaps we should go and join the others inside.

"Hmm," mused Louisa. "I must agree. There can't possibly be a clue out here."

Unanimous in their defeat, the pair was about to turn around when something caught Louisa's eye. "Oh, look," she gasped, pointing to one of the crumbling headstones. "Is that a hedgehog?"

Harry peered over to where she was pointing. "I don't think so, Miss Winchester. It looks more like a—"

"Oh, the poor thing. It's entangled in some rope. We must go and help it." She began marching purposefully toward her target.

Harry stood watching her, amusement pushing at the corners of his mouth. All at once, though, Louisa tripped, falling flat on her face on the grass.

Harry was by her side in a flash.

"Oh," she muttered, gazing up at him. "I do believe I tripped, sir."

"I do believe you did, Miss Winchester," he agreed, his

lips twitching. "Do permit me to help you up." He bent toward her, his arm outstretched.

Louisa placed her hand in his and allowed him, in one effortless movement, to pull her to her feet. For several seconds they stood staring at one another. All signs of humor vanished from Harry's face as their eyes locked. Louisa's head began to swim at the intensity of his and the way his thumb was gently caressing the back of her hand. All at once, though, he dropped her hand, bringing her back to her senses with a rude start.

She averted her eyes. "The, er, hedgehog, sir," she muttered, glancing over to the crumbling headstone.

Harry continued staring at her. "Wh-what?"

"Th-the hedgehog. That I was about to rescue. From the rope."

"Oh," said Harry, finally tearing his eyes away from her. "Oh, yes. The hedgehog." He marched over to the headstone and retrieved a piece of old brown sacking. "I think you will find, Miss Winchester," his mouth broke into a wide smile, "that it was not a hedgehog after all."

A deep flush crept over Louisa's cheeks but, before she had a chance to dwell on her embarrassment, something else caught her eye. "Oh, my word," she gasped. "Have you ever seen a more beautiful sunset, sir?"

Harry spun around and regarded the evening sky, streaked with a stunning combination of fiery red, burnt amber, and deep purple. "No, Miss Winchester," he replied. "I honestly don't believe I have."

Several minutes later—exactly how many, Louisa could not say—the companionable silence in which the pair had watched the setting sun, was broken by Lady Allenby's cheery calls for her son. It was only then Louisa realized how close she had been standing to Harry. So close, that she had been all but nestling against the man's side. She could only pray that he had been so engaged in the sight nature had presented them, that he had not noticed her unconsciously wanton behavior. By more twitching of his lips, though, she had a strong suspicion her prayers had not been answered.

"Oh, Harry, you will never in a million years guess who we met wandering about the church," proclaimed Lady Allenby, bustling over to her son and Louisa as they joined the rest of their party.

"Hmm. Let me think," smiled Harry, scratching his head as though giving the matter a great deal of consideration. "I would hazard a guess at perhaps...your cousin, Viscount Winston, Mother."

Louisa's eyes grew wide as she, too, observed the viscount leaving the church alongside her mama. She had, of course, gathered from their exchange at the Merchistons' ball that the two men knew one another. She had had no notion that they were related.

"Are you acquainted with my cousin, Miss Winchester?" beamed the duchess.

"Indeed I am, ma'am," replied Louisa shyly.

"Well, now isn't that convenient," enthused Lady Allenby. "Although, I confess that, even with the help of dear William, not one of us found anything remotely resembling a clue inside the church. I'm afraid there was little else for it but for us to engage in a lovely chat instead."

Louisa's eyes shifted again to her mother. The word "lovely" was not one she would have chosen to describe Lady Winchester's disapproving countenance. Neither would she have applied the word "chat" to her tight-lipped, unmoving mouth. She felt a twinge of sympathy for the poor viscount who, despite this lack of interaction, was obviously doing his utmost to engage Lady Winchester in conversation. Louisa could only conclude that the man must be exceedingly partial to a challenge.

"Please, can we go now," moaned a shivering Maria Dove as Lady Winchester and the viscount joined the group. "I am on the verge of freezing to death."

"Perhaps if you wore a little more clothing," retorted Lady Winchester brusquely, "you would not feel the effects of the evening temperature quite so much, Miss Dove."

~ * ~

The day of the Sabbath dawned fair and bright, casting a blanket of good spirits over the residents of Diddington as they made their way to Sunday worship.

Despite this general air of buoyancy, his grace, the Duke of Wolsington and her grace, the Duchess of Wolsington could not hide their surprise. They had already taken their seats in the family pew next to the altar, when they noticed their eldest son entering the church, accompanied by two dour women in plain gray cloaks. They watched as the unlikely trio seated themselves on a bench near the back of the rapidly filling place of worship. And, as Toby glanced over to them, they found they could do nothing more than raise their hands in bemused acknowledgement.

"Pray tell me what on *earth* our eldest son is doing in church, Charles?" the duchess muttered to her husband through her disbelieving smile. "*And* in Diddington?"

"No idea," whispered the duke, as he regarded his offspring. "One can only deduce, Arabella, that something is amiss. Couldn't get the boy anywhere near a church when he was a youngster, and I don't think he's been near one since, except for the odd funeral or wedding."

A sudden horrific thought occurred to Lady Allenby. "Oh, perhaps he is ill, Charles," she gasped, pressing a hand to her chest.

Through narrowed eyes, the duke studied his son, who appeared to be absorbed in his hymn book. "Looks well enough to me," he muttered.

Lady Allenby's rejoinder rang with rising panic. "Oh goodness, I don't think he looks well at all. See how pale he is? And those dark shadows beneath his eyes. He looks positively ghastly. Oh, if he has caught some dreadful illness I shall never forgive myself. I should have noticed sooner but I was so preoccupied with Aunt Millie that I—"

"There's nothing wrong with the boy other than too many late nights and over-familiarity with the whiskey bottle, my dear," assured the duke.

The duchess was not convinced. She began fanning herself furiously with her hand. "He *must* be ill, Charles. What other reason could there possibly be to explain Toby attending church—and with two missionaries?"

~ * ~

Toby Allenby was so tired he could scarcely keep his eyes open during the church service. His fatigue had not been helped by the predictably dreary Fothergay colloquy during the carriage ride to Diddington. It had borne very little of the characteristics normally present in a conversation, and much more of those found in a sermon. The only positive he could glean from the whole painful fiasco was that Caroline, rightly assuming Toby's parents' suspicion may be aroused if she appeared with him again in Diddington, had thought it prudent not to join the outing.

Following the service, Lord and Lady Allenby were amongst the first to file out of the church. Although the pair affected pleasant smiles as they passed him, Toby did not fail to notice the look of disbelief etched upon his father's face, nor the look of concern on his mother's. This did nothing to lift his low spirits or quell his rising anxiety.

He forced up the corners of his mouth into what he hoped was a carefree grin. A great deal more effort would be required to convince his mother that Miss Lucinda Fothergay would make him the perfect wife. As he walked down the steps toward his parents, a heavy cloak of dread draped itself about his shoulders.

"Toby, darling," exclaimed his mother, reaching up and planting a kiss on his cheek. "What a lovely surprise. You are not ill are you, darling?"

"Ill?" repeated Toby. "Whatever gives you that idea, Mother?"

"You are looking awfully pale, dear," fluttered Lady Allenby. "And you cannot possibly be feeling yourself. The last time we managed to drag you to church—kicking and screaming, I might add—you were but twelve years old."

At this observation, Toby observed a sweep of horror settle over the insipid countenances of the Fothergays. "How you jest, Mother," he declared with a hollow laugh. "Now do permit me to introduce my two companions—Lady Fothergay and her daughter, Miss Lucinda Fothergay."

"Delighted to make your acquaintance, ladies," beamed the duchess, shaking hands with both women. "However, as lovely a morning as it is, I own I am a little puzzled as to what brings you all the way out to Diddington on a Sunday."

"It is the only free day we have, your grace," replied Lucinda. "We are engaged in the Lord's good work every other day of the week. It was suggested that, on our day of rest, a ride into the country might do us the world of good."

Toby noticed the questioning look his parents exchanged. "I, er, see," continued his mother. "And you engage in these good works *every* day, you say, Miss Fothergay?"

"Every day except Sunday, ma'am. On Sunday we spend all day in prayer and at our Bible studies."

Lady Allenby raised a dubious eyebrow. "May I ask how old you are, child?"

"My nineteenth birthday was last month."

"And do you not engage in a little, um, light entertainment in London? A ball or two?" enquired Lady Allenby.

"Indeed we do not," snapped Lady Fothergay.

"The Lord frowns on such frivolous undertakings, my lady," clarified Lucinda solemnly. "There are much more worthwhile causes to attend to, other than wasting time floating about a ballroom."

"Really?" murmured the duchess.

"Much more fulfilling tasks, Lady Allenby, as your son will confirm," added Lady Fothergay. "Lord Toby's help in the soup kitchen this last week has proved invaluable. We are hoping he may see fit to also helping us at the orphanage."

"Toby? In a soup kitchen?" repeated the Duke of Wolsington, staring at his son bewilderedly. "Are you *quite* sure you are not ill, man?"

Following the uncomfortable exchange outside the church, Lady Allenby suggested they all take a stroll along the banks of the river. This was the Fothergays' first trip to Diddington and, evidently impressed at the town's beauty, Lucinda had launched into a long soliloquy on the wonders of nature and how man should learn to love all God's creatures. The duke's merry quip that he certainly loved his weekly leg of lamb had not met with a particularly favorable response from either of the female visitors. Indeed the pair had subsequently increased their pace, walking some way ahead of the Allenbys.

"Now you know I am not one to normally interfere in your business, Toby dear," began the duchess, the moment the Fothergays were out of earshot. "I fully appreciate you are a grown man and have your own life to lead. However, I must say, I was astounded to hear of you working in a soup kitchen. Not, I hasten to add, that it is not a most worthy cause. But even you must confess, darling, that it is somewhat out of character."

Toby took a deep breath. "Since meeting Miss

Fothergay, Mother, I have realized that there are much more important things in life other than the pursuit of self-gratifying amusements."

"There undoubtedly are," concurred Lady Allenby. "But you were always so fond of self-gratifying amusements, Toby. I find it hard to believe that you now find them so abhorrent."

"Miss Fothergay has shown me a different route," replied Toby, suspecting that, even with the help of the Almighty, or in a whole month of Sundays, there was no way he was ever going to convince his mother that Lucinda Fothergay was his ideal match. And, to make his task even more daunting, his father seemed equally incredulous.

"Road to misery if you ask me," chipped in the duke. "Never seen you looking so down at heel, boy."

"I have never been happier since meeting Miss Fothergay, sir," countered Toby. "In fact, I am considering asking her to—"

The duchess stopped in her tracks. "If you say marry you, Toby, I shall have a fit of the vapors on this very spot. Why, the very notion of such a thing is—"

"I was about to say, Mother," cut in Toby, recognizing there was no point in pursuing the matter and hoping to save what was left of his rapidly diminishing dignity, "that I was considering asking Miss Fothergay to join me in a visit to the old Norman church at Little Hampton."

Lady Allenby gave an embarrassed chuckle and patted her son's arm. "Of course you were, darling. How silly I am to have even contemplated the other idea."

"Yes, Mother. Very silly indeed," muttered a defeated Toby.

Twelve

The fact that they had so far discovered no clue to the Diddington Diamond's whereabouts did not dampen the group's spirits when it came to organizing their visit to the next destination. This was, according to Lady O'Hare's list, the rose garden at Diddington Hall. Again, it was to be an evening visit—no earlier than eight o"clock.

"Well, in that case," Lady Allenby had enthused, as her carriage had dropped off the residents of Hartley House following the Little Hampton trip. "You must all come to dinner at the hall first. Let us say…Sunday evening."

~ * ~

Maria Dove accepted the invitation with particularly effusive enthusiasm, which quite overshadowed the graceful agreement by Lady Winchester and Louisa.

Maria had to confess to feeling somewhat infuriated at Harry Allenby's lack of interest in her, and his deal of interest in the tiny, flat-chested Miss Winchester. If she were honest, she was now despairing of her plan completely. Progress was non-existent, although the evening of the dinner party, she swiftly reminded herself, all that could change. This could be just the opportunity she had been waiting for. If she could just lure Harry into the garden alone…

~ * ~

Louisa Winchester could scarcely wait for the Diddington Hall dinner party. While she would never dare admit it, she now felt quite at home at the hall. Not only did she take great delight from its wonderful library, she also enjoyed the company of its residents. Harry Allenby, although still obviously one of what her mother would term "that wicked breed of gentlemen", had not once given her cause to doubt the sincerity of his nature. Indeed, if she were honest, it was now her mother's opinion of the opposite sex that Louisa doubted.

Due to recent experience, she was convinced that not all men could possibly be as callous and devious as Lady Winchester insisted. The Allenby contingent, for example, had awarded her nothing but the utmost respect. And Lady Allenby's cousin, Viscount Winston, appeared kindness personified.

Kindness personified he may be, but Louisa did not know what to make of the fact that Lady Allenby had invited the viscount to join them for dinner. To make matters worse, she had also placed him next to her mother. Lady Winchester, looking particularly beautiful that evening despite the austerity of her mauve gown, succeeded in maintaining, her daughter noticed, a polite—if somewhat aloof—façade.

Lady Winchester, though, wasn't the only person Louisa had observed that evening. Maria Dove, sporting an indecent amount of rouge, had been acting very strangely. On more than one occasion, Louisa had noticed her pouting across the table at Harry, with an almost predatory-like expression on her face.

"Now," proclaimed Lady Allenby, when they had come to the end of the excellent meal. "I know it is customary at this point for us ladies to leave the gentlemen to their cigars and brandy but, as the purpose of this evening is to further our pursuit of the elusive Diddington Diamond, and as it is now well past our instructed hour of eight o"clock, may I suggest that we all take a stroll around the rose garden and see if we can find whatever it is Aunt Millie intended us to."

"A marvelous idea, your grace," piped up Maria Dove. "Although surely there is no need for us *all* to go rooting around the garden at this late hour. I'm sure it would suffice if only a couple of us went. Myself and—" she cast an innocent look about the table "—Lord Harry, for instance."

Harry choked on his wine.

Lady Allenby favored her with a gracious smile. "How very magnanimous of you to consider us all, Miss Dove. But I find myself rather in the mood for an evening stroll. Now, gentlemen, please do permit us ladies a moment to collect our shawls and we shall see you outside in five minutes."

Louisa made to follow Lady Allenby out of the dining-room. She stopped for a moment at the empty chair at the head of the table where a strange, yet pleasant, smell hit her nostrils—an aroma that put her very much in mind of lavender.

~ * ~

The delightful picture composed by Diddington Hall's rose garden failed to impress Maria Dove. Not only was she unimpressed, she seethed with fury. Determined to fulfill her mission of having Harry to herself that evening, she had been completely robbed of any opportunity to drive forward her plan by the old Duke of Wolsington. The man had completely monopolized her with his tedious chat about Yorkshire. Maria had little enough interest in her home county at the best of times.

This evening, the ghastly place had been the last thing on her mind. Particularly as she'd observed Harry and that flat-chested chit, Miss Winchester, walking companionably across the lawn together, deep—as usual—in conversation. Just when Maria had thought the situation at its worst, the duchess arrived on the scene and announced to her husband that she should like him to accompany her and Miss Dove back to the house forthwith. The evening was far chillier than she had first imagined and Miss Dove must be positively freezing in her thin gown.

Left with no choice but to acquiesce, Maria had reluctantly allowed herself to be dragged back to the hall. But not before she had caught the look of satisfaction on their hostess's face as the woman had turned back and observed Lord Harry and Louisa Winchester wandering around one side of the garden, and Eliza Winchester and Viscount Winston around the other.

~ * ~

As tempting as it had been not to return to London with the Fothergays that Sunday afternoon, Toby knew he would merely be postponing the inevitable. He would also, had he stayed in Diddington, been forced to endure one of his mother's ghastly dinner parties and engage in some ridiculous hunt for a jewel. Toby was in no mood for games. He had therefore returned to his lodgings and, having bolstered his courage with a little help from his friend the whiskey bottle, gone to call on Caroline. He found her in the middle of a whole host of female preparations for a ridotto that evening.

Although the woman was a veritable thorn in his side, Toby had to admit that she looked divine in a spangled gown of gold silk, one lock of auburn hair falling over her shoulder in the most sensuous of manners. He quickly checked himself. That was not the reason he was here. Besides, her flawless appearance notwithstanding, Caroline appeared in extremely high dudgeon. She dismissed her maid the moment Toby appeared. He immediately broke the news of his ignominious visit to Diddington with the Fothergays. As expected, the news was not well received.

"Look Caroline, it's not my fault if my parents consider the girl unsuitable," he slurred.

"Well, whose fault is it then?" snarled the countess.

"I don't suppose you have considered that it may be yours," countered Toby. "If you would only allow me to choose my own wife, I could find someone of whom they would approve in a matter of days."

"That," snapped Caroline, "is out of the question."

Noting her murderous expression as she moved toward him, Toby shrank back in his chair. His blood ran cold as she placed her face uncomfortably close to his.

"Be warned, Toby Allenby," she hissed. "If you so much as look at another woman, I will find out. My spies are *extremely* reliable." She straightened and, much to Toby's relief, moved over to her writing desk. "No," she sighed, as she plopped down on the chair there and pulled out a list from the drawer. "There is nothing else for it. We shall simply have to do better."

~ * ~

The morning following the Diddington Hall dinner party, Louisa Winchester awoke in remarkably good humor. The sunshine streaming through the window further enhanced her good mood. Yet again, she mused, she had spent another enjoyable evening in the company of Harry Allenby. A most congenial evening indeed. That they had failed to discover a single clue to help them with their search for the Diddington Diamond did not dampen her spirits one jot.

Unfortunately, she was to discover, as she entered the

breakfast-room a little later, that the spring sunshine was not having such a positive effect on other members of the household.

"Good morning, Miss Dove," she chirruped, as she breezed into the room and assumed her seat opposite their houseguest. "What a beautiful day it is."

Maria Dove, engaged in the furious buttering of a slice of unsuspecting toast, stopped this activity to glower at Louisa.

"Beautiful day?" she sniffed, reverting, much to Louisa's astonishment, to her almost indecipherable Yorkshire accent. "It's nowt o' t" sort."

Sensing the younger girl's disgruntlement, Louisa determined not to allow her to spoil her good spirits. Making another sanguine attempt at conversation, she asked, "How did you enjoy the dinner party at Diddington Hall yesterday evening, Miss Dove?"

Maria Dove narrowed her eyes. "Yer asking *me* if I enjoyed that boring old dinner party?" she sneered. "Well, let me tell yer, Miss-butter-wouldn't-melt-Winchester, I've "ad more amusement mucking out pigs."

Despite her resolution, Louisa spirits nose-dived. Completely taken aback, she stared open-mouthed at Maria Dove, who had not yet finished her tirade.

"It don't take a genius t" guess what's put t" smile on *your* face. Don't think I didn't notice what yer were up t" while I was lumbered with that boring old...*duke* last night."

Louisa gulped. Was Maria Dove referring to the time she had spent alone in the garden with Harry? She was aware that it wasn't at all the done thing, but the situation had been none of her own contriving. It had all happened quite by chance. Nevertheless, a guilty flush crept over her cheeks. She made a faltering attempt to steer the conversation in another—less embarrassing direction.

"Well I, um, know that we did not find another c-clue, Miss Dove, but we mustn't lose heart. There are, after all, two others we are yet to—"

"It weren't clues I were thinking o"," interjected Maria who, to Louisa's growing dismay, was now holding her knife in what could only be described as a threatening manner.

Much to Louisa's relief, the door to the dining-room suddenly burst open. A disheveled Lady Winchester staggered into the room looking, for all the world, as though she were on the verge of apoplexy.

"Mama!" gasped Louisa. "Whatever is amiss?"

Lady Winchester all but toppled into the chair at the head of the table. "I do not wish to cause a scene, Louisa," she sighed, "but I think it only fair to tell you that I have scarce closed my eyes all night."

"Why ever not, Mama?"

Lady Winchester yanked a lace handkerchief from her sleeve and dabbed at her forehead. "Because, child—" she paused for breath, "—every time I closed my eyes I experienced the most appalling nightmares."

Louisa furrowed her forehead.

"Nightmares of myself, alone in the garden with that ghastly…that ghastly…*viscount*."

Louisa drew in a sharp breath. "Are you referring to Viscount Winston, Mama?"

Lady Winchester's shudder was followed by an affirmative nod.

"But Viscount Winston is not at all ghastly," protested Louisa. "In my opinion the man is all that is consideration."

Lady Winchester flashed her daughter a look that implied she thought her all about in the head. "That viscount is nothing more than a…a…*man*, Louisa. And we all know what they are capable of."

A sardonic snort came from Maria Dove. Lady Winchester, having tossed the girl a disapproving glare, continued her speech.

"I am afraid, Louisa, that I shall be forced to decline any other invitations that come our way. My nerves simply cannot stand another ordeal like that of yesterday evening. I confess, I think it may be more advantageous to be considered a social pariah than endure another such torturous evening. I only trust you will agree with my sentiments."

Louisa did not agree. Not in the slightest. Despite her concern at her mother's distress, she was flooded with disappointment. How ironic it all was. If Lady Winchester had informed her only a few weeks before that they were never again to grace Diddington's social circuit, Louisa would have eagerly welcomed the decision. In marked contrast, she was now on the verge of tears. The reason for her disappointment was as disturbing as the emotion itself. The truth of the matter was that she had thought she might, in future, find such occasions diverting—depending, of course, on whether a particular Harry Allenby was present.

Louisa had never enjoyed herself quite so much as she had since making Harry's acquaintance. At the same time, neither had she ever felt quite so odd. Something very strange seemed to happen to her whenever she was around Harry Allenby—and at no time more so than in that magical rose garden yesterday evening.

She recalled observing, out of the corner of her eye, the duke and duchess—and a reluctant-looking Maria Dove—returning to the hall. The trio were swiftly followed by her mother who had quickly distanced herself from the viscount at an impressive rate of knots. Despite the fact that she had then been alone in the garden with Harry, Louisa had had no compulsion to follow her mother's example. Although she would never dare admit it—especially not to Maria Dove—she had rather liked being alone with him. That fact notwithstanding, the man had such a strange effect on her senses that Louisa was at a loss as to what to make of it. Every time he looked at her, she tingled from head to toe. Every time she caught the scent of his soap, she became light-headed and, whenever their hands touched, which, remarkably, was not always an accident on her part, her stomach somersaulted. In addition, she hadn't slept for days and her appetite had completely vanished.

What it all meant, she had no idea. Whatever it was, something told her it would be prudent to keep it to herself. She was only relieved that Harry had informed her yesterday evening that he would be absent from Diddington for several days on some business in London. A little while away from the man would give her time to think straight and, hopefully, to work out exactly what was wrong with her.

~ * ~

In London, Lord Toby Allenby had not enjoyed such high spirits for a long time. He had, by what means he could not recall, managed to wangle a whole ton out of one of his oldest friends, Lord Wells. Toby was particularly proud of this achievement given that it was his oldest friends who had first joined forces and announced they would not be lending him another penny. Then again, he reflected, perhaps he had taken advantage. He couldn't recall ever paying one of them such much as a bean back.

Today, though, old Welly had submitted. The fact that the man's acquiescence was due more to the bottle of vintage brandy the two of them had supped, than Toby's own persuasion tactics, did not bother Toby in the least. He was off to a very discreet gaming house. He would have a little fun there before the theatre closed and then a little more fun with his obliging actress.

Taking his leave of the club—and of Lord Wells, who was now slumped in a drunken heap on the floor snoring raucously—Toby staggered out into the street and looked about for a hackney cab. To his great amazement, one appeared immediately.

"First time that's happened, I don't mind telling you," he slurred to the jarvey. "Take me to John Street, there's a good man."

Toby then settled himself on the cracked leather seat and fell into a very deep sleep.

He awoke with a jolt, but it was several seconds later before he made any sense of his surroundings. He appeared to be in the middle of a derelict building that stank of rotting fish. He was tied to a wooden chair, his hands behind his back. And he was staring down the barrel of a loaded pistol. Other than that, he had no idea what was going on, but had the distinct impression he was about to find out.

"Now then, Lord Allenby—"

Toby whipped his throbbing head around to find Jack Wilmott sitting in an incongruous high-backed velvet armchair a few yards from him. He was a short stout bald man with a penchant for garish waistcoats. This evening, though, he sported one of plain funereal black. It did not bode well. Terror pulsed through every one of Toby's veins as he watched Mr. Wilmott take a languid draw of his cigar. Was this it? Was this the end of his life? If it was he hoped they wouldn't torture him. He'd rather they got it over with quickly. Just one accurately aimed bullet would do it. He gulped as the cold steel tip of the pistol pressed against his cheek.

Mr. Wilmott broke into Toby's terrifying musings. "It seems a positive age since we last saw one another, does it not, sir?"

Toby took a deep breath, which could, he realized, be one of his last. "I-it does indeed, sir. Time has a ha-habit of passing extremely quickly."

Mr. Wilmott nodded pensively. "Very true. Very true. Before we know it, we shall all find ourselves six feet under."

At the knowing chuckle that followed this remark, Toby's guts twisted.

"But we are not here to talk about such depressing matters," declared Mr. Wilmott, drawing in another mouthful of smoke.

"We-we aren't?" stammered Toby.

"No, indeed, sir. In these hard times, we all have enough to concern ourselves with making our way in the land of the living. Do we not, Lord Allenby?"

"We-we do, sir," muttered Toby. "Times are very hard. Very hard indeed."

Mr. Wilmott nodded again. "Although, I own, my lord, poor Mrs. Wilmott is finding it harder than most."

"She-she is?"

"A lot of mouths to feed, you see."

Toby said nothing, sensing the conversation's general direction.

"*Jack*, she said to me the other day, *if we're not careful those poor babes will starve to death.*"

Toby gulped.

"Now, it has come to my attention how you've been easing the plight of the poor, Lord Allenby. Been helping out in the soup kitchen, so I hear."

Toby nodded, the tip of the pistol grazing his skin.

"A very worthwhile cause," mused Mr. Wilmott. "Very worthwhile indeed. I don't mind admitting, I didn't take you for the caring sort, Lord Allenby, most of the Quality not giving a damn what happens to anyone outside their little circle."

"N-not me, sir," stammered Toby.

"Well, I'm very pleased to hear that, sir. What with me being a very caring man myself. And because I'm so generous, I thought it only fair to give you a little advance warning of our new terms. Another month you have, sir, before I shall require the whole sum—plus interest. Now is that not generous?"

"Ex-exceedingly, sir," murmured Toby realizing, with some relief, that he had another month to live at least.

"Good, good," concluded Mr. Wilmott, rising to his feet. "Now, please do be excusing me, my lord. It's been very pleasant sitting here chatting with you an" all, but I'm sure you understand I have other business to attend to. Not everyone is as obliging as yourself, sir. Mr. Mac here will be showing you out, if that's agreeable to you."

As the door swung shut behind Jack Wilmott, Toby dared to turn his eyes very slowly to the aforementioned Mr. Mac. The ruddy whiskered face and the smell of the man's fetid breath were not evoking good memories. He was about to find out exactly why.

Thirteen

Ever since the dinner party at Diddington Hall, Maria Dove had continued to exhibit all the signs of a young woman in the darkest of humors. Although her hosts and their servants were not excluded from her torrents of invectives, it was the doors of Hartley House that bore the brunt of the girl's ill will. Never, in all their years, had they been closed quite so fervently.

Due to the gloom surrounding their houseguest, Louisa had made no attempt to hide her relief when Maria Dove had informed her that she would not be accompanying her to Diddington Hall.

It was, therefore, due to the absence of both Maria and Harry, that the butler found Louisa alone in the library that afternoon and informed her that her presence was required in the crimson drawing-room forthwith.

"But whatever for?" a bemused Louisa had asked.

"I believe there has been an incident, miss."

"An incident? What kind of an incident?"

"One, I believe, involving your mother and a cutthroat."

Unable to believe her ears, Louisa had run to the appointed room as fast as her legs would carry her. There she had found Lady Winchester reposing on a chaise-longue, with a very concerned Viscount Winston and Lady Allenby fussing about her.

"Whatever has occurred, Mama?" she gushed, heading directly to her mother.

Lady Winchester rested the back of her hand against her

brow, striking a most dramatic pose. "Oh, Louisa, I am quite overcome. It being such a pleasant day, I decided to take a little air and walk into Diddington. On my return, I had just passed Diddington Hall, when…when—" She broke off at exactly the same moment a tear streaked down her cheek.

Louisa gazed imploringly at the viscount, now perched on the window seat.

"I believe what your mother is trying to tell you, Miss Winchester, is that she had just passed the hall, when out of the bushes sprang a young man brandishing a knife."

Louisa gasped and threw an astounded look at her mama before turning her attention back to the viscount. "Whatever did he do?"

"Thanks to dear William here chasing off the blackguard, I am pleased to report that the man did nothing more than make a futile demand for your mother's purse," replied the duchess.

Louisa swung her head back around to the viscount. "You-you chased him off, sir?"

"I did nothing more than any law-abiding man would have done had they encountered the same scene," informed the viscount with marked diffidence. "I am only grateful that I happened to be there when I was."

"As are we all," concurred Lady Allenby. "It is beyond contemplation what might have happened."

From her supine position, Lady Winchester emitted a little whimper.

"And so, contemplate it we will not," continued Lady Allenby, skillfully steering the conversation onto a more positive note. "Now, Eliza dear, may I suggest a nice dish of hot tea and a slice of currant cake? A very reliable combination, I always find, for soothing one's nerves."

"A marvelous idea, Cousin," agreed Viscount Winston. "Then perhaps, Lady Winchester, you would allow me to escort you back to Hartley House in my cousin's carriage?"

Lady Winchester, who, at the mention of tea and cake, had managed to bring herself to a sitting position, regarded the viscount with an unfathomable expression on her face.

"I'm sure my mother would appreciate that greatly, sir," proffered Louisa, breaking the embarrassing silence. "Would you not, Mama?"

Her eyes still fixed on the viscount, Lady Winchester nodded her beautiful head.

~ * ~

Contrary to clearing her head and making some sense of her symptoms, several days apart from Harry Allenby had left Louisa exhausted. Even more perplexing was that, despite her looking forward to some respite from the man, he had persistently occupied every one of her thoughts. She had even preferred to sit in his chair in the library while she had carried on her work there—his lingering scent making her feel paradoxically close to him, yet yearning for him at the same time. If she did not know better, she would say that she had missed him. But, with the exception of Miss Wilson, her old governess, she had never missed anyone in her entire life.

She had already decided to feign the headache after dinner and retire early to her bedchamber. There she would give the matter a great deal more concentrated thought. To her amazement, though, she discovered her mother had made arrangements of a quite different nature.

"But I don't understand, Mama. Why on earth do you suddenly wish to attend Lady Silverdale's ball? A matter of days ago, you stated quite adamantly that we were to accept no further invitations."

"I am quite aware of what I said, thank you, Louisa," retorted Lady Winchester, fiddling with the clock on the mantel. "However, I spoke with Lady Allenby this morning and the woman all but insisted upon my attendance. The occasion would, she assured me, be the perfect tonic to that dreadful incident with the cutthroat."

From her chair by the fireside, Louisa noted the flush creeping up her mother's neck. "But whatever shall you do if Viscount Winston is present, Mama? We do not, after all, wish you to have another bout of recurring nightmares."

Lady Winchester continued to avoid her daughter's gaze. She left the mantel and moved over to the sideboard. She began rummaging in a drawer there. "If the man is in attendance, then I shall simply ignore him," she replied, her attempt at nonchalance not fooling her daughter at all.

Louisa wrinkled her brow. Before she could continue her

line of questioning, Korbett, the butler, appeared in the doorway, bearing an elegant bouquet of white lilies bound with green silk ribbon.

"From Viscount Winston, Lady Winchester," he informed. "With a note."

As the recipient all but ran over to accept the offering, Louisa noted the woman's cheeks were now a deep shade of scarlet.

"What does it say, Mama?" she asked, as her mother ripped open the note and began reading it.

Keeping her back to her daughter, Lady Winchester put down the note on the sideboard and resumed her drawer rummaging. "Um, nothing more than he trusts I, um, have recovered from my dreadful ordeal."

"Is that all?"

Lady Winchester gave a strange little cough. "Well, um, I believe he may, er, also have mentioned something about a ball."

"Lady Silverdale's ball this evening?" enquired Louisa, increasingly mystified by her mama's behavior.

"Perhaps," replied her mother. "I-I really can't recall." Then, swapping her embarrassed tone for one of attempted vexation, "Really, Louisa, I know the man saved me from that dreadful criminal, but the truth of the matter is, he is becoming something of a nuisance. I have a good mind not to attend the ball this evening as an indication of my irritation."

Somehow, Louisa concluded that that circumstance was as unlikely to occur as Maria Dove attending the occasion in a high-necked gown.

Louisa could not deny that the unexpected turnaround in her mother's decision *vis-a-vis* their social situation was something of a relief. Nevertheless, she remained devoid of any inclination to attend the Silverdales' ball that evening. The reason for her lack of enthusiasm required very little deliberation. Yet again, as she began making her half-hearted preparations, her thoughts turned to Harry Allenby. How different her mood would be if he were back in Diddington and attending the same function that evening. But he was not. He was still in London. Which meant that, should she meet with an unseasonably early wasp, fall into a pond, or slip down a ladder, there would be no one there to rescue her.

~ * ~

Harry Allenby had never ridden so fast in his entire life. Although London had never ranked highly on his list of favorite locations, this time he found he could barely stand the place. The dirt, incessant hustle-and-bustle, noise and traffic had all conspired to make the trip particularly unbearable. He could scarcely believe, in just a few days, how much he had missed the peace and tranquility of Diddington—amongst other things. He spurred his horse on, noting the position of the sun. If they carried on at this pace, he calculated he should arrive in Diddington in ample time to attend Lady Silverdale's ball.

~ * ~

"Whatever is the matter, Louisa?" asked Lady Winchester, as the two women and Maria Dove climbed into their carriage that evening. "You have looked quite out of sorts for several days now."

"Nothing is the matter, Mama," muttered Louisa. "I am a little tired, that's all."

"Maybe it's all that *'ard work* at t' library," suggested a sneering Maria Dove.

At the younger girl's insinuation, Louisa's cheeks flew scarlet—a shade that was not at all reduced by her mother's next comment. "I do hope Lord Harry is not expecting too much of you, Louisa. In my experience, gentlemen are prone to take advantage of the fairer sex in as many ways as they can contrive."

Maria Dove's subsequent knowing snort prompted a disdainful glare from her hostess.

"You must let me know, child," Eliza continued, "if your work at the hall is proving too much for you. I am sure Lady Allenby would understand perfectly and would have no hesitation in speaking with her son."

"It's not my work at the library, Mama," admitted Louisa, longing to confide in her mother. "It's—" Catching the expectant look hovering over Maria Dove's countenance, she broke off. "It's nothing more than a good night's sleep will cure."

"Well then, may I suggest retiring to bed a little earlier," sniffed Lady Winchester.

Louisa bit back the urge to say that that was exactly what she had been planning.

Upon their arrival at the Silverdales' large country mansion, Louisa could barely conceal her amazement. As they handed their cloaks to the footman, she discovered her mother had discarded her usual gray and mauve attire, in favor of a gown of emerald-green silk, edged with gold lace. And that was merely the first surprise. As the evening progressed, Louisa observed that, for the first time she could ever recall, her mama actually appeared to be enjoying herself. In fact, she would have gone as far as to say that the woman may even have reveled in all the attention the cutthroat drama was awarding her. As she watched her mama talking animatedly with Lady Allenby, Louisa could not help but wonder at her parent's loveliness. Her pride, though, was tempered with another emotion—that of resentment. For the first time in her twenty years, Louisa resented her lack of inherited beauty and, most of all, her spectacles.

She recalled quite clearly how, two years earlier, she had smiled when the optician had nervously delivered his prognosis. Her unexpected reaction—which had thrown the man into a fit of sixes-and-sevens—had been primarily due to relief. The diagnosis had coincided exactly with her entry into Diddington Society. A society in which she would be forced to make the acquaintance of that terrifying breed known as "gentlemen". Gentlemen, it was widely appreciated, were never attracted to ladies in spectacles.

Thanks to her mother's many homilies over the years, Louisa had always found the notion of a gentleman's attentions quite repugnant. Now, however, her feelings on that matter had undergone a dramatic about-turn. If only she were spectacle-free and even half as lovely as her mother, then perhaps there may be a chance Harry Allenby would find her something more than a source of amusement. Not, of course, that she wanted him to fall in love with her or any such nonsense. But an elevation of her status in his eyes would do her confidence the world of good.

Swamped by despondency, and with her mother deep in conversation and Maria Dove nowhere to be seen, Louisa sought out a relatively quiet corner of the ballroom, as far away as possible from the eager musicians. She sank down on a chair there, where she resolved to remain until it was time to go home. She was in no mood for small talk, even with the delightful Lady Allenby. She was tired. Very tired. In fact, despite all the activity going on within feet of her, she could not prevent her eyelids closing. All at once, a familiar voice startled her—to such an extent that she almost toppled from the chair.

"Miss Winchester," said Harry Allenby, a smile playing about his lips. "Whatever are you doing hiding here?"

Shocked at both his unexpected presence and the fact that, in his immaculate evening attire he looked even more devilishly handsome than usual, Louisa's mind was wiped completely blank.

"I'm, er—I own, I'm, um, really not sure, my lord," she stammered, wishing he would stop staring at her in that disconcerting manner.

Harry's smile broadened. "Well," he said slowly, "perhaps, if you have nothing better to do, you might care to join me in a dance."

Louisa's brows shot to her hairline. "Dance? But I-I have never danced in my entire life, sir."

Harry's eyes twinkled. "I can assure you it is really not so difficult,
Miss Winchester. If you would permit me to show you..." He held out his hand to her.

Panic surged through Louisa. "But I-I couldn't possibly, sir. I shall be a laughing stock. And...and there is my mother. She would not—"

"Your mother is very well occupied in the supper-room."

Louisa cast desperately about for another excuse, but the determined look in Harry's navy-blue eyes told her he was in no mood for arguing. Admitting defeat, she tentatively placed her own hand in his large one, overwhelmingly aware of the difference in size, and could not resist a gasp as, with the minimum of effort, he pulled her from the chair, directly into his arms.

"May I have the pleasure of this waltz, Miss Winchester?" His gaze burned into hers.

With a hammering heart, and in a hushed whisper, Louisa found herself replying, "You may, sir."

Dancing, Lady Winchester maintained, was not only a waste of one's energy, but yet another cunning ruse employed by gentlemen to tempt and trick the fairer sex. Well, a cunning ruse it might be, mused Louisa as Harry swung her smoothly around the dance floor, but it was certainly a very effective one. So tempted and tricked was she that she had given no thought at all to the steps. The steps were, in fact, the very last thing on her mind.

Instead, every one of her senses was swamped by the realization that she was in Harry's strong arms, her head pressed to his broad chest, breathing in his delicious scent. In such a mesmerizing trance was she, that she did not, at first, realize the music had stopped and, for several seconds afterwards, remained in Harry's arms. The sound of Harry clearing his throat brought her back to reality. She jumped back from him, flooded, once again, with embarrassment.

"Would you, er, care to join your mother in the supper-room, Miss Winchester?" he asked, his lips twitching.

Noting his evident amusement at her absurd behavior, a mortified Louisa averted her eyes from his and mumbled, "I, um, I think I should prefer to retreat to my corner, if you don't mind, sir."

"Then allow me to escort you."

Silently chiding herself for her foolishness, Louisa could not think of a single thing to say to him as they made their way around the room. Harry, too, seemed lost in thought. Consequently not a word passed between the pair until they reached their destination.

"Thank you, for the, er, dance, sir," muttered Louisa, her eyes firmly fixed on a spot on the floor.

Harry did not reply. To Louisa's astonishment, he placed a finger beneath her chin and tilted up her head. Gazing into his eyes, her heart stopped. She was suddenly breathless. Her lips ached. Whatever did that mean? That she wanted him to kiss her? But she couldn't possibly. She had never been kissed in all her twenty years. She didn't have the first idea *how* to kiss. She would have to escape from the situation immediately, before she made an even bigger fool of herself. But, as Harry lowered his head to hers, all thoughts flew from Louisa's mind. Instinctively she closed her eyes and parted her lips, wanting nothing more at that precise moment than to feel his mouth upon hers.

"Good night, Miss Winchester," she suddenly heard him say.

Louisa snapped open her eyes to discover him marching away from her with unprecedented haste.

Never in her life had she felt more disappointed—or more foolish. And for a young lady as prone to accidents as herself, that was a remarkable feat indeed.

~ * ~

Mr. Gerald Hinds, Great Aunt Millie's solicitor, happened to be passing the corner of the ballroom at the precise moment Harry Allenby had tilted up Louisa Winchester's head to him. This intimate moment had brought forth a smile to the solicitor's lips. He didn't know what it was about Millicent O'Hare and her matchmaking skills but, even from the grave, they appeared to be most effective.

If he didn't know better, he would think the woman some kind of witch.

~ * ~

Red-hot anger surged through Harry's veins as he marched toward the supper-room. He was furious. Furious that he had, for the first time since Clara's death, allowed his resolve to slip. Not that he had ever really looked upon it as resolve. In the last five years he had not experienced the slightest temptation to so much as dance with another woman. This evening, in contrast, he had found himself employing every ounce of his restraint not to sweep the tiny Miss Winchester off her feet and kiss her to distraction. He was not sure what was happening to him but, whatever it was, he did not like it one bit. And he knew exactly what he needed to do to bring himself back to his senses.

~ * ~

In Lady Silverdale's supper-room, a bored Maria Dove had just helped herself to her third éclair. What else, after all, was there to do? There were no gentlemen here with whom she would even dream of amusing herself. Nor was there any chance of furthering her plan given that Harry Allenby was still in London. Or was he? Maria did a double-take as a man, bearing a strong resemblance to Harry, entered the room. No, she had not been mistaken. That was definitely Harry Allenby, marching directly over to his mother.

Maria crammed the remains of her éclair into her mouth, tossed her china plate into a nearby plant-pot, tugged down her bodice, and began sashaying over to Lady Allenby, who was deep in conversation with Eliza Winchester. She reached the pair at exactly the same moment as Harry. She greeted him with her most dazzling smile. It was returned with a stony glare. Before Maria could utter a word, Lady Allenby exclaimed, "Harry darling, we did not expect you back from London this evening."

Harry turned his unsmiling face to his mother. "I managed to escape a little earlier than planned, Mama. Having paid my respects to Lady Silverdale, however, I am now about to return to the hall."

"Oh, but surely not," protested Maria Dove, abolishing all signs of the Yorkshire accent to which the Winchesters had, once again, become accustomed. "Why, you have only just arrived, sir. Surely you would not be so heartless as to begrudge a poor, lonely girl one dance."

"I am sorry, Miss Dove," he intoned. "But I am exhausted from my journey. Perhaps Viscount Winston would be happy to oblige you."

"What's that?" asked the viscount as he joined the group. "Are you taking my name in vain, young Allenby?"

"Merely suggesting you may wish to dance with Miss Dove, sir. I am about to take my leave. Goodnight ladies. Sir."

As Harry whisked around, Maria Dove was so vexed that it was all she could do not to stamp her foot. All at once, however, a mischievous idea occurred to her.

"Please do forgive me, sir," she said, turning to the viscount, "but it quite slipped my mind that I have promised this set to another. Perhaps Lady Winchester would like to take my place."

At this impudent suggestion and the viscount's subsequent expectant expression, Eliza Winchester flushed the same color as the red gilded chair on which she was seated.

~ * ~

Harry arrived at the churchyard the following morning at what generally would have been considered something of an ungodly hour. The sun had just announced its ascent by streaking the sky a vivid pink and yellow, while the grass glistened with heavy dew. Harry paid the scene little heed as he marched purposefully toward Clara's grave. The only sensation of which he was aware, was a strong, vice-like grip of guilt, which had been tightening its hold on him all night.

How could he have behaved so abominably the previous evening? So abominably that he had almost betrayed Clara? Clara Walpole was, he reminded himself for the umpteenth time in the last few hours, the only woman he had ever loved and the only woman he ever intended to love. The fact that he had imagined he may be experiencing similar feelings for the diminutive, bespectacled Miss Winchester appeared now, in the cold light of day, nothing short of preposterous. It had served no other purpose than to demonstrate the strange effect the manic ride back from London must have had upon him.

After some forty minutes chastising himself thus, and feeling suitably penitent, Harry was on the verge of leaving when he found himself drawn, once again, to the grave of the mysterious stranger. What would this person have thought, he wondered, if they had known they would eventually lie in a forgotten grave? Would that harsh fact have made any difference to the way they had lived their lives? Would they have made different choices? Ensured they had no regrets? Or would it have made no difference to them at all?

That Harry had no intentions of marrying, and was almost assured to die childless, meant that he, too, could end up in such a lonely deceased predicament. Given the size of the Allenby family crypt, of course, this was unlikely. But, had he been of a different class, then the choices he had made could easily have led to him being an abandoned soul. Did that matter to him? Should he be doing something different with his life? Was how we ended up in death a reflection of how we ended up living our lives? Harry didn't know, nor was he sure he even wished to.

Fourteen

In London, Lady Backfield's Spring Ball had long been heralded as one of the major events of the Season. Ever since that coveted declaration, people had been known to go to extreme and bizarre lengths to gain an invitation. No such inventive efforts were required on the part of Lord Toby Allenby or Lady Caroline Levington, both of whom featured highly on all of the capital's guest lists. Despite the auspiciousness of the occasion, though, and the ease with which he gained entry, Toby was not at all desirous of attending Lady Backfield's ball. Caroline, according to the note she had sent demanding his attendance, was evidently of a different mind.

Toby had not been near Caroline since his run in with Mr. Wilmott. He had not, in fact, been near anyone. He had remained in his bedchamber where he had consumed a vast amount of alcohol—purely, of course, to dull the pain of his battered and bruised body. How he could have been so naïve as to even consider that Jack Wilmott might have let him off with just a warning now beggared his own belief.

The time alone with his bruises and bottles had done nothing to raise Toby's spirits. Never, in his entire life, had he been more miserable. The seriousness of his situation had been brought home to him with every one of Mr. Mac's punches. Toby needed money—lots of money—and he needed it soon.

During his self-induced confinement, he had given a great deal of thought to his options in achieving this goal. The first, to which an inordinate amount of consideration had been directed, had revolved around his father. If the duke thought for one moment that his son's life was in danger, surely he wouldn't hesitate in bailing him out. But in asking for his father's help, Toby would be admitting failure, condemning himself to the same depressing chapter of family history as his dissipated grandfather. More significantly, he would also be throwing away the dukedom. His father would have no hesitation in stripping him of his future title—and all that accompanied it—if he suspected Toby incapable of bearing the responsibility.

No, if Jack Wilmott was going to spare him his life, then Toby wanted it to be a life worth living. He wanted his birthright, title and all. He therefore *had* to get his hands on Diddington Hall—and sell it. And, while he knew his parents would strongly oppose the sale, Toby had mentally prepared his defense. Great Aunt Millie's will had contained no stipulation regarding the keeping of the house. Nor had his father's infamous contract mentioned anything about monies Toby might receive from other sources.

Naturally, Toby had no intention of revealing to his father why he needed the money. He intended merely to say that, as the country held little interest for him, he wished to invest the proceeds in a more lucrative scheme. Before any of that could happen, however, there remained the not insignificant detail of his finding a wife.

Damn Caroline! If only she wouldn't insist on complicating the matter. But complicating it she was and Toby now had very little choice but to go along with the cursed woman's plans. He only hoped that the next girl she had lined up for him was a vast improvement on Miss Bott and Miss Fothergay. Not that it signified. Whoever she was, Toby would have to marry her anyway and use every one of his persuasion tactics to convince his parents that he was head-over-heels in love. He pulled the counterpane up over his head. Perhaps he should add another, easier option to his list—that of death.

~ * ~

The third young lady on Caroline Levington's list of potential brides was one Miss Charlotte Ray, who, Toby was delighted to discover, was a deal more presentable than her predecessors. Not exactly pretty, with pale red hair and a smattering of unfashionable freckles, the girl was certainly not unappealing enough to turn the milk sour. But perhaps, pondered Toby, he had been a little too critical of the other two candidates. Perhaps they had not been so bad after all. Or perhaps, and much more likely, he had imbibed so much whiskey before he left the house that he seemed to be viewing everything in a more favorable light.

Neither Miss Ray, her mother, nor Caroline, appeared to be looking on Toby Allenby quite so auspiciously. An understandable circumstance, perhaps, given all his staggering and swaying. Oblivious to the disapproving nudges and winks surrounding him, Toby had followed his calamitous entrance by drunkenly informing the trio that he hoped the fashion for low-cut gowns would continue until he was cold in his grave. He was just about to move on and share his opinion on hemlines, when Caroline grabbed his arm.

"Please do excuse us, ladies," she beamed to the astonished Lady Ray and her daughter. "I have just recalled a matter of the utmost urgency which, I regret, I must discuss with Lord Allenby in private."

Leading Toby firmly away, her smile evaporated the moment she turned her back to the two women. "For God's sake, Toby," she hissed, as she steered him out onto the terrace. "If I had thought for one moment that you might turn up in this state, I would not have even considered introducing you to Miss Ray."

"What, hic, state are you referring to, my angel?" enquired Toby, affecting his most innocent smile.

Caroline's violet eyes glinted dangerously. "You know fine well what state I am referring to. Not only are you so drunk you can hardly stand up, but you look as though you have done ten rounds in the boxing ring—and lost."

A swaying Toby reached for the balustrade to steady himself. "If you, hic, are referring to my black eye, then I, hic, thought it suited me rather, hic, well."

"It does not suit you at all," snapped Caroline. "And I am assuming you did not acquire it in any sporting venture."

"Fell down the, hic, stairs."

Caroline fixed him with an icy disparaging glare. "I really do wonder why I am bothering, Toby," she huffed. "I have invested a great deal of my valuable time in trying to find you a wife and you have, yet again, squandered an ideal opportunity. I had a perfectly timid, pliable little chit lined up but, once again, you have ruined everything. Not only have you frightened the ninnyhammer—and her mother—half to death, but you have completely humiliated me and in front of the entire *haut ton*. I recommend you remove yourself from this house forthwith, before you embarrass yourself, or indeed me, any further."

"If you, hic, insist, my sweet," replied Toby, a much more welcoming scene occurring to him. "I shall go straight, hic, home."

"It is for the best, sir," concurred Caroline sanctimoniously.

"Of course it, hic, is, darling."

Not daring to risk a ride in another hackney, Toby opted to walk to the theatre to visit his little actress. The chilled night air had a sobering effect on him. Whatever had he been thinking turning up in such an inebriated state? Caroline was right. He had ruined any chance he might have had to woo the meek and freckled Miss Ray.

The girl's appalled mother would not now allow him within ten feet of her daughter—and who could blame her? Certainly not the daughter, who would no doubt be equally undesirous of having him within ten feet of her. The worst of it was, the chit really hadn't seemed so bad, if one ignored the fact that so much as a sneeze would have scared the wits out of her. Well, no good dwelling on spilt milk. He only hoped that Caroline had another suitor lined up—and soon. Throwing a look over his shoulder, he breathed a sigh of relief. There appeared to be no one following him—for this evening at least.

At the theatre, Toby made his way directly to the actresses' changing room via the usual warren of bustling corridors. The buzz which filled the building never ceased to have an uplifting effect on him as, indeed, did the antics of his little thespian. To his bewilderment, though, he found the chair she usually occupied empty—and no sign of her things on the dressing table. A seed of worry took root.

"Where's Francesca?" he asked one of the other girls, who was applying a thick coat of red paint to her lips.

The girl's eyes grew wide. "She's gone, sir."

"Gone?" repeated Toby, his worry sprouting at an alarming rate. "Gone where?"

"Dunno, sir," shrugged the girl. "All we know is some note arrived telling her if she valued her pretty face, she'd be out of London by tonight."

Toby stood motionless.

"And that's not the worst of it, sir," continued the girl, wrinkling her nose. "The note was delivered in a box—a box containing a dirty stinking dead rat."

At this revelation, Toby Allenby turned around and promptly vomited all over his polished shoes.

~ * ~

Toby was at his wits' end. He could not sleep. He could not eat. He could not even think straight. And thinking straight ranked well above both eating and sleeping at this particular time. Caroline refused to see him. Whether this was a good thing or a bad thing, Toby couldn't decide. There was not a scrap of doubt in his mind that she had arranged for the note and the dead rat to be sent to his little actress. As if that were not worrying enough behavior, the matter of how she had found out about the affair also weighed heavily upon him. He could only assume that she had people constantly watching him. The thought made him shudder.

Caroline Levington's spies, though, were not the only ones apparently monitoring Toby's movements. Notes from Jack Wilmott, providing daily reminders as to his payment date, had started to pop up in the most unlikely places. Toby's nerves were in tatters. He needed a wife and he needed one quickly. But what decent woman—of whom his parents would approve—would even consider him as a husband given the state he was in? And, introductions to prospective daughters-in-law aside, how could he even face his parents in his current condition?

Toby was squeezed into a very tight corner. So tight, he could hardly breathe.

~ * ~

For all Lady Eliza Winchester's extensive library at Hartley House included a catholic and impressive range of reading matter, its distinct lack of romantic material would undoubtedly have caused disappointment to a less distinguishable young lady. That Lady Winchester would have blithely tossed such works into the fire was not the only reason this circumstance had occurred. It was rather that Louisa

Winchester had never been remotely inclined to read such frivolous fiction. It was, therefore, with some trepidation and a great deal of curiosity, that she found herself surreptitiously borrowing Maria Dove's copy of Miss Jane Austen's *Sense and Sensibility* that evening.

After three full hours of reading Miss Austen's novel, Louisa sat bolt upright in bed, horror surging through her. It had only at that moment occurred to her—she was in love with Harry Allenby—totally and utterly and hopelessly in love. She flopped back onto her pillows, suddenly feeling extremely nauseous.

~ * ~

Toby had not left his lodgings for two whole days. He had had neither the inclination nor the courage to relinquish the safety of its four walls. Those four walls, though, were not feeling quite as safe as they used to. Over the past forty-eight hours, two of Jack Wilmott's reminders had turned up in the apartment—one pushed under the door and the other— much more terrifyingly—under his pillow. The mere notion of how the note had come to be in his bedchamber sent a shard of ice slithering down Toby's spine. His nerves were in pieces. Every noise caused him to jump, and something as innocuous as a knock at the door, propelled him to the edge of apoplexy.

His fragile state notwithstanding, the knock at the door that morning had brought with it a mixed blessing in the form of a note from Caroline, demanding his presence forthwith. Toby wasted no time deliberating his feelings. Instead, he ordered his carriage and, keeping a wary eye out of its window all the while, arrived at the Levingtons' townhouse not thirty minutes later. Caroline received him in her bedchamber. So out of sorts was her visitor that the fact she was wearing only a white silk robe, so thin it was almost transparent, barely registered in Toby's befuddled mind. In contrast, Caroline's powers of observation appeared distinctly sharper.

"Good lord!" she exclaimed, the moment she set eyes upon him. "Whatever have you done to yourself?"

Toby did not answer. Instead, he plopped miserably down into an armchair which, quite by chance, awarded him an unhindered view of the three-part mirror on the dressing table. A disheveled man, with greasy, too long hair, three days' growth of beard, and heavy black bags underlining each of his red eyes, stared back at him.

"Jesus," he muttered, running a hand over the thick stubble on his chin. "I didn't think I looked quite as bad as that."

"*Bad* is something of an understatement," sniffed Caroline. "I don't mind telling you, Toby, that had you presented such a pitiful sight the first time I met you, you would not have held my interest for a second."

At this admission, Toby wished vehemently that he had neither shaved nor bathed before that fateful weekend house party all those months ago. Unfortunately, he, like many others before him, lacked that much-coveted ability to turn back the clock. The timepiece concerning him presently was much more important, ticking off the minutes, hours and days with terrifying speed—as Mr. Wilmott's notes insisted on reminding him. Rather than wasting more of this valuable time worrying about the state of his appearance, Toby seized the bull by the horns.

"I wish to apologize for my behavior at Lady Backfield's ball, Caroline. I was completely out of order and can assure you there will be no repetition of such a shameful scene."

Caroline's eyes held a knowing glint. "My, my, what a change of heart you appear to have had, my lord. Such a change, in fact, that one cannot help but wonder if Mr. Wilmott has his infamous screws in you."

Toby dropped his head into his hands. "Enough of these games, Caroline. No doubt your *contacts* have informed you that Mr. Wilmott *is* turning up the heat. Well, all right. I admit defeat. You win. Go ahead and choose whomever you like to be my bride and, if it is the last thing I do—which it may well be—I shall do everything possible to convince my parents that she is the woman for me."

To Toby's amazement, this speech was not greeted with an air of victory, but with one more akin to boredom. "Hmm," mused Caroline, smoothing her eyebrow with the tip of her index finger. "The business of finding you a wife, Toby, has become more than a little tedious. Perhaps I should just leave the matter to you as you first suggested."

"But you can't!" barked Toby. "Not now. Look at the state of me. I'm not eating. I'm not sleeping. I'm living on my wits. There is no way I can find a wife of my own now. Please, Caroline, you've got to help me."

Caroline gazed pensively out of the window, before turning to look at him once more. "Very well," she sighed at length. "But I am warning you, Toby. If you let me down again, I shall be very *very* upset."

~ * ~

In accordance with Lady Winchester's meticulously planned timetable, the three residents of Hartley House were to be found in the drawing-room just before dinner that evening— Lady Winchester and Louisa bent over their embroidery and Maria Dove paying more surreptitious attention to the window than the book she was assumed to be reading. Noting the hour, the younger girl resisted a smile as she threw another sly glance outside and saw exactly what she had been expecting.

"Goodness, Mama," declared Louisa, upon spotting a green carriage rattling up the drive. "I do believe it is Viscount Winston come to call upon us."

All color drained from Lady Winchester's face. "V-viscount Winston? At this hour of the evening? W-whatever can he want?"

"Well," smiled Maria Dove beatifically, "I expect we shall soon find out."

"Lady Winchester," beamed the viscount, executing a bow in the doorway a few minutes later. "May I say how very gracious it was of you to
invite me to dine here this evening."

Lady Winchester's dark eyes grew wide. "I-invite you? To d-dine? Here? Th-this evening?"

"Why, yes," the viscount said. "The invitation arrived two days ago…" He trailed off, the look of stupefaction on Eliza Winchester's face leaving him in no doubt that she had not the first clue to what he was referring. "You did send me an invitation, did you not, ma'am?"

A dumbstruck Eliza shook her head.

The viscount appeared ready to sink. "Oh," he muttered.

Louisa, almost as stunned as her mother, gathered her wits. Thrusting to her feet, she declared, "Obviously, sir, there has been some misunderstanding. But, now that you are here, there is no reason why you should not join us for dinner. Cook is always over-generous with her portions and I'm sure there will be more than enough for the four of us."

The viscount scratched his head. "Well, I'm not, er, sure," he mumbled, casting a questioning look in the direction of Lady Winchester. "After all, my turning up completely unexpectedly must seem like the greatest imposition. I cannot, I own, contrive how the misunderstanding has occurred. I received an invitation only two days ago and sent a reply forthwith, informing you that I should be delighted to attend."

Louisa glared at Maria Dove who was listening to the exchange with an air of angelic innocence. "Well, it does not signify in the slightest, sir," she continued. "Please do say you will join us."

The viscount bit his lip, slanting another look at Lady Winchester.

"Well, I suppose that as you are here," muttered the older woman, addressing her hushed tone to a spot on the carpet, "you might as well stay."

Although having long since considered Viscount Winston a kind and considerate man, Louisa had had no idea just how interesting he was. He had, of course, been present at the dinner party at Diddington Hall, but Louisa had been so preoccupied with Harry, she had paid the viscount very little attention. He had, so it transpired, spent a great deal of time overseas and related several amusing stories of his foreign exploits.

Lady Winchester contributed very little to the conversation. Nonetheless, Louisa had noticed a marked change in the woman's behavior toward their dinner guest and could only attribute this to his heroic actions in saving her from the cutthroat. The distant and aloof manner she had maintained during the dinner party at Diddington Hall, had now been replaced by something altogether softer. On several occasions, Louisa had even noticed her casting a furtive look at their guest from under lowered lashes and, when he spoke directly to her, color flew to her cheeks. Was it possible that—? But no, it couldn't be. Could it?

~ * ~

The following morning, Maria Dove remained in her bedchamber chewing her nails. Although she had denied any part in Viscount Winston's suspicious dinner invitation, it had not stopped Lady Winchester from giving her a stark piece of her mind. But Eliza Winchester's ranting was not paramount on Maria Dove's list of concerns. Something much more pressing was on her mind. A certain monthly event was, she had calculated with mounting apprehension, almost three weeks late. She glanced down at her assets, resplendent in scarlet silk—and feeling, she suddenly acknowledged, decidedly tender. As dark clouds of gloom began gathering over her head, Maria Dove reached for her chamber pot and emptied into it the entire contents of her stomach.

Fifteen

Much to Harry Allenby's politely concealed delight, Miss Maria Dove once more failed to appear at Diddington Hall that morning. Louisa had informed him that the girl was not feeling at all the thing.

Wasting no time worrying about Maria Dove's health, it did not pass Harry by that Louisa did not look at all the thing either. While still undeniably pretty, she had lost something of her sparkle; the normal bloom in her cheeks had disappeared; and there were dark smudges beneath her eyes.

"Are you feeling quite well yourself, Miss Winchester?" he asked, as she stood before the desk in the library.

"Quite, um, well, thank you, sir," she mumbled, in a manner that implied to Harry quite the opposite.

Harry felt a niggle of worry. Had he done something to upset her? Perhaps it had been the way he had left her so abruptly at Lady Silverdale's ball. But no, it couldn't possibly be that. Miss Winchester could not have had the first idea that he had had to employ a mountain of restraint not to kiss her. He had acted in a most gentlemanly manner. Perhaps, then, she had no wish to carry on the search for the Diddington Diamond—particularly as they seemed to be getting no further forward with it.

The third instruction on Great Aunt Millie's list was a visit to the willow tree at the bottom of Buttercup Meadow—to be made before noon. Harry's heart had sunk when he had read it. Given the emotions he had experienced the last time he had visited the meadow, he did not relish the thought of another visit. The place held far too many memories for him and he would hazard a confident guess that being there with Miss Winchester would only exacerbate his state.

Half hoping that her answer would be of a negative nature, he tentatively asked, "Are you, er, happy to continue with the search for the diamond today, Miss Winchester?"

"Perfectly happy, sir," muttered Louisa. Her lack of eye contact and mournful tone leaving Harry in no doubt that "happy" was not a word one could associate with Louisa Winchester today.

~ * ~

Contrary to what she had told Harry, Louisa did not feel at all the thing. She desperately wished she had had the foresight to feign some illness and had not had to face Harry today. It was the first time she had seen him since her embarrassing behavior at Lady Silverdale's ball and, more significantly, the first time she had seen him since she had realized she was in love with him. This "condition", as she was now referring to it, was not one she was happy with. Nor was it one her mother would be happy with. And today, of all days, Harry had announced that he intended investigating the third clue on his great aunt's list; a clue that just happened to take them to the willow tree in Buttercup Meadow—Louisa's favorite place in the whole of Diddington.

Well, Louisa had made up her mind. This was to be the last day she would spend in the company of Harry Allenby. She would invent an excuse that meant she could no longer assist him with the cataloguing of the library. She had no wish to exacerbate her condition and putting some distance between the two of them could only expedite her recovery.

In spite of Harry's bright chatter as they crossed the flower-strewn meadow, Louisa had a strong suspicion that something worried him. He seemed a little on edge as he handed her over the stile, and had demonstrated no sign of humor when the string of her reticule had caught on the wooden post dragging her backwards. But, whatever Harry Allenby had on his mind, she concluded, it could be nothing to her own humiliation and despair. She could not wait for the day to be over when she could return to the safe confines of Hartley House—and not venture forth from them again until she had made a complete recovery.

"Well," sighed Harry, as they arrived at their destination. "Here we are, Miss Winchester."

"Indeed." Louisa plumped down onto the grass.

Harry remained standing, looking about him bewilderedly. "And, yet again, I have absolutely no idea what we are looking for," he confessed, sitting down next to her. "What do you make of this apparently wild goose chase my relative has sent us on?"

The Diddington Diamond being the last thing on Louisa's mind at that moment, she directed her reply to the abundant patch of daisies beside her. "I really don't know, sir."

"Well, I think it's all very odd," said Harry. "I hate to say it, but I think Miss Dove may well have been correct when she suggested my great aunt was mad. The exercise makes no sense at all."

At that moment, a family of ducks came waddling toward them with five fluffy brown ducklings.

Louisa's spirits immediately soared. "Oh, look!" she cried. "Are they not adorable?"

They both watched as the parents led their squawking offspring down to the waterside. Four of them immediately followed their elders, taking to the water with ease. The fifth remained on the riverbank.

"Oh!" exclaimed Louisa. "She must be afraid. She'll have to join them soon or she'll be left behind."

"I'm sure she'll be fine," assured Harry.

"But what if they leave her behind? What will happen to her?" gasped Louisa.

"She will be straight in the water the moment she sees them leaving," Harry assured her calmly.

Louisa observed the scene with mounting agitation as the four water-borne ducklings copied their parents and dived underwater. All at once though, the diving lesson complete, the little family began heading downstream. Still the fifth duckling remained on the bank.

"No, it is no good," asserted Louisa, tugging off her slippers. "I cannot bear to see her left behind. I shall coax her into the water myself."

Harry lifted a dubious eyebrow. "I really don't think,

Miss Winchester, that is a very good idea."

"And why not?" challenged a clearly affronted Louisa.

A faint smile hovered over Harry's lips. "Without wishing to be rude, your recent history in the area of animal rescue has not been what one would call a roaring success."

Noting his amusement, Louisa turned her attention back to the patch of daisies, plucking at them furiously. "Perhaps not," she sniped. "But at least I mean well. At least I try. I didn't know that it was not a hedgehog outside the church at Little Hampton. And it certainly wasn't my fault that that poor frog in Lady Merchiston's pond—"

"Ah, yes. The frog with the, er, damaged femur," cut in Harry.

"Yes, the frog with the damaged femur," confirmed Louisa.

Noting his strangled tone, she whipped her head around to him and found his broad shoulders shaking with constrained laughter. Quite what was so amusing, she had no idea, but, overcome with a combination of tiredness, humiliation at her condition, and anger that Harry was, once again, laughing at her, a tear escaped her. Quickly she wiped it away and turned her attention back to the daisies.

"Oh, Miss Winchester," said Harry, his tone suddenly serious. "I am so sorry. I didn't mean to upset you. It's just that the note you sent me, when you included that description about frogs' legs…it was…well, it was…" he burst out laughing.

Anger surged through Louisa. "Obviously you found it highly amusing, sir," she snapped, her eyes bright with the combination of fury and tears. "Obviously, you find *me* amusing. Well, let me tell you, Lord Allenby, that I am not amusing. I am not amusing at all. In fact, I have it on good authority that I am actually very clever and I—"

She had no opportunity to expand on her impressive list of credentials because, before she could take stock of what was happening, Harry Allenby had drawn her to him and was kissing her.

~ * ~

As Harry strode furiously along Diddington's country lanes, he could not believe what he had just done. Not only had he kissed Louisa Winchester, but he had done so under the willow tree at the bottom of Buttercup Meadow—the same place he had first kissed Clara Walpole.

And that was not the worst of it! The entire time he had been holding Louisa in his arms—which must have been at least five minutes—he had not given Clara a single thought. He had been thinking of no one other than the adorable Miss Winchester.

Well, it would not do. It would not do at all. Louisa Winchester affected him in the most peculiar way—a way he was not at all comfortable with. The only escape he could see out of the embarrassing situation was for him to return immediately to London. He would inform Miss Winchester that she could carry on with the cataloguing of the library and the search for the Diddington Diamond if she so wished, but Harry could not bear to be around her a moment longer. The girl had somehow wriggled her way under his skin, occupying every one of his thoughts, and stirring up feelings he had long considered dead. Feelings that should be dead—just like Clara.

He pushed open the gate to the graveyard and marched directly over to Clara's grave. Crouching down, he traced her name in the slab of marble. A shiver ran down his spine. The marble—the only thing he had to remind him of her—was cold and hard; the very antithesis of Clara who had been so warm and soft. He read the epitaph—"Loving Daughter & Sister"—no mention of "Wife". She had been taken from Harry before he had had the chance to make her his completely. That did nothing to ease Harry's conscience. He had kissed another woman and, by doing so, he had betrayed his beloved Clara Walpole.

~ * ~

Louisa Winchester, her head still spinning from that kiss, had not returned directly to Hartley House. Instead, she had wandered, in something of a daze, along the riverbank trying to make some sense of what was happening to her. The fact that Harry had caught her completely off-guard had not, of course, helped the situation. At least if she had had time to prepare, had had some inclination of what was about to happen, she could have…

She could have what? She had no idea what. She would not have changed a single thing. The kiss had been everything she had dreamed of—and more. And she had returned it every bit as eagerly. Then it had stopped. And, muttering something inaudible, Harry had jumped to his feet and run off, leaving Louisa's insides churning and her head reeling—a state which had not altered by the time she passed the churchyard—just in time to see Harry disappearing inside.

By the time Louisa reached Hartley House, she was emotionally and physically drained. She found both her mother and Maria Dove in the drawing-room—her mother scribbling a letter at her writing desk, and Miss Dove seated before the fire sipping a cup of tea.

"Are you all right, child?" asked Lady Winchester, noting her daughter's flushed cheeks and glazed eyes. "You are not looking at all the thing."

"I'm quite well, thank you, Mama," Louisa said, in no mood for fussing.

"Well, you certainly don't look it," countered a concerned Lady Winchester. "I only hope you are not coming down with the same thing as Miss Dove."

Maria Dove choked on her beverage.

~ * ~

Despite an early night, Louisa awoke the next morning feeling ten times worse than when she had retired. Her body ached and her head pounded. Not wishing to be alone with her miserable thoughts, she dragged herself out of bed and down to the breakfast-room. There she found her mother at the table engrossed in a letter, the contents of which, if the expression on her face was any indication, were not particularly uplifting.

Lady Winchester put down the note and heaved a heavy sigh.

"Whatever is it, Mama?" croaked Louisa.

"It is Cousin Olivia," replied Lady Winchester. "My one and only relative. She has, so her neighbor has written to inform me, met with an accident and broken her leg."

"Oh, the poor dear," exclaimed Louisa. "And her widowed only six months ago. However will she cope on her own? Has she employed a nurse?"

"Apparently she refuses to even contemplate the idea. She has no wish to have a stranger in her home and is, instead, asking for me."

"For you? But you haven't seen her for years."

"Indeed I have not," concurred Lady Winchester. "Nonetheless, the woman is family and, unlike me, is not fortunate enough to have a daughter for—"

She broke off at Louisa's racking cough. "Goodness, child," she exclaimed, taking in her daughter's clammy skin and glazed eyes, "you really are not looking well. If I'm not mistaken, you are developing a fever."

She placed her hand on Louisa's burning brow. "Well, that is decided," she declared. "You do have a fever. I shall write immediately to Cousin Olivia and inform her there is no way I can even contemplate leaving you."

"It is just a cold, Mama," dismissed Louisa. "I think poor Cousin Olivia is likely in far greater need of your services."

Lady Winchester was not convinced.

All three residents of Hartley House were partaking of tea and cake in the drawing-room when Lady Allenby came to call a little later. Lady Winchester wasted no time in outlining the situation to her.

"Well, I can see no problem at all," pronounced Lady Allenby. "The solution is as clear as day. You must go to your poor cousin, Eliza, and the two girls must come and stay with me at Diddington Hall."

Immediately following Lady Allenby's proposed solution, which Lady Winchester accepted with only a polite amount of demurring, the two girls had been instructed to pack their belongings. Devoid of both the inclination and the energy to participate in the task, Louisa had delegated it wholly to her maid. Although she had not dared to object, lest she raise suspicion, the mere thought of removing to Diddington Hall filled her with dread and, she was convinced, had already increased her temperature by several degrees.

How could she possibly face Harry Allenby after that kiss yesterday? The kiss she had scarcely been able to put out of her mind. Conversely, Harry Allenby had obviously put it out of his mind—and very quickly too. Running off as he did showed that he must have regretted his actions immediately. And, if that were not humiliating enough, he had then gone directly to visit another woman—albeit a dead one. Did that, Louisa wondered, make him any better than the men her mother had constantly warned her against? She didn't think so. And if Harry Allenby thought, for one moment, that he could treat Louisa Winchester like a used slipper, then he had better think again.

~ * ~

Lady Caroline Levington was silently congratulating herself. Not only did she have Toby Allenby exactly where she wanted him—begging her assistance in his search for a wife—but she also had the perfect girl for him—Miss Alicia Flowers. Although a little prettier than her three predecessors—which was why Caroline had placed her last on her list—Miss Flowers was certainly no competition for Caroline's outstanding beauty. The girl was also of a slightly more balanced nature than the others and should, she reflected, find more favor with Lord and Lady Allenby, but hopefully not too much favor with their son.

What was more, the meeting was to take place at a garden party just outside Diddington which, Caroline was assured, would be attended by both the Duke and Duchess of Wolsington. Toby would therefore have the opportunity to introduce the girl to his parents that same day. Everything was falling into place perfectly, Caroline concluded with a smile, as she swiped up her parasol and her reticule and headed downstairs to her waiting carriage.

~ * ~

Toby Allenby had invested a great deal of time in his appearance that morning. Thanks to his valet's assiduous attentions, he almost resembled his old self.

"Not bad," mused Caroline, as he climbed into her carriage. "Not bad at all." She puckered her lips to him.

Toby planted a perfunctory kiss upon them. As ravishing as Caroline looked in her fashionable white gown, ravishing the woman was the last thing on his mind. He had no desire to lay another finger upon her. But how to escape his mistress's evil clutches was a problem that would have to wait until later. Much later. First, Toby had to find a wife, sell off Diddington Hall, and remove Jack Wilmott from the equation. And to do all of that, he required Caroline's help.

Toby's spirits soared the moment he set eyes upon Miss Alicia Flowers. With her dark blond hair and large blue eyes, he found her refreshingly pretty. Moreover, his positive opinion could not be attributed to the whiskey bottle. He had not touched a drop that morning. The girl also seemed perfectly normal, with a distinct lack of snorting, religious fervor, or surfeit of nerves. He could scarcely wait to introduce her to his parents, who, to add to Toby's optimism, seemed particularly pleased to see her.

"Ah, Miss Flowers," beamed Lady Allenby. "How lovely to see you today. And may I pass on my felicitations on your betrothal—I heard of it only yesterday."

Horror crept over Toby's face. "You are b-betrothed, Miss Flowers?"

Alicia Flowers colored up. "Yes, my lord. To the Duke of Beesley. The announcement was in yesterday's *Morning Post*. Obviously you did not see it."

"No," muttered a devastated Toby. "Obviously I did not."

~ * ~

Hidden from the rest of the throng, in a small copse of trees, Caroline Levington appeared equally as surprised as Toby at the news—and equally as unimpressed. "The Duke of Beesley?" she spat. "The man is the biggest dullard in England."

"I'm afraid your opinion matters little, Caroline," snapped Toby. "The chit seems more than happy with the match. Dullard or not, I think you may safely scratch Miss Flowers's name from your list."

"Which leaves us with precisely... no one," pronounced Caroline.

Toby stared at her aghast. "No one? But I need a wife, Caroline. And I need one quickly. If you can't find me one, then I shall have to take matters into my own hands."

"And we all know where that will lead us," said Caroline with a knowing smile. "I shall have to give the matter further reflection, Toby. When I have, I shall let you know." With that, she whisked out of the trees in a haze of perfume, leaving a distraught Toby staring after her.

~ * ~

Looking about her very large and very comfortable room at Diddington Hall, Maria Dove could only conclude that fortune was, once again, shining down on her. Now that they were ensconced in the same house, she would have the perfect opportunity to seduce Harry Allenby. This time there would be no distractions. This time Maria Dove would go straight for the kill—and she had the perfect strategy for doing so. She dug out the fourth of her set of little hard-backed books and turned to page forty-six.

~ * ~

Downstairs in Diddington Hall's library, Harry Allenby poured himself another brandy. He had no desire at all to retire. He attributed this circumstance to Miss Louisa Winchester's presence in the house. Although he had seen the girl only fleetingly that afternoon, before his mother had whisked her straight up the stairs, the wrathful look she had flashed him had made up his mind. Despite his ability to think of very little else, the kiss they had shared had obviously done nothing more than offend the girl. His mother had muttered something about Louisa being unwell. Harry considered it more likely the girl was taking refuge in her room—refuge from him. Well, that was fine by him. It wasn't as if he was hoping she had fallen in love with him or anything. He most certainly was not in love with her. And, to prove it, he planned to remove to London the very next day. There he would lose himself in the hectic whirl of the Season. With that decision made, he reached for the brandy decanter and poured himself another large glass.

By the time Harry made it upstairs, he was in a much mellower frame of mind. Perhaps he wouldn't go to London tomorrow. After all, he really couldn't stand the place. Besides, why should he allow his feelings for a woman—and a tiny, bespectacled one at that—force him out of Diddington? He would face the situation head on tomorrow. He would confront Miss Winchester and tell her there was no need for her to hide from him. He would explain that the kiss had been a mistake, that he had not been himself and that he was deeply sorry for taking such liberties. With that resolution firmly in mind, he slipped into bed and into a deep, inebriated slumber, only to wake with a start.

It took a few minutes for him to figure out exactly what was happening. Someone was under the covers of his bed. And that someone was performing a rather impressive trick with their tongue, and a very delicate part of Harry's anatomy. Harry lay quite still for a moment, contemplating how best to handle the situation. First, his blood being as red as any of his male counterparts, he considered simply lying there and enjoying the experience. It was a long time since he had had such intimate contact with a woman. Naturally he visited the odd ladybird now and again. He was, after all, a man in his prime. But that was nothing more than a business transaction. Perhaps then, a business-like approach may be just the tack to adopt now. He cleared his throat.

"Miss, er, Dove," he exclaimed in a hushed whisper. "What on earth are you about?"

Maria Dove's heavily rouged face peeped out from beneath the covers and grinned. "I just thought you might like a bit of fun, sir. Given how we've never had the chance to be alone."

Harry rolled his eyes. "And what, pray, gives you the impression I wished to be alone with you?"

Maria batted her lashes. "You're a man, sir. And there's not many who would say no to being alone with a pretty girl." She sat up, allowing the bedcovers to slide from her back. "What's more, how can you resist *them*?" she asked, thrusting forward her naked assets.

Harry gulped, and promptly averted his eyes to the ceiling. "They are indeed very, um, *impressive*, Miss Dove. Nonetheless, I am afraid I shall be forced to resist. I think it perhaps best if you put on some clothes and return to your chamber."

A look of stupefaction fell over Maria Dove's painted countenance. "But don't you want to—"

Harry held up his hand. "No, Miss Dove. I certainly do not."

No sooner had a furious Maria Dove pulled on her robe and stomped out of the room, than Harry buried his head in a pillow and groaned. That embarrassing incident had made up his brandy-befuddled mind. He was *definitely* going to London tomorrow. Whatever dangers lurked in the streets of the capital, he was certain to be safer there than he was at Diddington Hall. At least there, there would be no risk of losing his heart—or his virtue.

Sixteen

If Maria Dove had not had more pressing matters on her mind, she could have spent weeks, nay—months, indulging her humiliation at Harry Allenby's rejection, and equally as long plotting her revenge.

Maria's immediate concerns, though, were of far greater importance. Having given her predicament an inordinate amount of thought, she had still made no decision. Harry Allenby had well and truly scuppered her Plan A. She now needed a Plan B. She could, of course, go back to Yorkshire and marry Ned Stickleback but that would be her last resort. If she was with child, and it was looking increasingly as if she were, she could be no more than six weeks. If she acted quickly, she could still find herself a rich gentleman and pass off the child as his.

Time was of the essence and, as Harry Allenby had been her only hope in Diddington, the one option left to her was to make her way to London. She was still mulling over the finer details of this plan when an interesting development occurred at Diddington Hall leading Maria Dove to conclude, once again, that she was a very blessed young lady indeed.

~ * ~

Toby Allenby could not face returning to London. The mere thought made him ill. A few days at Diddington Hall would allow him a little respite from Jack Wilmott's terrifying notes. And, with his brother absent, at least his mother seemed pleased to see him.

Toby could not fail to notice that Lady Allenby's

pleasure at her eldest son's unexpected presence was far outweighed by that of another member of the household—a very comely young wench by the name of Maria Dove. The girl had made no attempt to conceal her eagerness to sit opposite him at dinner that evening. Finding her blatant admiration a refreshing and welcome change, and being decidedly relaxed thanks to the four large glasses of wine he had imbibed, Toby felt the urge for a little flirtatious banter.

"So, Miss Dove…" He fixed the girl with a lascivious stare. "My mother informs me you are to stay awhile at the hall with a friend of yours."

From beneath a sweep of dark lashes, Maria returned his look with equal lasciviousness. "Yes, sir. Although I am afraid poor Miss Winchester is suffering the affliction of a cold and is unable to join us this evening."

Toby ran his tongue along his bottom lip and focused his eyes on the deep tantalizing valley between Maria Dove's magnificent breasts. "Oh, what a pity," he murmured, his tone implying quite the opposite. "Still, every cloud has a silver lining. The fact that Miss Winchester is unable to join us, permits me the opportunity to focus all my attention on you. Now, tell me, what do you wish to talk about?"

"Oh, do tell me all about London, my lord," gushed Maria Dove. "I own, I am most desirous to visit there soon."

All at once, Toby's features hardened. "London is no place for innocent young ladies, Miss Dove. It will suck you up and spit you out as though you were nothing more than a piece of chewed fat."

A horrified Lady Allenby set down her wine glass. "Toby! Pray do not frighten the girl so. And what on earth are you referring to? You have always adored London."

"Not any more, Mother. In fact, if I never set foot in the place again, it will be a day too soon."

The duchess shook her head despairingly. "Really Toby, I do not know what has got into you lately. You have been acting most peculiarly. You would tell us if you were in any sort of trouble, wouldn't you?"

Toby contorted his mouth into a disingenuous smile. "Of course, Mother," he slurred, raising his glass to her. "But what sort of trouble could I possibly be in?"

Lady Allenby regarded her son through narrowed navy-blue eyes. "I own, I cannot even begin to think, Toby."

"And for that, we thank God," snorted her son, before bursting into a manic fit of laughter.

~ * ~

Maria Dove had found her dinner with Toby Allenby most interesting and the man himself most handsome—in a much more rugged way than his younger brother. She had also intuited that Toby Allenby was in some sort of trouble. And quite what that trouble was, Maria intended to find out—that same evening.

Feigning the headache, she retired to her chamber early after dinner. Seated at her dressing table, she preened herself for some thirty minutes, touching up her rouge and teasing her ringlets. She had then patiently observed the hands of the clock until they reached half past eleven, by which time, she was confident, Lord and Lady Allenby would have retired. Adjusting her assets so that they were displayed to their full advantage, she then slipped out of her room and made her way downstairs.

She headed first to the crimson drawing-room. Upon finding both it and the small room adjacent to the dining-room empty, she racked her brains as to where else her prey might be. She turned in the direction of the library. Easing open the door, her heart began hammering when she spotted Toby in the chair behind the desk, his long muscular legs stretched out atop it. In front of him was a full glass of whiskey, a decanter and a box of cigars, one of which he puffed on. So lost in his thoughts did he appear, that Maria had time to make one last check of her assets before breezing into the room.

"Good evening, my lord," she announced, adopting a guttural tone which she hoped would add to her appeal.

Startled from his reverie, Toby's cigar smoke caught in his throat. "Miss, er, Dove," he spluttered, whipping his legs from the desk. "What are you doing wandering about the house at this late hour?"

"I...couldn't sleep, sir," lied Maria. "I thought, perhaps, I would come down and select a book to read."

"Oh, I can recommend a much more effective remedy than a book." He indicated the decanter. "Would you care to join me in a drink, Miss Dove?"

Maria Dove, who had never tasted so much as a sip of whiskey in all her eighteen years, tossed him a seductive smile. "I should be honored to join you, my lord."

While Toby jumped up to fetch another tumbler, Maria sank down in the chair opposite his silently congratulating herself on the successful progression of her plan thus far.

"Now then," declared Toby. He resumed his seat and poured an obscene amount of liquor into the empty glass. "Tell me the truth, Miss Dove. What, in heaven's name, is a young beauty like you doing stuck out here in Diddington?"

Maria regarded him coyly as she pretended to sip at her drink. The very smell was enough to make her vomit but, given her condition, that was not at all unusual lately. Briskly, she swept all thoughts of vomiting aside.

"It is rather a long story, sir," she replied enigmatically. "Although, I own, I am becoming increasingly bored here and have been considering removing to London for what remains of the Season."

"Have you now?" Toby's eyes moved languidly down to her cleavage. "May I enquire if you are acquainted with anyone in London, Miss Dove?"

Maria refrained from mentioning Harry Allenby. She had no desire to see him again—ever. "Er, no, sir. Not yet." She ran a finger along the edge of her bodice.

Toby's navy-blue eyes grew a shade darker as they followed the suggestive movement.

"Well," he smiled. "I should have been only too happy to have offered you my services in the capital, Miss Dove, but I'm afraid I have no intention at all of returning there."

As he averted his gaze from her cleavage to his whiskey glass, Maria detected a shift in mood. Her spirits dived. Desperate not to stray from the topic, she blurted, "Oh, but I have heard that London is all that is diverting, sir."

Toby gulped down the contents of his glass. "Diverting is one word for it. There are a great many others that apply equally as well—none of which are suitable for a lady's ears." He set down his glass.

Maria Dove panicked. Sensing he might, at any moment, decide to leave, she sprang into action. "Goodness," she sighed, swiftly removing the stopper from the decanter and replenishing his glass. "From the way you talk about the city, sir, one can only assume that you have been having rather a bad time of it there."

Toby picked up his newly-replenished glass and knocked back a large slug. "A bad time, does not even begin to describe it, Miss Dove. Something more akin to the worst time of what I fear may be my very short life—is definitely more apt."

Now Maria was getting somewhere. "Well, perhaps there is something I can do to help," she purred, running her tongue over her lips.

Toby regarded her intently. "I doubt that very much, Miss Dove," he intoned, raising his glass. "You see, I am in dire need of a wife."

Maria Dove attempted to quell her excitement. Fluttering her lashes, she breathily exclaimed, "Why, how very fortuitous, sir. You see, I am in dire need of a husband."

~ * ~

As Toby Allenby, accompanied by the most pounding head he could ever recall, staggered down to the breakfast-room the following morning, he hoped and prayed Maria Dove would not be present. The girl had caught him completely off-guard in the library the previous evening where he had been attempting, yet again, to fathom some way out of his mess. The mess that consumed him—nibbling at his innards like a greedy, bloodsucking parasite.

Still he had reached no solution, which may, he conceded, have something to do with the vast amount of alcohol he had consumed—again. He would have to stop drinking. If he had a clear head, he was sure to come up with a solution. He only hoped that he could do so before Maria Dove let anything slip to his parents.

Somehow he had managed to humorously dismiss the line he had blurted out about needing a wife. Somewhat worryingly, though, there had been no hint of humor when Maria Dove had declared her need for a husband. Despite her attempts at resistance, Toby had managed to change the subject. He had said far too much. The less people who knew about his mess—and his plans—the better, and, more importantly, the safer. If his father caught so much as a sniff of what he was up to, Toby could kiss goodbye to his dukedom.

No, all he needed was a few days' respite, a few uneventful days in which to pull himself together and come up with a plan. There had to be some way to drag himself out of this mire without going to such extreme lengths as marriage and selling off the hall. He just had to give it more—sober—consideration. He would start today. He would banish Jack Wilmott, Caroline Levington and Diddington Hall from his mind for the next four-and-twenty hours. That, if nothing else, should allow him to breathe more easily.

Less than an hour later, Toby's positive resolve had shriveled up and disappeared in a puff of smoke. Returning to his chamber after breakfast, his blood had run cold the moment he spotted a note lying atop his counterpane. A note from Jack Wilmott, informing him of the remaining time he had left to come up with the money. How it had come to Mr. Wilmott's knowledge that he was sojourning at Diddington Hall, and how the note had come to be in his bedchamber, Toby did not dare to think. All he was certain of was that there was to be no let-up. Jack Wilmott was turning his infamous screws tightly. So tightly, Toby could almost feel them. There was nothing else for it. He had to get married—and sell Diddington Hall—as soon as possible. Scrunching up the missive and shoving it into his breeches' pocket, he flew out of the room and down the stairs.

~ * ~

If Maria Dove had been of a more credulous nature, she may have been persuaded that she was some kind of heavenly angel, upon whom good fortune continually shone. After spending the entire night deliberating the next stage of her plan, she could scarcely believe it when, after breakfast, Toby Allenby had sought her out and bid her accompany him to the rose garden. There, he presented her with a most attractive proposal. A proposal that just happened to suit every one of Maria's needs perfectly.

Lord Toby, just as she had suspected, was in trouble. So much trouble—and so much debt—that he dared reveal nothing of his desperate circumstances to his parents. The only apparent hope he had of extricating himself from the mess was to satisfy the bizarre condition of his great aunt's will. By taking a wife, he would inherit his relative's ancestral home, which he would sell to the eager buyer he had waiting in the wings, pay off his debts and free himself of London's most notorious moneylender who was, he explained falteringly, breathing heavily down his neck.

For Maria's part, he assured her, there would be sufficient money left over for them both to live comfortably; he would not interfere at all in her life; and, as the future Duchess of Wolsington, she would enjoy all the reverence that accompanied such a lofty position.

Maria deemed it best not to add that she would also have a father for her unborn child which she would, naturally, insist was Toby's. A child that would, if it were male, be a duke in waiting himself. Despite this proposal being better than even she could have expected, Maria judged the situation wisely. Toby's desperation was clear. If she dared exploit it, there could be even greater rewards—not least of which would be the man's fawning appreciation.

"So what do you say, Miss Dove?" asked Toby, standing before her. "Now that I have laid all my cards on the table, so to speak, would you agree to marrying me and helping me out of this mess?"

Maria, seated on a bench beneath the arbor, sighed dolefully and fiddled with the folds of her skirt. "Oh, I'm not sure, my lord. I had hoped to marry for love."

Toby regarded her with an air of incredulity. "*Love*, Miss Dove? What on earth has love to do with anything?"

Maria rearranged her countenance into one dripping with wholesome concern. "But it all seems dreadfully...*calculated*, does it not, sir?"

"Well, of course it does, woman. That's because it is."

Maria pressed a finger to her lips as though contemplating the matter further.

"Lud, Miss Dove," puffed Toby, plopping down onto the bench alongside her and running a hand through his already disheveled hair. "I thought you would have jumped at such an offer. I have it on good authority that most women would happily swap one of their own legs for the chance to become a duchess."

Maria regarded him innocently. "But *I* am not most women, sir."

"*That*, Miss Dove," sniffed Toby, "is perfectly obvious."

Noting the irritation creeping into his tone, Maria slanted him a sly look. She found him staring miserably at a spot on the ground. A heavy silence fell over the pair as Maria wondered if she had pushed him too far. His next words confirmed that she had gauged him perfectly.

"I am not suggesting for one moment that it will sway your decision, Miss Dove, but, in addition to all the other benefits you would enjoy should you agree to my proposal, I shall insist that my mother make you a present of my late grandmama's ring."

Victory surged through Maria. "Is it a diamond, sir?"

Toby cast her a look of disbelief. "It is an emerald, Miss Dove. Not that I imagined the type of stone to signify in the slightest."

Sensing his impatience, Maria realized she had best stop toying with the man and accept his offer before he withdrew it.

"Oh, well," she exhaled wistfully, reverting her attention back to her skirts. "I find emeralds pleasing enough. So I suppose in that case…"

Toby pinned her with an expectant gaze.

"I shall, after all, marry you."

~ * ~

Toby's relief at Maria Dove's acceptance of his proposal was tempered with resentment as he made his way back to the house. He didn't know why he had blurted out the offer of his grandmother's wretched ring—a jewel his mother held in great sentimental regard. Surely he could have talked Maria Dove into the match without resorting to such extreme measures.

Or could he? She had certainly proved a deal more reluctant than he had imagined. He had envisaged the chit practically swooning at his feet at such a mutually beneficial proposition. Not that it mattered in the least now. All that did matter was that the chit had accepted. And all that remained, was for him to inform his parents of his marriage plans—and hope that they would approve them. He was confident. Maria Dove was, after all, a guest in their house, which must count for something. He would settle the matter straight away, before approaching the bishop for a special license. A satisfied smile touched his lips. Despite a discouraging start, this was turning out to be a most propitious day.

As soon as he entered the house, Toby spotted his mother scurrying down the stairs. Her cheeks were flushed and she emitted a palpable air of anxiety. Toby, though, was not at all desirous of involving himself in his parent's problems. He was far too intent on sorting out his own.

He awaited her at the bottom of the staircase. "Mother," he began, affecting his most earnest tone. "May I speak with you on a matter of the utmost importance?"

To his astonishment, Lady Allenby scarcely even glanced at him as she reached the bottom of the stairs and began scuttling toward the drawing-room. "Not now, Toby dear," she muttered.

Indignation swept over Toby. Determined to put his dismal affairs in order, he had no intention of being dismissed quite so lightly. He made to follow the duchess, arriving at the doorway to the crimson drawing-room just in time to hear the cause of her apparent distress.

"Charles!" She bustled over to the writing desk in the corner at which her husband was seated. "I own, I am most dreadfully worried about Miss Winchester. She has taken a distinct turn for the worst. No doubt you will dismiss my sentiments as fussing, but I should be much happier if Dr. Pike were to examine her."

The duke glanced up from his correspondence. "I doubt it's anything more than a case of influenza, Arabella," he assured her. "A lot of it about what with this unseasonably warm weather. Still, by all means have the doctor take a look at her, my dear, if it will make you feel better."

As the duchess scuttled out of the room, paying her hovering son no attention at all, Toby's spirits lifted still further. With his mother so obviously distracted by Miss Winchester's influenza, there could not be a more perfect time for him to announce his marriage plans. He just needed to wait for exactly the right moment.

~ * ~

Harry Allenby was having the most marvelous time in London—or so anyone observing him might have thought. His brief absence from the city appeared only to have heightened his popularity. His presence was in great demand and this, for once, appeared to be a circumstance in which he reveled. Harry had not declined so much as one invitation since his arrival in the city. He had attended a stream of balls, routs and soirées every evening. This uncharacteristic gregariousness had not gone unnoticed. It had whipped up a great cloud of excitement amongst the capital's hostesses, the majority of who welcomed this apparently revised personality with newfound optimism. Some, however, were a tad more wary, even going so far as to suggest that Harry might be following in his brother's footsteps. Not only had his consumption of vast amounts of alcohol in his club been noted, but so, too, had the fact that he had requested the hand of eight different dancing partners the previous evening.

Regardless of the general opinion of his jovial, pleasure-seeking exterior, the façade was doing nothing to ease the dull ache in Harry's heart. He had imagined being away from Diddington might have some effect. It had not. He had imagined alcohol might have some effect. It had not. He had imagined taking an interest in other chits might help. It had not. As futile as it was, it seemed that, whatever else he did, he could not wipe the picture of Louisa Winchester's beautiful, bespectacled face from his mind.

Harry had left Diddington without saying goodbye to Louisa. If she insisted on hiding in her room under the pretext of being ill, then he would not force his company upon her. Obviously, she did not wish to see him. Well, now that he was out of the house—and indeed the town—the girl could do whatever she liked, with whomever she liked.

Meanwhile, Harry would continue his campaign to eradicate his memory of her. He might not even stay in London. He might go to… Italy. He had thought it quite beautiful when he had visited the year after Clara's death. Or he could go to Paris. He had several acquaintances there who would be happy to see him again. He had a whole host of means at his disposal to help him forget Louisa Winchester. He need never set eyes on the girl again. After all, when Toby eventually inherited Diddington Hall, it would likely be sold within a matter of months. And, by bidding farewell to the hall, Harry would also be bidding farewell to his reason for ever visiting Diddington again.

~ * ~

Toby Allenby was on a mission. A mission he was

determined to accomplish.

"Mother..." he began, as the duchess slipped out of Miss Winchester's bedchamber, bearing a large pile of towels.

"Not now, Toby dear," she retorted as she swept past him and began marching along the corridor. "I am extremely busy."

"It won't take a moment," protested Toby, scurrying after her. "I was just wondering, if, um, if you would mind if I married—"

Lady Allenby came to an abrupt standstill, spinning around to face her son. The disparaging glint in her eyes left little doubt as to her mood.

"I can scarce believe that you wish to discuss the matter of your marriage now, Toby," she retorted stiffly. "Perhaps you are unaware that our houseguest, Miss Winchester, is extremely ill. Not, I imagine, that that unfortunate circumstance would give you so much as a minute's concern. Obviously you are incapable of considering anyone other than yourself. Frankly, at this precise moment, Toby, I do not care a button who you marry. In fact, I feel nothing but sympathy for the poor girl who has the misfortune of having to tolerate you. Now, if you are quite finished, I have much more important matters to attend to."

Deciding that he had indeed finished, Toby mumbled a brief apology to his mother, awarded her a courteous bow, and retreated down the stairs.

Toby eventually located his father in the stable block. Huddled around one of the stalls with three grooms, he was anxiously awaiting the birth of a foal. Approaching from behind, Toby gently tapped the old man on the shoulder. "Father," he began in a hushed whisper.

The duke flicked him a cursory glance before turning his attention back to the horse. "Not now, Toby. I'm busy."

Quelling his frustration, Toby took a calming breath. "I appreciate this is not the best time to approach you on a matter of some delicacy, sir. But I wondered if you might have any objections to my marrying—"

From over his father's shoulder, Toby caught sight of the leggy foal slipping effortlessly out onto the hay. While he shuddered at the bloody sight, the other men present gave rise to an almighty cheer and an enthusiastic round of congratulatory handshakes and pats on the back.

Toby remained resolute. "Father, I would be much obliged, sir, if you could let me know—"

"What's that, son?" beamed the duke distractedly.

"Something about me minding you marrying?"

"Yes, sir. Would you mind if I marr—?"

"Well, of course I don't mind," chortled the duke. "Every man needs a good woman behind him, isn't that right, Dodds?"

Dodds nodded effusively. "Place wouldn't be the same without them, sir," he chuckled.

At this observation, the duke broke out into raucous laughter. "Now then, that answered your question, son?"

Toby did believe it had.

Seventeen

Although not a word he would have expected to employ when describing Mrs. Danderton's evening soirée, Harry had found the occasion most...*interesting*. This he attributed more to the startling proposition he had received than anything of a remotely musical nature. The issuer of the daring offer had been a very attractive young widow, known affectionately amongst her friends as Lou-Lou. She had invited Harry to call upon her the following evening, the glint in her dark eyes providing him with some indication as to exactly what the visit might entail. During the carriage ride back to his lodgings, Harry had concluded that the diversion could prove exactly what he needed. If that didn't help him wipe Louisa Winchester from his mind, then nothing would.

The following evening, as Lou-Lou's butler led him up the stairs of her decadently decorated townhouse, Harry attempted to quell his rising doubts. In the intervening hours following the proposition, he had convinced himself that a willing, beautiful, young widow was the perfect remedy to his situation. Besides, wasn't it time he had a little fun? Hadn't he been miserable for far too long? If nothing else of a positive nature had emerged from his acquaintance with Miss Winchester, then at least she had taught him, however inadvertently, to smile again.

He shook his head as if to clear it. This was not the time to be thinking of Louisa Winchester. Moreover, was not the obliteration of Louisa Winchester from his mind, the very reason he was here? Still following the servant, he reached the top of the staircase and began making his way along a sumptuously carpeted corridor.

Deep in contemplation, he started as the butler came to a halt before a white paneled door. The man rapped sharply upon it before inclining his head to Harry and marching directly on. Harry turned his nervous attention to the door. He gulped as he observed the turning of the gleaming brass knob. Very slowly the door began easing open, to reveal a languorously smiling Lou-Lou. The black lace negligee adorning her body did not even pretend to disguise the outline of her full pert breasts or long shapely legs. Harry's eyes grew wide. His chest constricted. Was this how it felt to be on the verge of a fit of the vapors? He endeavored to pull himself together.

"Good, er, evening, madam," he uttered, executing a formal bow.

Lou-Lou shook back her mane of glossy dark hair and gurgled with affected laughter. "Surely there is no need for such formalities between...*friends*, my lord. Please do come in." She stepped back, gesturing to him to step inside.

Harry lacked the ability to comply. His feet were frozen to the spot. Haplessly, he stared into the room, his gaze landing on an enormous four-poster bed, draped with black silk and scattered with an array of crimson cushions. His heart began an uncontrollable bout of hammering, while beads of sweat sprinkled his forehead.

"My lord?" prompted Lou-Lou, staring at him with questioning dark eyes.

His tongue proved as ineffective as his feet. Harry said nothing as he turned on his heel and flew out of the house, completely forgetting, in his haste, to collect his hat or his gloves.

Returning to his lodgings, Harry believed the results to be conclusive. Nothing would help him forget Miss Louisa Winchester. Or at least nothing in London. There had to be something seriously lacking in a man who could not muster the wherewithal to seduce a beautiful, willing woman dressed only in a lace negligee. Well, there was nothing else for it now. He would *have* to go abroad. That had to be the solution. Italy first and then Paris—and he would remain overseas for a year at least—perhaps even two.

His mind had quite settled upon the idea when he alighted from the carriage. His butler greeted him at the door, before handing him a letter that had, so the servant informed, arrived not thirty minutes after Harry had left the house. The note was addressed in his mother's hand. He sensed instinctively that it was bad news. What he could not predict, was just how bad.

No sooner had he finished reading the letter informing him of Louisa's illness, than a surge of panic had forced Harry to dash to the bathroom where he had been violently sick.

During the ensuing carriage ride to Diddington, he found himself enduring exactly the same helter-skelter of emotions he had experienced when Clara had been ill. Only this time it was worse. During Clara's illness, he had lacked no conviction that she would recover. That a young, strong, normally healthy girl, who had never ailed another thing, could not have her life snatched rudely away. Now, though, he knew differently. And Miss Winchester's frailty merely fueled his anxiety. Yet another overwhelming desire to protect her consumed Harry, but this time, as he knew from experience, there was very little he could do. Very little, except pray.

Harry arrived at Diddington Hall a little before midnight. He wasted no time exchanging inanities with the servants, but bounded directly up the stairs to Louisa's chamber. The heat, courtesy of an enormous fire blazing in the grate, hit him the moment he entered. Seemingly oblivious to the stifling temperature, Lady Allenby stood directly before the flames, nervously twisting a handkerchief around her fingers as she talked, in hushed tones, with the doctor. Silent tears streamed down her cheeks.

"Oh, Harry," she gasped, visibly starting as she set eyes upon her son. "Thank goodness you are come." She held out both hands to him.

Harry took them briefly, before turning his attention to Louisa. His stomach lurched at the wretched picture she presented—a deathly shade of white, her eyelids were closed, her long dark hair strewn about the pillows, her brow covered in sweat and her breathing shallow and labored. So vulnerable and tiny did she look, that something tugged at his heartstrings.

With a deal of hesitation he steeled himself to ask, "How is she, Doctor?"

The physician pulled a rueful face. "I confess I am at something of a loss as to what it is she is suffering, my lord. I can only suggest that we attempt to break her fever and hope, in the process, that she does not take a turn for the worst."

"Oh, Harry, it's all my fault," whimpered Lady Allenby. "This house is so draughty. She really ought to have stayed at Hartley House."

"Don't be ridiculous, Mother," chided Harry softly. "The girl was ill before she came here. I'm sure you have given her the very best of care."

"But I could have given her equally good care at Hartley House," sniffed the duchess. "I should have removed there to look after her, not have her—"

"Such thoughts will not help anyone," interjected Harry firmly. "Now why don't you and Dr. Pike go and have a nice dish of tea? I shall stay here and call you immediately if there is any change."

"I do think a little rest would do you good, your grace," concurred the doctor.

Lady Allenby made a feeble protest but, nonetheless, allowed the physician to gently lead her from the room.

Alone with Louisa, Harry dropped down into the armchair at the side of the bed. Her hand lay lifelessly atop the covers. Instinctively he reached for it. Resting it in his, he noted just how slender and dainty it was. His mind flashed back to the host of other occasions that very same thought had occurred to him.

When, in Buttercup Meadow, their hands had briefly touched in the search for her spectacles; when he had pulled her from the pool at the Merchistons' ball; when she had toppled into his arms from the ladder in the library; when he had pulled her to her feet following her fall at the church at Little Hampton; and, finally, when she had wound her arms around him during their kiss under the willow tree.

Having finished picturing every one of this series of events, Harry found the corners of his lips curving upwards. No one, it occurred to him, had ever made him smile quite so much as the accident-prone Miss Winchester. And if anything happened to her, he had the worrying presentiment that no one would ever make him smile again.

Harry spent the entire night slumped in the chair at the side of Louisa's bed. He had snatched no more than an hour's sleep, but still remained unwilling to leave her in the morning.

"You must partake of a little breakfast and some fresh air, Harry," insisted a still anxious Lady Allenby. "It will be nothing but a dreadful inconvenience if you fall ill too. And it will not help Miss Winchester in the least."

Reluctantly, Harry acknowledged his mother's concerns. He dragged himself down to the breakfast-room where he could stomach nothing more than half a cup of coffee. In his pursuit of fresh air, he then ventured out onto the front steps, only to find himself several minutes later, dazedly heading down the drive.

For all it was a little before eight o"clock, there was no sign of the sun which had been so evident over the past few weeks. Instead, the sky was dark and menacing, the air heavy with the threat of rain. Harry remained oblivious to the meteorological conditions as he entered the forbidding gray churchyard and headed directly for Clara's grave. There, just as he had left it a short time ago, was the posy of pink roses. They were wilting. Soon they would be dead.

As he studied them, a cold harsh fact struck Harry. Everything died. Everything had to die. And was it not that fact that made life so precious? As our time on earth was so obviously fleeting, surely we should endeavor to make it worthwhile, to give it some purpose. Even the roses had had a use. Their beauty had brought pleasure to others. Just as Clara's beauty had done. For all the brevity of her life, Clara's existence had nonetheless served a purpose. She had been the apple of her parents' eye, had made Harry the happiest man alive, and had forfeited her own future to ease her mother's suffering.

What difference, by contrast, had Harry ever made to anyone? What was his purpose? He couldn't answer. Because his existence was meaningless. He did nothing other than flounder in self-pity. Would Clara, if things had been the other way around, have spent her life moping? Would she have wasted every day wallowing? Or would she have picked herself up and got on with the rest of her life?

As Harry marched decisively out of the graveyard and

back up to Diddington Hall, he knew, quite definitely, what he wished his purpose to be. He only hoped that, this time, he was not too late.

~ * ~

Toby Allenby was furious. The bishop of the Diddington diocese was not available. He was, so his disobliging butler informed, in Spa taking the waters.

"Well, what deuced good is that to me?" Toby had raged on the man's doorstep. "I can't wait three weeks for banns to be read. I need a special marriage license and I need it now."

"I can only suggest, sir," sniffed the unimpressed servant. "That you go directly to his grace, the Archbishop of Canterbury."

"Can't do that," snapped Toby, a shudder overtaking him at the mere thought of returning to London. "That is entirely out of the question."

"Then, I'm afraid, sir," intoned the butler haughtily as he made to close the door, "the only other option is Gretna Green."

~ * ~

Seated at the writing desk in her bedchamber, Lady Caroline Levington ran the tip of her finger along the blade of the letter-opener, exerting just the right amount of pressure to draw blood. She watched, with morbid fascination, as the dark red liquid dripped onto her clean white handkerchief, instantly transforming it from an object of purity and innocence, to one of filth and repulsion.

Blood was definitely what Caroline had a taste for—but not her own. It had come to her attention that Toby Allenby had been attempting to procure a special marriage license. Obviously the man had found someone to marry—some blonde chit from Yorkshire with a large bosom, Caroline had been reliably informed. But the size of the strumpet's bosom did not signify in the least to Caroline. What did signify—and a great deal—was that Toby had reneged completely on their agreement. He had ignored her threats and chosen the girl himself. The latest news of which she had, just minutes before, been made aware, was that the pair planned to elope to Gretna Green. In yet another fit of pique, Caroline squeezed the lesion on her finger, forcing out another drop of thick crimson liquid.

Since their last encounter at the garden party, Caroline

had realized just how much she enjoyed Toby Allenby's dependence upon her. Reveling in this position of superiority, she had resolved not to contact the man for a while, but to allow him to sweat a little. An assured tactic that would increase her power and make Toby appreciate the extent to which he relied upon her. All of this, Caroline had carefully planned with her ultimate aim in sight—that of her future marriage to Toby and her subsequent rise in status to the giddy, much coveted, heights of duchess.

Now, though, with blatant disregard for any of her plans, the blasted man and his impatience had gone and ruined everything. Perhaps she had not made herself quite as clear as she had intended. Perhaps Toby had deemed her threats idle. Well, if that was the case, he had grossly underestimated her. Caroline Levington had never made an idle threat in her entire life. And she was certainly not about to start now.

She knotted her handkerchief tightly around her bleeding finger, dipped her quill in the Standish and began to write…

~ * ~

Maria Dove had never experienced such a whirlwind of excitement. Wait until they heard about this back in Yorkshire. A marquis, so desperate to get a ring on her finger that he was whisking her off to Gretna. Naturally, Maria would not bother to mention the reasons for the man's desperation. Nor would she bother to mention her own, rather pressing, need for the marriage to take place. *That* would never be mentioned at all—to anyone. After all, had not many a babe been conceived on a wedding night, and had not many a babe come into the world a little earlier than the calculated date?

To firmly affix the final piece of her plan, all that remained was for her to seduce Toby Allenby as soon as possible. And that, from the way the man continually eyed her assets, should be the easiest part of all.

Just as Toby had made her swear, Maria had not divulged a word of their scheme to anyone. She had even hidden her portmanteau—into which she had crammed a few essential items— in the back of her wardrobe, out of sight of the servants. All other arrangements had been undertaken by Toby. At midnight, he was to await her in his carriage at the entrance to Buttercup Meadow. And, only days later, plain old Maria Elsie

Dove would emerge as Lady Maria Allenby, Marchioness of Yarm—with an emerald ring, a future as a duchess, and a timely—just about—father for Ned Stickleback's unborn child. Let's see who dared to jeer at her then, when she next visited Yorkshire.

Diligently following every one of her future husband's instructions, Maria slipped out of Diddington Hall twenty minutes before midnight. She congratulated herself on achieving the task without being spotted by a single servant. Not that she thought it likely that anyone—servants or otherwise—would have been remotely interested if they had seen her. The entire household, including Harry Allenby—who she had thankfully managed to avoid ever since the incident in his bed—was far too preoccupied fussing about Miss Winchester. The girl, so her maid had informed her, was laid low with influenza or some such.

Maria had taken little notice—she had enough matters of her own to occupy her, without wasting time on that flat-chested ninny. Well, wait until she and Toby returned to the hall as husband and wife. Then they would all—including Harry Allenby—sit up and pay her some attention, and some respect, in her new role as marchioness; even the duke and duchess who had not *actually* approved the match. That, as far as Maria was concerned, was a minor detail. She could win the Allenbys around easily enough. Then, when Toby sold off Diddington Hall, she could buy a house in London and go about town exactly how she pleased. By the tender age of nineteen, Maria Dove would have achieved every one of her high-flying ambitions. Could there be a luckier girl?

In her dark, hooded cloak, Maria crept down the drive, keeping to the shadows. The night sky was pitch-black with a perfect half-moon throwing out a hazy silvery hue. At the bottom of the drive, she turned right and began marching along the wide country lane, lined with thick yellow gorse bushes. Excitement bubbled in her veins. She could scarcely wait until the next time she traveled along this road, as the new Marchioness of— The snapping of a twig broke her thoughts. With a hammering heart, she spun around, her eyes darting about in the dim light. Nothing. It was nothing. She was being a wet-goose. Whisking around, she took a deep breath and resumed her marching—a little more quickly this time. The rustle of a nearby bush caused the hairs on the back of her neck to stand on end. Again she spun around. Again she saw nothing.

Picking up her skirts, Maria hurried on, giving a faint murmur of relief when the outline of Toby's waiting carriage came into view.

Toby's driver opened the carriage door and pulled down the steps as Maria approached. In a flash, she had tossed him her bag and scrambled inside. Sinking gratefully down on the seat opposite Toby, she noted that he appeared in remarkably high spirits.

"Are you ready, Miss Dove?" he grinned, his eyes twinkling in the dark of the conveyance.

"Indeed I am, sir," purred Maria, untying her cloak and pushing it back from her shoulders to reveal an expanse of creamy flesh. "Ready for anything."

~ * ~

As the carriage pulled away, Toby congratulated himself on his scheme. Although he had not actually informed anyone of his intentions before leaving the house, he had left behind a note for his brother, advising him that he would be returning to Diddington in a week or so, with Miss Maria Dove as his bride.

Due to the level of secrecy—and the speed—with which it had been formed, Toby was confident that Caroline could know nothing of his plan. Nevertheless, he had spent the greater part of the day shrouded in uneasiness. On more than one occasion, he had even imagined he was being followed. Thankfully, his suspicions had remained unfounded. Besides, even if someone *had* been following him, they had obviously done nothing to thwart his actions, because here he now was— on his way to Scotland—with a very comely young wench in tow.

Studying Maria Dove's ample cleavage, Toby considered that perhaps the journey to Gretna might not prove quite as tedious as he had imagined. After all, in only a matter of hours, Miss Dove would be pledging herself to him. Was it not natural, therefore, that he should wish to further his acquaintance with the girl? He was on the verge of voicing such a suggestion, when the carriage drew to a shuddering halt. Before its two occupants had time to comprehend what was happening, the door had been whipped open to reveal a large masked figure with a tri-corn hat and a pointed pistol.

Maria Dove squealed. She shuffled along the seat and pressed herself tightly into a corner. Toby, conversely, breathed a sigh of relief. The moment he had realized something was amiss, his first thought had been that it must be some ploy of Caroline's. But it wasn't. It was only a highwayman. If he tossed over a couple of coins, they could be on their way in no time. Fortunately, he always kept a few at hand for this very event, the rest hidden where no self-respecting highwayman would dare to look.

Toby regarded the highwayman with a rueful smile. "I'm afraid I don't have much on me, sir," he explained, patting his various pockets. "I hope this will suffice." He proffered three gold sovereigns.

The highwayman did not award them so much as a glance, but continued to point the pistol at the middle of Toby's forehead. At exactly that moment, niggling suspicion began gnawing at Toby that perhaps this was no ordinary hold-up after all.

"I, er, believe I may have a, er, couple more somewhere," he mumbled, frantically searching about his person. "And Miss Dove, I'm sure you could spare the gentleman your pearl earrings."

A quaking Maria Dove began fiddling with the clasps of her jewels. But, before she had had time to remove even one of the earrings, the highway commanded, in a startlingly gruff voice, "Step out of the carriage."

Toby quaked. "But s-surely there is n-no need for that, sir. Surely we can—"

"Out!" boomed the man.

~ * ~

In a now familiar picture, Lord Harry Allenby was, once again, to be found by the side of Louisa Winchester's bed, stroking her fragile hand. He had partaken of no more than a couple of mouthfuls of toast over the last few days. But, while his appetite had been sadly lacking, his resolve had strengthened. He had made the most momentous decision of his life. If Louisa recovered, he would ask her to marry him. The very notion of spending the rest of his life with this diminutive girl suffused him with a warm glow of optimism. He dared not even imagine the pleasure in waking up every day to her. Of course, if Harry had had the nerve to put this proposal to her a few days before, instead of continuing to deny his feelings, they would—had Louisa accepted—have had the added advantage of being able to make Diddington Hall their home. But, although the hall being filled with the sound of their children's laughter conjured up another tempting image, it signified little. Harry would live in a cave if it meant he could be with Louisa. And, if Toby was a brave enough man as to wed Maria Dove, then he deserved the house a great deal more than Harry.

Had circumstances been different, Harry had little doubt that he would have been appalled at his brother's intentions regarding Maria Dove. With his mind on much more important matters, though, he had awarded Toby's letter no more than a cursory scan before tossing it into the fire. The contents of the missive, he had opted to keep to himself. With the household already in such turmoil, he was grateful his mother did not appear to have noticed that neither Toby nor Maria Dove was in residence. With the duchess in such an anxious state over Louisa, Harry had no intentions of adding to her worries. What was the point when it was too late to stop Toby anyway? No, the time to deal with the newlyweds would present itself upon their return to Diddington. Before then, Harry would not give either of them a second thought. His mind was focused on one thing, and one thing only—Miss Louisa Winchester and her recovery from this mysterious illness. Gazing at her pale thin face, he had to acknowledge that that happy eventuality seemed increasingly unlikely.

Eighteen

Miss Elizabeth Wilson felt fit to sink. Since receiving Lady Winchester's letter earlier that morning, which had included a very long and very detailed description of her niece's antics in Diddington, Miss Wilson's headache had grown to one of excruciating proportions. Needless to say, the rocky road of emotions she had traveled in the intervening hours—beginning at amazement; passing through disbelief; stopping briefly at shame; and ending in mortification—had not helped her fragile state at all. Yet all of these emotions were being rapidly overtaken by another—that of red-hot anger. Although one might be forgiven for assuming the target of this rage to be the lady's errant niece, such a conclusion would be erroneous.

Every bit of it was aimed at none other than Elizabeth Wilson herself—for allowing the very thing she had vowed, at the tender age of thirteen, she would never allow again. Even though she had known it was wrong, and even though it had gone against every one of her better instincts, Elizabeth had allowed herself to be bullied into submission by her older sister, Mrs. Elsie Dove, thereby inflicting her niece upon the Winchesters.

This bullying predicament was not new. It had been a regular occurrence during the girls' childhood. Elsie had reigned supreme over a set of equally spiteful peers and had never failed to exploit an opportunity to taunt, intimidate or ridicule her younger sister. Although similar in physical appearance, the characters of the two siblings could not have been further apart.

Elizabeth had liked nothing more than to tuck herself away in a quiet corner, her head in a book. Elsie's pleasure had been derived from a long menu of daring and dangerous ruses, including stealing loaves from the bakers; setting fire to the hen house; and torturing the youngsters from the "big houses" until they handed over every penny of their pocket money.

With Elizabeth resigned to her miserable fate, this state of affairs continued for many years. Then, one day, quite by chance, she had ended up confessing all to kindly Miss Hudson who ran the Sunday school.

Last to leave the church that particular morning, Elizabeth had tripped over one of the pews on her way out. Her fall had revealed a colorful band of bruises around each of her calves. Miss Hudson, in her unassuming manner, had gently probed her as to the cause of these marks. Amidst a tide of tears, Elizabeth had told her the truth—that her sister and her cronies had tied her down and forced her to eat earthworms. She had expected Miss Hudson, like her mother, to merely dismiss it and the other "pranks" she found herself relaying, as nothing more than childish antics. What she had not expected was the old woman's horror and sympathy.

"Tell me, child," she had asked, when Elizabeth, with the aid of a restorative glass of lemonade, had eventually stopped sniffling. "What do you see yourself doing when you grow up?"

Elizabeth confessed that she had given the matter very little thought. She would end up doing, no doubt, what all the women of her acquaintance did. Marrying one of the local boys and popping out a babe each year. Not that, she hastened to add, she had the remotest interest in any of the local boys.

Why then, the woman had continued, did she not consider doing something different? Something where she could use her brain? For it had apparently not escaped Miss Hudson's notice, just what a remarkable brain Elizabeth had. She could do so much more with her life, she insisted, than settle down and become a breeding machine. She could even, if she wished, leave Yorkshire completely.

Elizabeth had laughed at the suggestion. Leave Yorkshire? The idea had never once occurred to her. Besides, what would she do? What *could* she do?

"You could become a governess," Miss Hudson had

asserted. "A good governess is rarely without employment. You would have your choice of places in which to work. You might even go abroad."

As she had crawled into bed that night, only to be awarded a sharp kick from Elsie with whom she shared the uncomfortable straw mattress, Elizabeth had determined that she would follow Miss Hudson's advice. She would steer herself away from the dreary predictable path every one of her peers was destined to follow. She would become a governess. And with the money she earned, she would build a new life for herself—one far away from Yorkshire and, more importantly, far away from her bullying sister.

The progression of her plan had necessitated a great deal of hard work. All her learning had been done with the unfailing aid and encouragement of Miss Hudson who never once, despite her many other charitable commitments, had denied Elizabeth so much as a minute of her time.

Although little was generally known about Miss Hudson's past, Elizabeth never ceased to be amazed at the woman's energy and zeal for helping those less fortunate than herself. But it was her phenomenal font of knowledge that had impressed the youngster the most.

"How is it that you know so much about everything, Miss Hudson?" she had dared to ask one day.

Miss Hudson had not replied immediately. A cloud of sadness had settled over her features before she had admitted, "Because, child, I, too, always wanted to be a teacher."

With the insouciance of youth, Elizabeth had asked, "But why ever did you not then? I think you would have made the best teacher ever."

Miss Hudson's eyes had flooded with tears as she had regarded the younger girl. "Thank you, child," she had replied with a faint smile. "I had certainly hoped so. But I'm-I'm afraid my father had other ideas."

Noting the abrupt way in which she had then changed the subject, Elizabeth had not pressed her further. Moreover, it had seemed a perfectly reasonable reason.

Elizabeth had not discussed her teaching ambitions with her mother or her sister. By doing so, she would have been subjecting herself to a never-ending stream of taunts and ridicule. The first time the pair had gleaned so much as an inkling of her plan, was the day Elizabeth had announced that she had procured a position at a seminary in Bath and that she would be leaving forthwith. By that time, Elsie had been married and widowed and Maria was a child of seven. Nevertheless, the look upon her mother and sister's faces as they had absorbed her news had awarded Elizabeth an even greater thrill than her receipt of the letter offering her the position.

Elizabeth Wilson was not one to bear grudges. As well as keeping in regular contact with Miss Hudson, she had forwarded a monthly missive to her family, enquiring about their health and providing amusing snippets of her new life. Not once had she received a reply. In fact, Elizabeth had received no communiqué whatsoever from her family until the letter had arrived requesting her help in procuring her niece a sponsor.

Naturally, Elizabeth had empathized with Maria's predicament. The child had grown, so her sister had informed, into a quiet, bookish girl, keen to improve her mind and expand her knowledge of the world. Elizabeth was relieved to hear this. At the time of her departure from Yorkshire, she had secretly found Maria a little precocious and outrageously vain. But the poor child had, so Elsie related, spent her entire life putting the needs of her widowed mother before those of her own. As a sign of her gratitude and devotion, Elsie was, therefore, eager to help her daughter realize her potential; to make a better life for herself than she had done.

Elizabeth understood perfectly. She would do everything within her limited power to help the girl. Why, if Miss Hudson had not been obliging enough to help her, then she, too, would have been forced to trudge the same well-trodden, miserable path as her sister and so many other Yorkshire lasses before and after her.

To that end, Elizabeth had offered a number of suggestions as to how young Maria might improve her situation. She had recommended a host of books and courses of study which would open her mind and encourage her to broaden her horizons. All such suggestions had been rejected out of hand. The only route—on which Elsie had remained resolutely focused—was to find a sponsor for Maria. Preferably one who resided in "a big house in London."

Elizabeth had explained that her acquaintance of people who resided in "big houses in London" was distinctly lacking. She knew of no one who made their home in the capital. Why, she had only ever been there twice herself—when in the employ of the Winchesters of Diddington.

To Elizabeth's dismay, Elsie had pounced on this nugget of information with all the zeal of a ravenous lion on a carcass of fresh meat. Having obviously made some enquiries as to the exact whereabouts of the little market town, she had concluded that, if Maria couldn't go to London, then Diddington, being the nearest thing, would have to do. She would therefore be much obliged if Elizabeth could write to this Lady Winchester and request that she take Maria in for a few weeks—or months.

Elizabeth had replied that it was her biggest regret, but her most recent position in Scotland had kept her so busy—and the postal system was so irregular—that it was now quite some time since she had corresponded with the Winchesters. Consequently, she should not feel at all comfortable approaching them out-of-the-blue and requesting such a huge undertaking.

But Elsie Dove had persisted. And persisted. And persisted. Until, as the older woman had known she would, Elizabeth had capitulated.

How Elizabeth could have been so naïve, she did not know. Her sister had obviously succeeded in pulling the wool completely over her eyes. No doubt the woman would be congratulating herself on how, a decade on, she was still able to manipulate her younger sibling so easily.

The question now, was what Elizabeth should do about the unfortunate circumstance? Maria Dove, who, from Lady Winchester's note, sounded the very antithesis of a shy, bookish, and unworldly miss, could not possibly be allowed to remain under the Winchesters' roof. Elizabeth cringed as she noted the date on the letter. It had taken almost two weeks to reach her having been directed first to her previous address in Scotland.

Well, there was simply nothing else for it. Immediate action had to be taken. Elizabeth would have to travel to Diddington herself, extricate her niece from Hartley House, then accompany the girl back to Yorkshire where she intended, in no uncertain terms, to give both Maria and her sister, a very large piece of her mind.

~ * ~

Unbeknown to her furious aunt, Maria Dove was, at that moment, already winding her way northwards. On the public stage, crammed between a sweaty, leering octogenarian and an incessantly chattering tabby, she had never been so cast down in all her eighteen years. Every one of her plans had been ruined. And how. She had no idea who had been behind the hold up of Toby Allenby's coach the evening of their planned elopement. What she did know was that being tied to a tree all night with a dead rat strapped to her chest was an experience she had no wish to repeat. The note, which had been pinned to the stinking rodent, had said, quite definitively—*Go home*. Maria Elsie Dove did not need to be told twice.

~ * ~

At Diddington Hall, Toby Allenby jerked bolt upright in his bed, his heart racing ten-to-the-dozen, cold rivulets of sweat streaking down his face. Recognizing his comfortable surroundings, he flopped back down onto the pillows and heaved an enormous sigh of relief. Relief that he was no longer trapped in a coffin with a dozen stinking rats clambering all over him. He had had no idea how long he had been there before a farmer had come upon him and his hysterical traveling partner the following morning.

Although Toby had said nothing to Maria Dove on the matter, he was convinced that this was one of Caroline's schemes. Clearly, in assuming her ignorant of his elopement plans, he had completely underestimated the woman. Somehow—and he did not like to dwell on the finer details of that point—his intentions had come into her knowledge and she had put an end to them in her own inimitable way. More worrying still, was that Toby suspected this would not prove the end of the matter; that Caroline's vengeful campaign had only just begun.

~ * ~

Alighting from the stagecoach in Diddington's market square, a pleasant tingling sensation swept through Elizabeth Wilson as she absorbed all the sights with which she had become intimately acquainted during her six years in the Winchesters' employ. The scene was just as delightful as she had remembered, with the cobbled streets, pretty shops and profusion of flowers.

But it was not only Diddington's aesthetic appeal that made it so special. There seemed, to Elizabeth Wilson, to be something in its clear, fresh air, in the way its inhabitants went about their cheery business, that gave the town a unique atmosphere. For all she loved the grandeur of Bath and the wilderness of Scotland, never once had she experienced that same fizzle of pleasure as when in Diddington.

The same could also be said of Elizabeth's teaching posts. Although she had enjoyed working at the seminary in Bath, and for the family in Scotland, never had she established the same close affinity with her pupils as with Louisa Winchester. The girl had proved an exceptionally bright and willing student and, in many respects, had put Elizabeth a little in mind of herself. If there was to be a lining of silver surrounding the dark cloud of her visit to Diddington, it would hopefully be that she would have the pleasure of seeing her former student again.

Her meeting with Lady Eliza Winchester, though, was quite another matter. The woman's cool and distant manner had been the one thing that had blighted Elizabeth's time in Diddington. Despite her efforts to break through the ice, Elizabeth had failed to make a single chip in it. After weeks of such efforts, she had concluded that Eliza Winchester bore a raft of deep emotional scars—courtesy, no doubt, of her philandering husband. If she chose to shun Elizabeth's offer of friendship, treating her as nothing more than a member of the hired help, there was very little Elizabeth could do about it. The reason for her visit today would certainly do nothing to improve matters between the governess and her former employer. However reluctantly, Elizabeth had forced her wayward niece upon poor Lady Winchester and could therefore be assured of a very frosty reception indeed.

Accepting her portmanteau from the driver of the stage, Elizabeth took a deep, fortifying inhalation before heading in the direction of Hartley House.

~ * ~

A short while later, Toby Allenby had just reached the bottom of Diddington Hall's branching staircase. He almost jumped out of his skin as the chime of the doorbell reverberated around the walls of the entrance hall. His heart racing, he frantically looked about for a hiding place. He nipped behind a suit of Tudor armor just in time to observe the butler heave open the front door. To his immense relief, Toby saw neither Jack Wilmott nor Caroline Levington hovering on the threshold, but rather a young woman wearing a dark-green traveling gown and matching high-crowned bonnet, from under which peeped several strands of wheat-gold hair.

"Begging your pardon," she said respectfully to the manservant, "but I have been directed here from Hartley House. I am Miss Elizabeth Wilson. I am here to pay an unexpected call on my niece—Miss Maria Dove. I believe she is staying here with Miss Winchester."

Before the butler had a chance to reply, Lady Allenby, who just happened to be making her way across the hall at that moment, made an unforeseen detour toward the stranger.

"Do forgive my butting in, my dear, but I am Lady Allenby. Did I hear correctly? That you wish to see Miss Dove?"

The young woman dipped a polite curtsy. "Yes, your grace. I am Miss Wilson—Miss Winchester's former governess. I have traveled from Bath with the express purpose of speaking with my niece. I did think to find her at Hartley House but the servant there informed me that she had removed here a while with Miss Winchester."

"Indeed she has," confirmed Lady Allenby. "But, do you know, Miss Wilson, it is dreadfully remiss of me, but I'm afraid I have been so preoccupied of late that I am quite unsure of the last time I set eyes upon your niece." She turned and directed her next comment to a suit of Tudor armor. "Toby darling, have you any idea where one might find Miss Dove?"

From his—obviously ineffective—hiding place, Toby cringed. Trust his mother to catch him doing something so ridiculously stupid—and to make him feel, with that meaningful tone of hers, less like a man approaching his thirtieth year and more like a child approaching his fifth. Desperate to save some face before appearing before his bemused audience, he cast about for a reason which might explain his absurd position. In the absence of one, he attempted to feign breezy nonchalance.

"Do you know, Mother," he replied airily, slipping out from behind the military relic and brushing down the sleeves of his jacket, "now that you mention it, I recollect Miss Dove received an, er, an unexpected note a few days ago. From...from Yorkshire."

Miss Wilson clapped a hand to her chest. "Oh goodness, I hope there is nothing amiss there. Was it bad news, sir?"

"Oh, I, er, I certainly don't think it was anything of that sort," replied Toby, making haste not to alarm the pretty creature. "I think it more likely that it simply made the girl realize how much she missed her home county."

Lady Allenby looked a little bewildered at this revelation. "Are you suggesting, Toby, that Miss Dove has returned to Yorkshire? Without sharing with me one word of her intentions?"

Toby felt as though he were digging a very large hole. "Oh, how very remiss of me, Mother," he said, with a self-deprecating tut. "I recall that you were, um, so preoccupied that day that I reassured Miss Dove that it would be best not to disturb you and that I would pass on her thanks and farewell. I own, though, what with all the kafuffle in the house, it quite slipped my mind." He finished this speech with what he hoped was a rueful smile.

Lady Allenby looked far from convinced. Before she could continue her questioning, Miss Wilson gave a deflated sigh.

"Oh, well. If my niece is not here, then there has been little point to my visit. I suppose I shall return to Bath forthwith."

This remark appeared to bring the duchess, who had been studying her son through narrowed eyes, abruptly back to the present situation. "Oh, gracious me," she fluttered. "Where on earth are my manners? You really must excuse us, Miss Wilson, but, as Toby mentioned, the house is quite at sixes-and-sevens at the moment. Please do come in and join us in some refreshment."

Miss Wilson broke into a grateful smile. "That is most kind of you, ma'am. I would be delighted to do so. And please do forgive my impertinence, but I don't suppose, perchance, that Miss Winchester is at home. I should like very much to see her again."

Lady Allenby heaved a shuddering sigh. "I am afraid, Miss Wilson, that the very reason we are at sixes-and-sevens is, unfortunately, due to Miss Winchester's illness."

"Miss Winchester is ill?" gasped Miss Wilson.

Tears pooled in Lady Allenby's navy-blue eyes. "I think it best if you come in and have a dish of tea, dear. Then I can tell you all about it."

~ * ~

So exhausted was he that, contrary to his initial reaction, Harry Allenby was now extremely grateful for Miss Wilson's help in looking after Louisa. And what a good help the governess had proved. She had dispatched a remonstrating Harry to his own bed last night, with the minimum of fuss. Once there, he had appreciated her no nonsense insistence and had fallen unconscious the moment his head had hit the pillow. The sleep had obviously done him good. He was feeling much more refreshed that morning. The same, unfortunately, could not be said of Louisa. Still her fever persisted. And still she remained sweating and motionless in her bed.

~ * ~

Pacing nervously about the crimson drawing-room, Toby was only grateful that his mother's preoccupation in caring for Miss Winchester, meant that, with the exception of the Tudor armor incident, she had noticed very little of his own strange behavior. He had considered his nerves to be in tatters before his ignominious elopement, but so on edge were they now that he could scarcely sit still. How envious he was of the ease with which Maria Dove had been able to extricate herself from the situation—by the simple action of jumping on a coach. In a few hours, the girl would be back in Yorkshire, without a care in the world. Toby's predicament had been going on for so long, he had quite forgotten what it was not to have a care in the world. At this rate, he doubted very much he would ever be reminded of it.

Exactly what his next course of action was to be, Toby had no idea. He had made an enemy of Caroline; his short reprieve with Jack Wilmott was almost at an end; and the chances of him finding a bride and inheriting Diddington Hall were slim to say the least. Alternative solutions were equally as depressing. The probability of his raising such a large sum of money from other sources was so low as to be non-existent. Or was it? Was now the time, with all his other options well and truly quashed, for him to approach his father? He stopped his pacing as the butler appeared in the doorway, a small brown package tied with string in his hand.

"Begging your pardon, my lord, but this has just been delivered for you. The messenger said it was most important."

As Toby eyed the item, he had the impression of something very cold and sharp pressing against his chest. Without saying a word, he accepted it from the servant and headed for the stairs.

In the safety of his chamber, Toby tentatively untied the string of the parcel. A mound of scandal sheets slid from the paper directly to the floor.

This was bad. Very bad. Having Caroline as an ally had been unsettling; to have her as an enemy was terrifying. Not daring to read the full contents of her vulgar pamphlets, in which he, obviously, was the starring attraction, Toby had flung them straight onto the fire. From the few details he had gleaned, it was apparent that he would not be welcome in London for a very long time. What semblance of reputation he had had was now, thanks to the poison of Caroline's pen, in tatters. Tatters that would make it impossible for him to find a bride of whom his parents would approve. Without a bride there was no way he could inherit Diddington Hall and pay off Jack Wilmott.

Damn! If only Caroline hadn't interfered, his plan with Maria Dove would be well on its way to fruition now. Instead, the girl, scared out of her wits, was well on her way back to Yorkshire—taking with her Toby's very last chance of escaping his mess. He plopped down on the bed. His one and only remaining option was to speak to his father. But how to even begin to broach the matter, Toby had no idea.

Nineteen

Miss Elizabeth Wilson had been at Diddington Hall only a few short hours before she had concluded that Toby Allenby was a very troubled man. Not only did he appear incapable of sitting still, but every time the clock chimed the quarter hour, he jumped almost as high as the ceiling. Toby Allenby's troubles, though, were of no concern to her. She had willing accepted Lady Allenby's kind offer to stay at the hall and help care for Miss Winchester. Having seen her former pupil in such a worrying state, there was nothing Elizabeth had wanted more. Her help seemed to be much needed. The doctor made frequent visits but Lady Allenby would not hear of employing a nurse. With the aid of two or three trusted servants, the duchess and Harry were sharing the burden between them—one of them constantly by Louisa's side. They both looked exhausted. This morning, however, Lady Allenby apparently had another worry to add to her list.

"Oh, Miss Wilson, perhaps you could offer me some advice," she fluttered. "I own, I am at quite a loss as to what to do."

"About what, ma'am?"

"About Lady Winchester, my dear. I sent a letter informing her of Louisa's illness the first day Dr. Pike visited. I have, however, received no reply and cannot but wonder if my note ever arrived in Cornwall."

Elizabeth Wilson, herself not a great proponent of the British postal system, could only agree that the missive had most likely not reached its destination. As cold and distant as she had always found Eliza Winchester, she did not suppose for a moment that the woman would not have returned to Diddington post-haste if she had had so much as an inkling of her daughter's condition.

"Perhaps, ma'am, you could send one of the servants down to Cornwall to collect Lady Winchester," she suggested. "After all, I have no doubt she will waste not a moment in making plans to return to Diddington the minute she hears the news."

Lady Allenby gave this suggestion a little thought before pronouncing, "What a first-class idea, Miss Wilson. But I shall not send a servant. No indeed. I know of a *much* more suitable person to conduct an errand of such import."

~ * ~

If Toby Allenby had been forced to select a phrase that most described his mood that day, "chomping at the bit" would have summed it up perfectly; chomping to escape the increasingly suffocating atmosphere of Diddington Hall. He was not chomping sufficiently, however, to dare to venture outside its confines. There, he feared, a very nasty surprise may await him—from either Caroline or Jack Wilmott—or both.

As a result, he found himself wandering about the rose garden later that evening. It had been a glorious day and, even though the sun was about to set, it was still pleasantly warm. This fact passed Toby completely by.

So wrapped up was he in his problems that everything passed him by—particularly what was going on in the house. Once again, he had found himself on the receiving end of his mother's sharp tongue for failing to enquire about Miss Winchester.

If he was perfectly honest, Toby, unlike every other member of the household, had given Miss Winchester's condition very little consideration. The only person with whom he was concerned, was himself. Not that he found himself a particularly interesting case. Far from it. He would be the first to acknowledge that he was a coward. Not only was he continuing to hide away at Diddington Hall, but he had also failed to summon sufficient courage to speak to his father. Another very apt phrase sprung to his mind, that of "burying one's head in the sand". He was pathetically clinging to a sliver of hope that if he did nothing, perhaps all his problems would magically disappear. As stupid as he had been, even he was not dense enough to believe that a likely scenario. And, as he discovered the following morning, it was not.

No sooner had Toby opened the box the butler had brought to him than, upon seeing the mutilated rodent within, he dashed out to the garden and deposited the contents of his stomach over the lawn—and, as she turned the corner at a most unfortunate moment—almost over Elizabeth Wilson's slippered feet.

"Sir, whatever is amiss? Are you ill?" she asked concernedly.

Toby, feeling exceedingly ill at that particular moment, assured her it was nothing serious.

"Well, forgive me for saying so, but you are not looking at all well," she remarked. "Please, come and sit down over here." She indicated to the group of four wicker chairs that had been set around a garden table. "Is there anything I can fetch for you?"

Toby resisted saying that a large amount of cash might go some way to relieving his symptoms. Instead, without thinking through the consequences, he found himself following Miss Wilson.

Blast! He'd thought the moment he sat down and his wits returned. Now she's going to quiz me on what is amiss and, once she's exhausted that topic, will most likely move on to prattle some inanities about the deuced weather.

But quiz him Miss Wilson did not. Nor did she make any reference to the meteorological conditions. Instead, she sat beside him, observing her pleasant surroundings. She did not say a single word.

Toby, unused to silence, felt a little awkward at first, suspicious even of such unfemale-like behavior. Turning his head slightly, he studied the woman out of the corner of his eye. Her day gown of pale green muslin was plain yet flattering. The loose knot of blonde hair atop her head was simple yet complimentary. Her eyes were a brilliant cornflower-blue and she had two small dimples in her pink cheeks. Confident that she did not seem at all the type of girl who might develop a penchant for posting small dead mammals, he began to find the refreshing combination of sunshine, silence, and a reassuring presence beside him, quite relaxing.

All at once, Elizabeth turned to face him causing Toby's cheeks, for the first time in his life, to flush a deep shade of crimson.

"Are you feeling a little better, my lord?"

Noting the concern in her voice, it occurred to Toby that it had been quite some time since he had had the impression that anyone cared for him. Not that he was worthy of anyone's care. He had been acting like a damned fool and his mess was purely of his own doing. To his amazement, he found he could suddenly see things clearly; enough to even consider making some important decisions. And all of this he could only attribute to the calming presence of Miss Elizabeth Wilson. A woman who had addressed little more than a handful of words to him.

~ * ~

Harry Allenby almost jumped out of his chair as the door to Louisa's bedchamber burst open and Eliza Winchester bowled in. The woman's distress was evident—her beautiful face pale, drawn and streaked with tears. Viscount Winston, whose concern appeared only marginally less, followed her.

Scurrying directly to her daughter, Eliza exclaimed, "Oh, thank goodness! She is still—" She broke off in a torrent of shuddering sobs.

Viscount Winston, at her side in an instant, said nothing, but wrapped a reassuring arm around her shoulders. Crying uncontrollably, Eliza Winchester turned toward him and buried her head in his broad chest.

~ * ~

Dressing for breakfast that morning, Toby discovered that, for the first time in a very long while, his thoughts were actually focused on someone other than himself. And, as he pushed open the door to the breakfast-room to reveal that same someone alone there, his stomach launched into a series of impressive somersaults.

Miss Elizabeth Wilson was seated at the table with a cup of chocolate before her and a half-eaten slice of toast. She was staring wistfully into space and did not at first notice Toby. Toby, on the other hand, noticed her. He noticed everything about her. The result was that he deemed her the loveliest, most unaffected, creature he had ever set eyes upon.

"Oh, good morning, my lord," she said, fixing him with her blue eyes.

Something strange tugged at Toby's heart. Good lord—what was the woman doing to him? He had no idea, but he resolved not to allow her the slightest hint of it.

"Good, er, morning, Miss Wilson," he said, a little more stiffly than he had intended. Remonstrating with himself for sounding so aloof, he made his way over to the sideboard to help himself to ham and eggs. To his amazement, he found his hands shaking as he lifted the silver dome.

"I hope you are feeling a little better this morning, sir," said Miss Wilson courteously.

"Much better, thank you, Miss Wilson," replied Toby. Still with his back to her, he pulled a rueful face. In his efforts not to sound pompous, he actually sounded the very epitome of the word.

"Er, well," said the woman, rising from her chair at exactly the same moment Toby reached his. "May I wish you a, um, pleasant day, my lord."

She bobbed a charming curtsy before whisking out of the room. Toby regarded his food for several minutes following her departure, before concluding he no longer had a scrap of appetite.

~ * ~

Elizabeth Wilson could only conclude that something very peculiar must have happened to Eliza Winchester. She had bumped into her former employer and Viscount Winston later that morning. In a most uncharacteristic gesture, Eliza had grasped both Elizabeth's hands and insisted on telling her, several times over, how much she appreciated her help in caring for her daughter. She had seemed to Elizabeth much less harsh than she remembered, softer around the edges. Of course it could be as a result of Louisa's illness. The poor woman had been forced to endure what must have seemed like an interminable journey back to Diddington, most likely fearing what she was to encounter on her arrival. Elizabeth was only grateful that the kindly Viscount Winston had broken the news to Eliza and had accompanied her on the return journey. Not only did the man appear a rock of support to the woman, but he was all that was charming.

"Charming" was not an adjective Elizabeth could ever imagine applying to Toby Allenby. She had never met a stranger specimen in her entire life. Not only was he afraid of his own shadow, hiding behind suits of armor and jumping ten feet in the air if anyone so much as clinked a teaspoon in their saucer, but he had a most disagreeable manner about him —verging on the pompous. For all she had had very little contact with the man, the few minutes they had been alone in the breakfast-room that morning had convinced her that the less she had to do with Toby Allenby, the better.

~ * ~

Sitting in the garden, beneath the window of the crimson drawing-room that afternoon, Toby was predictably wallowing in the misery of his situation. A butterfly, landing, with an audacious flutter on his knee, momentarily distracted him. He studied the insect's wings—a beautiful shade of lilac veined with shimmering threads of pink. At the sudden sound of voices in the room above him, it flew off.

"I'm afraid I must apologize, Eliza dear," Toby heard his mother saying. "If only I had removed to Hartley House to care for Louisa, rather than bringing her to the hall where it is so draughty—"

"I don't know how you can even suggest such a thing, Arabella," sniffed a tearful Lady Winchester. "The fault is mine. I should never have left the girl in the first place."

"But you had to, my dear. Your poor cousin was quite indisposed."

"I should have put Louisa first."

"Fudge! We all thought, including the child herself, that her affliction was nothing more than a cold," said Lady Allenby. "Now, there is little point in us both driving ourselves to Bedlam with such talk. What has happened, has happened. We must now pray that the child recovers."

There followed a brief hiatus, during which Toby could imagine several tears being shed. The clearing of noses shortly afterwards, confirmed his assumption.

"Now," sniffed the duchess. "Let us talk of more pleasant matters. I have been meaning to tell you for several days, Eliza, what a delightful woman I find Miss Wilson to be. Her very presence in the house has had the most calming influence on us all."

Lady Winchester agreed. "I did always find her a most marvelous governess. Although I doubt very much that I ever told her so. Dear Louisa thought the world of her."

"And one can quite understand why. Such a capable, strong young lady. And strikingly intelligent. The type of person one would have no hesitation in approaching if one had a problem."

As efficiently as if this last comment had been a well-rehearsed stage direction, Toby leaped to his feet.

~ * ~

Basking in the uninterrupted sunshine in the garden that afternoon, Elizabeth Wilson had spent a very pleasant few minutes observing a pink and lilac butterfly which seemed to have taken a liking to the puffed sleeve of her sprigged muslin gown. Despite her interest in the lovely creature, Elizabeth was slowly losing the battle to keep her eyes open. Perhaps she should submit and have a little doze. It would likely do her the world of good and she would be refreshed when she returned to the sickroom later.

Setting down her book on the table in front of her, she closed her eyes and settled herself in the high-backed wicker chair. If she could grab thirty minutes, it would—

"Good afternoon, Miss Wilson."

Elizabeth started. Shielding her eyes from the sun, her heart sank when she discovered Toby Allenby standing before her. Whatever did he want with her?

"A very pleasant afternoon, is it not?"

Elizabeth felt a surge of impatience. She was not an advocate of stating the obvious, nor of exchanging mundane inanities. "Er, yes, sir," she managed to reply. "Very pleasant indeed."

To her horror, Toby seemed to take this concurrence as a cue to plonk himself down in the chair alongside hers.

"How is Miss Winchester today?" he asked, not looking at her, but staring directly ahead.

"I'm afraid there is still no improvement, sir."

"Hmm. Then we must all continue to pray for her."

"Indeed we must." Elizabeth's impatience rose.

Really, what was this all about? she wondered, flicking him a look. Whatever it was, she was in no mood for it. She wished she was alone in her bedchamber, where she would be free to sleep without interruption. She was on the verge of inventing some excuse to bring that situation about, when, much to her astonishment, Toby turned to her and blurted out, "Miss Wilson, can I talk to you?"

Elizabeth fought the urge to say that she'd much prefer he didn't, but sensed that this retort may not be appreciated. "Of, er, course, sir," she faltered instead.

Toby leaned forward, his arms resting on the table, his hands clasped. Still he did not look at her. "What would you say, Miss Wilson, to someone who had managed to surround himself in the most awful mess and who did not have the first clue how to extricate himself from it?"

Elizabeth stared at him blankly. "Well, I, er, I suppose that depends on what type of mess you are referring to, sir."

Toby heaved a weary sigh. "A mess of inordinate proportion, Miss Wilson, and one entirely of one's own doing."

Sensing that no further details would be forthcoming, Elizabeth replied, "Well, I, um, suppose, if the unfortunate circumstances were entirely of this person's own doing, then I should tell him to stop feeling sorry for himself and to take whatever action possible to rectify the situation. In my experience, sir, there is seldom a problem one cannot resolve satisfactorily, if one allows it due consideration."

Toby turned to her, his eyes shining with something she could not decipher. "So, in other words, Miss Wilson, you would tell that person to cease moping around and to sort himself out?"

"Yes, sir," she confirmed, hoping desperately that that was to be an end to the matter. It was.

Toby stood up. "Good afternoon, Miss Wilson," he said, executing a bow before her.

Elizabeth observed him as he made his way across the lawn, toward the house. For all he had divulged very little detail in that brief conversation, Toby Allenby had, quite unwittingly, revealed a great deal about himself. A deal which lead Elizabeth to believe that she may have grasped completely the wrong idea about the man. There had been a distinct air of confused vulnerability about Toby Allenby that afternoon—combined with the very pleasant scent of his cologne.

~ * ~

With a pounding heart, Harry rose from the chair. Had he just imagined it or had Louisa actually murmured something? Hardly daring to breathe, he leaned over the bed to find her gazing up at him with huge brown eyes.

"Hello," she whispered.

Twenty

Following his conversation with Miss Wilson, Toby now knew exactly what he had to do. He had to face his problems head on, like a man. He had no one but himself to blame for his predicament, and no one but himself ought, therefore, to suffer the consequences.

Jack Wilmott wanted money from him but it was, in fairness—ignoring the astronomical interest the man had lumped on top—money that Toby had borrowed. Consequently, it was only right that the man be repaid. The only remaining solution open to Toby to raise the money to settle the debt, was to ask his father. If, in the process of doing so, he forfeited the right to his inheritance, then was that not also just? Had he not proved himself incapable of managing the Allenby estate? That he was cut from the same cloth as his notorious grandfather?

If the title was to pass to Harry then so be it. Harry would make a worthier duke and the Allenby fortune would be safe in his capable hands. Why, had not Harry selflessly nursed Miss Winchester every hour of the day and night? *That* was the type of man who should be heading up the family, not a womanizing, gambling, elbow-crooker like Toby.

Filled with his newfound zeal, Toby headed directly for his father's study. So intent was he on his target, that he collided directly with a footman coming around the corner. The servant's silver tray tumbled to the floor, as did the copy of *The Times*, which had been resting upon it. The newspaper landed face upwards, drawing Toby's eye to its astonishing headline.

In his bedchamber, Toby re-read the front-page article for approximately the tenth time. Jack Wilmott was dead! Found with his throat cut, in the same alley Toby had once, almost as unwittingly, spent the night. Although part of him was appalled at the gory attack, the greater part could scarcely believe it. Jack Wilmott's death meant that he was free. His ridiculously immature prayers had been answered. Of course Wilmott's lackeys might make some attempt to carry on the business, but it was unlikely any of them would possess a brain half as sharp as their predecessor. Toby would estimate a couple of weeks at most before they were chased out of London—or worse.

No, Toby was certain that his Wilmott association was as dead as the man himself—and he could only describe the feeling as one akin to having a ten-ton weight lifted from his shoulders.

In spite of his solitary rejoicing, Toby did not fail to acknowledge that he had been extremely lucky. His fortunate escape in no way excused his irresponsible behavior. Had he not spotted the newspaper when he had, then he could easily have confessed all to his father—and been subsequently stripped of his inheritance. He had escaped by the skin of his teeth. He would never, ever, he vowed, allow himself to fall into such a mess again.

All that remained for him to worry about now was Caroline.

~ * ~

From the moment Harry had flown down the stairs three days ago, announcing Louisa's recovery, the mood at Diddington Hall had been one of celebration. It would be quite some time until she was fully recovered but at least now she could, with the help of a mountain of pillows, sit upright in bed, and, best of all, her appetite had returned.

"Do you think anyone would mind if I had some more, sir?" she tentatively asked Harry, as he finished spooning her the last of her rice pudding.

Harry smiled broadly. "I shouldn't think so, Miss Winchester. Would you like me to enquire for you?"

"If it's not too much trouble, I should be much obliged, sir," she replied shyly.

Harry stood up and bowed to her. "Please be assured that

I shall give the matter my personal attention."

As he walked along the landing, it occurred to a chuckling Harry that he had never felt happier in his entire life. He had not yet plucked up the courage to ask Louisa to marry him. But something in the way she looked at him convinced him she was going to accept. Perhaps this afternoon…

~ * ~

The moment the butler had informed Elizabeth Wilson that a letter—postmarked Yorkshire—had arrived for her, she had known immediately that it must be bad news. Her first thought had been that it must be from her family. It was not. It was from a solicitor, who had evidently gone to great pains to discover her whereabouts. The note was brief—only three lines. Enough to inform her that her closest friend, Miss Desiree Hudson had passed away quietly in her sleep some two weeks ago.

A stunned Elizabeth sat stock-still for thirty minutes before the tears came, and came, and came. She attempted to console herself with the knowledge that Miss Hudson had enjoyed a long, healthy and fulfilling life—which was more than could be said for a great many other people. Her strategy proved ineffective. The cold truth was that the most influential figure in her life, and the dearest friend she had ever had, was dead.

Three hours later, Elizabeth's incessant sobbing had resulted in a pounding headache. Desperate for fresh air, but not for company, she drifted down the drive of the hall and, once at the bottom, turned toward the town. So absorbed was she in her reminiscing, and so oblivious to her surroundings, she failed to notice the runaway gig whose pair of lively colts had deposited their inexperienced driver on the roadside some ten minutes before and now appeared intent on putting as much distance between them and their master as possible. It was only when a strong arm yanked Elizabeth from their thundering path, that she had the faintest notion of the danger from which she had been plucked.

"Oh," she exclaimed, looking bewilderedly from the careering horses into Toby Allenby's handsome face. "Was I about to—"

Toby nodded. "I'm afraid you were, Miss Wilson."

Elizabeth gawped at him for several seconds, before

bursting into yet another torrent of tears.

~ * ~

Harry Allenby could not have felt more desolate if his heart had been viciously ripped from his chest and trodden to a pulp by a herd of cavorting elephants. Perhaps that served him right for being so confident. But his confidence had had very little to do with his ego. It had stemmed from the unmistakable twinkle in Louisa's eyes every time she looked at him. In spite of his conviction, Harry had been wrong. Louisa had refused his offer of marriage. She had turned him down—point blank.

~ * ~

"Louisa, child!" exclaimed Lady Winchester, the moment she entered her daughter's bedchamber. "Whatever is amiss? Is it the fever?" She rushed immediately over to the bedside.

A tearful Louisa shook her head. "No, Mama. I am feeling m-much better."

"Then what is it?" persisted the older woman.

Louisa began a fresh bout of sobs. "Nothing. Nothing at all."

"Well, if that is nothing, I cannot imagine how you should go on if it were something." Eliza plumped down on the side of the bed and took hold of her daughter's hand. "Now tell me, what is it?"

"I-it is Lord Harry, Mama."

Eliza wrinkled her brow. "Lord Harry? But I cannot imagine for one moment that the man would do anything to upset you so."

"Oh, he hasn't upset me intentionally," sniffed Louisa, jumping immediately to Harry's defense. "Quite the contrary. He has...he has asked me to...to—"

Lady Winchester's dark eyes grew wide. "To what?"

"To-to...marry him," muttered Louisa in such a subdued tone that Eliza could scarcely hear her.

Cringing at the mere thought of her mother's reaction, to Louisa's amazement, Lady Winchester clapped her hands together in delight. "But that is marvelous, child. I do hope you accepted."

Louisa gawped. "I did not, Mama."

Lady Winchester gawped back. "Why ever not? Anyone

can see the two of you are head-over-heels in love."

Louisa lowered her eyes and began fiddling with the edge of the counterpane. "That may be so, Mama. But I could never marry him. The institution of marriage is as advantageous to women as leeches on a cor—"

Lady Winchester tilted up her daughter's chin to her. "My dear girl, I own that was my opinion until a short while ago. Before...before—"

"Before you met Viscount Winston, Mama?"

Lady Winchester flushed to the roots of her hair. She stood up and began smoothing down her skirts. "Before I, er, realized it was unfair of me to inflict my own experience onto you. Now child, I am going to find Lord Harry and send him straight back to this room, where you will accept his proposal forthwith."

Louisa opened her mouth to speak, but Eliza held up her hand. "And I do not wish to hear another word of protest. Is that clear?"

Louisa's mouth stretched into a wide, grateful smile.

~ * ~

Harry Allenby had considered that the kiss he and Louisa had shared under the willow tree at Buttercup Meadow had been special. Nonetheless, it paled into insignificance when compared to the one that followed Louisa's acceptance of his proposal.

"Although it shall be quite some time before I am well enough to walk up the aisle, sir," she sighed, when their lips eventually parted.

"Good God, I suppose it shall," agreed Harry, employing a deal of restraint not to join her under the bedcovers. "In the meantime, I shall have to find something useful with which to occupy myself. Either that or go out of my mind with impatience."

"You could always continue the search for the Diddington Diamond," suggested Louisa, twining her fingers through his. "Perhaps you would have more luck without me and Miss Dove in tow."

"The Diddington Diamond?" repeated Harry, forcing his gaze from the laces of her nightdress, which he longed to untie. "Do you know, I had forgotten all about it."

"Well, you must not," insisted Louisa firmly. "Lady O'Hare obviously wanted you to find it and find it you should."

~ * ~

Meandering along the riverbank toward Buttercup Meadow, Eliza Winchester swiped a tear from her cheek. She had done the right thing by insisting Louisa wed Harry. The two of them were made for one other; their mutual adoration was clear for all to see. Eliza would be the first to admit that she had first used Harry and his library cataloguing as a means of injecting some distance between her daughter and the man-obsessed Maria Dove. That aside, even she was not prejudiced enough to deprive Louisa of that wonderful feeling she herself had experienced in her short marriage.

With the wonderful benefit of hindsight, she now realized how unfair it had been of her to inflict her bitterness onto her unsuspecting daughter. Still, there was little point dwelling on that now. Thankfully, all had turned out well—for Louisa at least. Quite how Eliza would cope without her daughter she dared not think. But she was a grown woman—and one of more than adequate means. She would cope very well alone. She started as a male voice interrupted her reverie.

"Good afternoon, Lady Winchester."

"Oh, Viscount Winston," she smiled, on a breath of relief.

While the man inclined his head to her, Eliza couldn't help but notice that he seemed uncharacteristically agitated, nervous almost.

"My, er, cousin informed me you were out w-walking, ma'am. And I-I wondered if I might be permitted the pleasure of joining you."

"Of course you may, sir," replied Eliza, aware of heat flooding her cheeks.

The viscount indicated the willow tree a little way ahead of them. "Perhaps you-you wouldn't mind if we sat awhile. I-I have something I should like to ask you."

Eliza's heart began hammering a tad faster as she observed a pink and lilac butterfly flutter from the top of Viscount Winston's head and land on the handle of her parasol.

~ * ~

If someone had informed Elizabeth Wilson that, within a

few short days, her opinion of Toby Allenby would rise from the lowly depths of pompous and irritating, to the giddy heights of charming and compassionate, she would never have believed them in a million years.

Nevertheless, that was exactly what had occurred. Since she had first gleaned a glimmer of his boyish vulnerability the day he had sought her out in the garden, Elizabeth had found herself increasingly attracted to the man. Indeed, she seemed to be finding new attributes to admire in him on an almost daily basis. Directly after he had wrenched her from the path of the runaway horses, for example, the poor man had been forced to endure a stream of ridiculously personal stories about Elizabeth and Miss Hudson that could not have held a scrap of his interest.

Yet, if her recounting had bored him to Bedlam, Toby had betrayed no signs of it. He had remained by her side for three hours while she had continued her ramblings and he had even offered some soothing words of wisdom.

"From what I now know of Miss Hudson," he had said, "I can only assume that the world will be a much poorer place for her loss."

This particular sentiment had echoed Elizabeth's own perfectly, yet, when she had turned toward him to share this fact, and his navy-blue eyes had locked with hers, Elizabeth had found all words flying directly from her head.

~ * ~

Harry Allenby stood before his family crypt at the front of Diddington's little church—the final destination on Great Aunt Millie's list of instructions in the search for the Diddington Diamond. Harry looked about him, nonplussed. The grounds were certainly pretty enough with a few other crypts and gravestones scattered about, but he failed to see how any of these could be a clue. He could make no sense of it at all. In fact, it now occurred to him that the entire exercise had been nothing more than a wild goose chase. He wasn't sure what Great Aunt Millie had hoped he would achieve in running about the countryside, but, whatever it was, she should have made herself clearer, or just simply bequeathed him the jewel in her will.

"Good day, my lord."

Harry spun around to find Mr. Gerald Hinds, Great Aunt Millie's solicitor, strolling up the winding little path, carrying a bunch of tulips."

"For my wife's grave," the man explained. "Ruby always loved her tulips."

Harry nodded understandingly. Then, in an effort to lift the mood he announced, "I am to have a wife myself soon, sir. Miss Louisa Winchester of Hartley House."

A look of incredulity spread over Mr. Hinds' features. "Not the pretty bespectacled young lady, sir? With the long dark hair?"

Harry beamed proudly. "The very same, Mr. Hinds. Although I'm afraid it shall be quite some time before we actually make it to church. You see—"

Gerald Hinds paid no attention to Harry's explanation of the delay of his nuptials. All he could think was that Millicent O'Hare really must have been a witch. A bee buzzing directly past his ear, brought him back to the present situation.

"—so to occupy myself in the meantime," continued Harry, "I have attempted to find the last clue in an infuriating puzzle which mysteriously came into my possession several weeks ago now-"

Color flooded Mr. Hinds' cheeks.

"It was a series of clues designed to lead us to the Diddington Diamond, however, I confess, I have come nowhere near finding the jewel."

"Oh, but you have, sir," countered the man of law, who was, Harry realized, staring at him in the most disconcerting manner.

~ * ~

Elizabeth Wilson was having the strangest of days. Not only had she received a very unexpected letter that morning—unexpected, but nonetheless wonderful—but now Lord Toby Allenby had requested that she accompany him to the rose garden. The air of awkwardness surrounding the man had not escaped Elizabeth's attention. She strongly suspected that her outstaying her welcome at the hall was at the root of it. With Louisa making a steady recovery, Elizabeth's reason for remaining at Diddington had long since expired. Yet, conscious of this fact for some time, she had done nothing to rectify it; had not encountered so much as a hint of motivation to rectify it. And it was not only the delightful company of her former pupil that had resulted in this apathy. If truth were told, it was actually the company of another member of the household that held Elizabeth a willing prisoner of Diddington Hall—the company of Toby Allenby.

Although she would never dare admit it, she now considered Toby every bit as charming as his much-esteemed relative, the viscount. And he was so kind and considerate to her that she had, on several occasions, battled a shameful urge to kiss him. Only yesterday, when a sudden gust of wind had whipped her bonnet from her head, Toby had chased it all around the garden, before returning it to a giggling Elizabeth with all the gallantry of a dashing knight.

Despite her growing feelings for the man, Elizabeth knew she was being fanciful—as well as postponing the inevitable. She would have to leave Diddington soon. And now, courtesy of the letter she had received that morning, she knew exactly where she would go and what she would do—which would, hopefully, not allow her a free moment to pine for Toby.

As Toby came to a halt before a stone bench under one of the rose arbors, Elizabeth was jolted back to the present. He gestured for her to sit down. She did so, but not without first noticing that he looked more anxious than ever. A strong compulsion to wrap her arms around him surged through her.

"Miss, er, Wilson," he began, running a finger under his pointed collar.

Elizabeth took a deep breath in and on the exhalation blurted out, "I can assure you there is no need to look so uncomfortable, my lord. I know exactly what you are about to say."

Toby regarded her aghast. "You do?"

Elizabeth nodded. "And I should like very much to spare you the embarrassment."

"You would?"

A tear rolled down her cheek. "I shall pack my things and take my leave immediately."

"Pack your things? B-but surely there is no need for that, Miss Wilson. If you do not wish to marry me, then surely we can still be friends. I have to admit that I have never before had a friend who I can-"

Elizabeth Wilson snapped her head up. "Marry you?"

she repeated, her blue eyes wide.

"Why, yes. That was what I was about to ask you. Before you announced your imminent departure."

"But I-I thought you were going to ask me to leave."

Toby's brows drew together. "Why ever would I ask the woman I love to leave? You must be all about in the head, Miss Wilson."

"You-you love me?"

Toby gave an embarrassed nod. "Have scarce been able to think about another thing since the moment I first set eyes upon you—from behind that curst set of Tudor armor."

A delighted but astonished Elizabeth took a moment to assimilate this information. Why on earth would Lord Toby Allenby, heir to a dukedom and quite the most adorable man she had ever encountered, be proposing to her—a humble governess? The very reason smacked her directly in the face.

She tilted up her chin to him. "I'm afraid I cannot marry you, sir," she pronounced haughtily. "I appreciate I am only a governess and, therefore, naïve regarding such matters, but I am fully aware of the terms of your great aunt's will, and I have no wish to be used as a pawn in a game which will allow you to inherit Diddington Hall."

Toby's previously distraught countenance suddenly broke out into a wide grin. "You think that is the reason I am asking you to marry me? So I can inherit the hall?"

"What other reason could there possibly be," retorted Elizabeth, trying desperately not to cry, "for a future duke to request the hand of a lowly governess? I may be of a different class from you, my lord, but I am certainly not stupid."

"Oh, but you are, Miss Wilson," countered Toby, dropping to his knees before her and clasping both her hands in his. "If you cannot see that I am head-over-heels in love with you, then you must be the stupidest woman alive. And as for being of a different class—well, you are certainly that all right. You are in a class far superior to mine. As well as being the most beautiful woman I have ever set eyes upon, you are intelligent and capable and strong and—"

"I still refuse to be used as a pawn, sir," said Elizabeth, a watery smile touching her lips.

"Oh, I can assure you, Miss Wilson, that using you as a

pawn is the last thing on my mind." He slipped onto the bench beside her. "Along, I hasten to add, with inheriting Diddington Hall. If it will make the slightest difference to your decision, we shall postpone our marriage until after that of my brother and Miss Winchester, which I hope will prove my sincerity. So, what do you say, woman? Will you marry me now?"

Gazing into his dark eyes, Elizabeth thought there was nothing she should like more, but then her loyalty rose to the fore. "I should like very much to marry you, sir," she replied, averting her eyes from his. "But I have had some unexpected news this morning—news that I still cannot fully comprehend. I have discovered that my dear friend, Miss Hudson, was actually a great heiress—and she has left her entire fortune to me."

"But that is wonderful," declared Toby.

Elizabeth nodded. "Indeed it is. And very surprising—I had not the

slightest notion of it. But, given how much of herself the woman dedicated to others, and how good she was to me, I should like very much to do something in her honor. I should like to return to Yorkshire and set up a school in her name."

Toby beamed at her. "Then that, Miss Wilson," he said, lowering his lips to hers, "is exactly what we shall do."

~ * ~

Louisa Winchester, propped up in bed against a mountain of feather pillows, could scarce believe what she was hearing. "So your great aunt instructed her solicitor to deliver you the note regarding the Diddington Diamond if he so much as suspected you had found another girl you could love?"

Harry nodded. "The note which we all thought was intended to lead us to a precious jewel, but which was actually just a guise for us to visit a list of romantic locations."

Louisa furrowed her brow. "But what did Mr. Hinds mean when he said that you had found the diamond after all?"

Harry began rubbing his thumb over the back of her hand in a gesture so sensuous it caused Louisa to tremble.

"He thinks, my darling, that as the objective of the entire exercise was to make me forget Clara and to fall in love again, that the diamond is actually you, Miss Winchester. Now, what do you say to that?"

Louisa could say nothing as Harry's lips claimed hers at

exactly the same moment a pink and lilac butterfly fluttered through the window landing, with an audacious flutter, on the vase of freesias at the side of Louisa's bed.

EPILOGUE

Two weeks later

At the writing desk in her bedchamber, Caroline Levington attempted to concentrate on another of her lists—a list of further surprises she could inflict on Toby Allenby. In truth, she had lost interest in the project. She was bored. Bored to distraction. And, to make matters worse, there was not a soul in London with whom she wished to amuse herself.

All at once the door burst open. Caroline was amazed to find her husband standing on the threshold, with a distinct air of purpose about him.

"E-Edmund," she spluttered. "Wh-what are you doing here?"

The earl drew up his broad shoulders. "I am here, Caroline, to claim you as my wife."

Caroline's violet eyes grew wide. She opened her mouth to inquire as to the nature of this assertion, but the man held up his hand.

"The matter is not for discussion, Caroline. Now, remove your robe immediately, madam. Unless, of course, you wish me to take my riding crop to you."

At his dominant tone, and the production of the riding implement from behind his back, something began fizzling deep in the pit of Caroline's stomach—something that told her that perhaps the afternoon may pan out a tad more interesting than she had imagined after all.

Several hours later, a satisfied Lady Caroline Levington flopped down on the bed. She was scarcely able to believe what she had just experienced. Wherever had her husband learned tricks like those? And that domineering manner he had taken with her... Not one of her lovers had ever dared to treat her so...*contemptuously*.

"Well, Caroline," demanded the earl. "It is time for an ultimatum. Either you stop treating me like an idiot and we start acting like man and wife or we part company. Which is it to be?"

Caroline affected her most beatific expression. "I own, I am really not certain, my lord. I think perhaps a little...*cajoling* may be required." She flicked a meaningful look at the riding crop lying atop the counterpane.

Interpreting her meaning perfectly, the earl's lips curved into a scornful sneer. Caroline quivered with anticipation.

"Very well," he announced. "I can see that I shall have to treat you like the willful mare that you are. Now bend over that chair, madam, and let me see if I can't whip some sense into you."

For the first time in her life, Caroline Levington did exactly as she was bid.

Two months later

Mrs. Clark, the milliner, ran an appraising eye over the hatted heads of the church congregation. She heaved a satisfied sigh. She had, although she said so herself, done them all proud—again. She was worn to a frazzle, but that was only to be expected, what with Eliza Winchester's wedding to Viscount Winston two weeks before, Louisa Winchester's wedding to Harry Allenby today and Toby Allenby's wedding to the lovely Miss Wilson next month. Her feet had scarce touched the ground.

And she was not the only one. Poor Mrs. Pike, charged with the ecclesiastical floral arrangements, had worked herself up into such a lather, that her husband, the doctor, had been forced to order extra supplies of Hartshorn and salts especially for his spouse.

In spite of the woman's nervous affliction, Mrs. Clark had to admit that Mrs. Pike had done almost as splendid a job as herself. The hundreds of cream and white roses adorning the building looked magnificent. But there was something Mrs. Clark could not quite put her finger on... Something that had her completely bamboozled. Despite the profusion of roses, it was not their perfume flooding the church, but rather the unmistakable scent of lavender.

Seven months later

In Yorkshire, a despondent Maria Stickleback gazed into the crib of the newly christened, sleeping Miss Aphrodite Stickleback.

"Ain't she just like her ma," enthused her husband, Ned. "A little diamond."

At the mention of diamonds, Maria felt a prick of optimism. "She'll 'ave assets yer know, Ned. Good assets. And we'll 'ave t' make sure she knows 'ow t' use "em."

"Well," muttered her husband, one hand sliding up to caress his wife's assets which, to his great delight, had increased their voluptuous proportions since the birth of their daughter, "as I recall, yer always knew exactly 'ow t' use yours. Although perhaps yer 'ad better remind me."

Maria trembled with pleasure at her husband's expert touch. She had been devastated when her plans had been dashed and she had been forced to return to Yorkshire. But the disappointing outcome was not without its advantages. His lowly farmer status notwithstanding, Maria could not imagine any man—titled or otherwise—keeping her quite as well amused as Ned Stickleback. Particularly since he, too, had been reading the set of little hard-backed books she had brought with her from the Diddington Hall library.

Almost two hundred years later

Dr. Alice Ross could not believe that, in all her thirty-three years, she had never visited Diddington. Having immediately fallen in love with the town, though resplendent in all its springtime glory, she had the strong presentiment that this first visit would certainly not be her last.

As she pushed open the smooth wooden gate to the

graveyard, she stood a moment in the warm April sunshine, observing the scene. She could imagine it had changed very little over the past three hundred years or so. Unlike Alice's own life, which had changed dramatically over the last three. Who would have imagined that she would be a widow at the ripe old age of thirty? Certainly not her.

But she was—courtesy of a reckless driver who had wiped out Carl and his bicycle in a matter of seconds.

Since that fateful day, Alice had thrown herself into her work as a GP in Bath. She had worked so hard that her parents had all but tied her to a chair until she had finally agreed to take a year off. She was still young, they had insisted. She should try something completely different. Travel, perhaps.

Neither lugging around a rucksack, nor lying on a beach held much appeal for Alice. Instead, she had attended a course at her local library—a course on exploring one's family history. That, decided Alice, was just what she needed—something that would occupy her brain, minimizing opportunities for it to meander, as it was prone, to all things Carl.

No sooner had this decision been revealed to her parents, than Alice's delighted mother had bounded up the stairs, only to reappear with a small wooden chest.

The contents of this chest had rapidly become the main focus of Alice's search. The dozens of hours she had spent poring over its correspondence, combined with the efforts of the library staff and the wonders of the Internet, had provided her with a fascinating insight into the life of her great-great-grandfather's younger brother, Robert Samuel Ross. The man's mountain of love letters, from a young lady by the name of Millie, had proved particularly fascinating and had revealed a very special courtship.

The letters made regular reference to locations where the pair had managed to snatch a few precious moments together before Robert's life had tragically ended at the age of twenty-one. These places—all around Diddington—included a little Norman church, a rose garden, and a meadow with a willow tree. So magical did they sound, Alice had felt compelled to visit them herself.

And so, from her base at the Diddington Hall Country Hotel & Spa, that's exactly what she was doing. She had now found all the locations mentioned in the lovers' letters—even the rose garden at the former Diddington Hall still remained. The only reference that still puzzled her was a bizarre joke regarding a stone and a fish. Had it been the lovers' secret code for something? She doubted she would ever know.

As she entered the graveyard, a large family crypt at the front of the church caught her eye. Alice walked over to it and studied the names inscribed on the marble. A Millicent O'Hare was buried there. Could that be the Millie her relative had loved so much? That was something else Alice would most likely never know.

She turned and was about to walk on, when she noticed a pink and lilac butterfly perched on the sleeve of her jacket. With a smile, she watched it flutter away. Intrigued, she followed it around to the back of the church and watched as it landed on the hand of a young man at one of the graves there. He appeared to be replacing some wilting blooms with a pretty bunch of pink rosebuds. He jumped as he noticed the butterfly. In the process he managed to spill the vase of water he had been holding all over his feet.

He turned toward Alice and grimaced. "Severe case of accident-prone-itis," he grinned. "Runs in the family, so I'm told. No known cure for it."

Quite uncharacteristically, Alice found herself giggling. "Do you need a hand?" she asked.

~ * ~

In the elegantly furnished lounge of the Diddington Hall Country Hotel & Spa, an old stuffed trout stared disconcertingly from its glass case above the bookshelves. Almost three hundred years on, the very valuable—and legendary—twinkle in its eye, still remained unnoticed.

About Wendy

Wendy Burdess lives in the north of England with her husband and one very pampered rescue dog. When not playing real-life *Monopoly* with houses, or writing at her holiday home in Northumberland, she attempts to play the violin in her local orchestra. Just in case anyone is looking for a new principal violinist, she is currently studying for her Grade Four exam and is available at very reasonable rates.

Visit our website for our growing catalogue of quality books.
www.champagnebooks.com